C0-AJV-889

THE COMMON SENSE OF MUSIC

THE COMMON SENSE *of* MUSIC

BY

SIGMUND SPAETH

GREENWOOD PRESS, PUBLISHERS
WESTPORT, CONNECTICUT

The Library of Congress has catalogued this publication as follows:

Library of Congress Cataloging in Publication Data

Spaeth, Sigmund Gottfried, 1885-1965.
The common sense of music.

1. Music--Analysis, appreciation. I. Title.
MT6.S69 1972 780'.15 74-163550
ISBN 0-8371-6210-6

Originally published in 1924
by Boni and Liveright Publishers, New York

Reprinted with the permission
of the Liveright Publishing Corporation

First Greenwood Reprinting 1972

Library of Congress Catalogue Card Number 74-163550

ISBN 0-8371-6210-6

Printed in the United States of America

THERE IS NO REASON FOR CONCEALING ANY LONGER THAT THIS BOOK IS DEDICATED TO K. L. S.

PREFACE

This book is written on the assumption that musically all men are created free, though not necessarily equal. It is addressed to potential listeners rather than potential performers.

If you think you are not a musician or even a music-lover, read it. And if you think you are a musician or a music-lover, or both, read it just the same.

It presupposes no knowledge on your part, and it admits no fundamental ignorance. It does not worry about the hair-splittings of the technical scholars, nor is it concerned with the maudlin exaggerations of the sentimentalists.

It merely tries to approach the subject of music in a common-sense fashion, analyzing the effects of this mysterious art upon the casual listener, the so-called man in the street. It tries to find a reason for some of your reactions to musical performance and composition. It assumes, therefore, a universal instinct for such response, which may also be called, without severely stretching the play on words, a "Common Sense of Music."

Least of all does it try to exhaust its subject,

for that would be impossible. It skims lightly over the sea of music, following no definite course, and merely dipping here and there into its endless flood. Every example will suggest plenty of others, and it is partly in the hope of stimulating such individual research that this book was written.

All it asks is that you read it, try it on your piano (or what have you?) and then go about with your ears open.

It is impossible to express here the conventional thanks to those who have helped make this book, for too many people have been concerned. The author should mention, however, his father and mother, both honestly convinced of the necessity of music in a home; his sister, a natural pianist, who kept music in the air for him long before science had simplified such matters; his musical friends and fellow-enthusiasts of many years in Philadelphia, Princeton, Asheville and New York; and finally the thousands of encouraging listeners to his recent talks on music, whose stimulating interest has compelled him to put his thoughts on paper and proved in advance that there is literally a "Common Sense of Music."

New York City,
Christmas, 1923.

CONTENTS

THE COMMON SENSE OF MUSIC

"When music and courtesy are better understood and appreciated, there will be no war."

—Confucius.

THE COMMON SENSE OF MUSIC

CHAPTER I

THE LURE OF MELODY

WRITERS on music have treated it in two ways. Either they have insisted on a highly technical scholarship which made music an inexpressibly dull thing, or they have turned loose an unrestrained imagination which left it wallowing in the ridiculous.

Music has been given plenty of publicity during its few centuries of real achievement, but most people are to-day still in the dark as to what it is all about.

The difficulty lies partly with music and partly with its hearers.

When a man wants to advertise an article, he tries to think up a slogan which emphasizes some constant quality in that article, something that the public is certain to recognize as permanent and distinctive.

For instance, there was the brand of soap which needed only the simple legend, "It floats." So long as the soap floated, it made good; and, so far as I know, it always floated, and still does.

Then there is the chewing gum, about which we are told that "The Flavor Lasts." Nobody stops to ask what the flavor is, or whether we want it to last. I am informed by experts that it does last, and so the slogan is justified.

THE USES OF ADVERTISEMENT

Why can't the same thing be done with music? Chiefly because it affects different people in different ways.

You might say of a beautiful melody, "It floats," or of a Hungarian Rhapsody, "The Flavor Lasts," but how many would recognize the piece by the description?

Similarly Schubert's "Unfinished" might be called "The Symphony without a Headache," and Brahms "The composer you will eventually use," but few would be the wiser.

What then are the constant factors in music, the things by which individual compositions can be recognized? Obviously, the tunes.

"THE TUNE'S THE THING"

When a piece of music has no words, and perhaps no title that you can remember, there is only one way of reminding someone of it. You have to hum or whistle or sing or play the tune or a part of the tune. "By their tunes ye shall know them." It applies equally to Beethoven and Berlin, to Josef Haydn and to Victor Herbert.

Recognition is the first step toward musical appreciation. We like the things that we recognize. "Popular music is familiar music," and the whole problem of making good music popular is simply that of making it familiar.

PERHAPS THIS IS TOO PERSONAL

Have you ever noticed how a concert audience will applaud a familiar encore after a few bars have been played? They are not applauding the performer or the music. They are applauding themselves because they recognized it. That is human nature, and this honest enjoyment of recognition marks the significant progress of the real music-lover.

But the mere fact that music is easy to recognize does not prove its value. In general it works quite the other way. Those pieces which are most quickly grasped by the memory are likely to be the weakest musically, and the ones of which we are sure to tire most rapidly. Conversely, those things which take a little more concentration at the outset, and require repeated hearings before they are remembered, usually have the greatest permanent value.

The weakness of most popular music is that it slides too quickly and easily into the memory. Incidentally it slides out again just as quickly and easily.

Actually no music exists which can stand constant repetition. The problem of musical taste is to steer clear of the obvious and at the same time avoid such slavish devotion to any one composition as may eventually create boredom, regardless of intrinsic merit.

The careful housewife solves the same problem in the arrangement of her meals. No matter how fond her clients may be of a certain dish, she sees to it that it does not appear too often on her bill of fare, and particularly not in succession.

"COME OUT OF THE KITCHEN!"

But to get back to the subject of tunes. Somebody once asked how many notes it took to make a tune. The answer is two. Any combination of two tones is enough for a whistle or a bird-call, and may be made the basis of an entire melody. One of the oldest and most popular is the two-note combination that the cuckoo sang in the Garden of

CUCKOO CALL

Eden. Listen to it on any of the cuckoo instruments that you can get in a toy-store.

You will recognize the whistle that every kid uses when he wants the kid next door to "come on over." It is the eternal "come hither" whistle of the human race.

TRY THIS ON YOUR EAR

Consciously or unconsciously a lot of popular composers have recently based their tunes on this universal combination. Do you remember the Japanese Sandman, that Nora Bayes sang so insidiously? The first eighteen notes of the chorus are nothing more than the cuckoo call:

JAPANESE SANDMAN

But by harmonizing them in Japanese fashion (or rather, the near-Japanese fashion of Puccini's Madame Butterfly), the composer made his song sound quite original. Listen to it on a record, or get someone to play it for you, if you can't manage it yourself.

Then there is that lilting melody that swept

the country even more recently: Carolina in the Morning. Again the essence of the tune is the cuckoo call, eight exact quotations in a row

JAPANESE SANDMAN HARMONIZED À LA BUTTERFLY

to start the chorus, seventeen notes altogether, without variation:

CAROLINA IN THE MORNING

But once more the harmonizing is important, and it is this that gives character to the song. Try it for yourself, and notice how the same trick is used again and again, creating what is almost literally a two-toned chorus.

The same thing happened in a song called "Toot, toot, Tootsie, good-by," in which, naturally, the leading phrase is the "come hither whistle," applied to a steam engine.

TOOT, TOOT, TOOTSIE

Most marked of all is the two-tone foundation of one of Irving Berlin's hits, "Pack up your Sins." He uses the same combination in groups of half-a-dozen at a time, merely switching the key and moving gradually up the scale, employing a rag-time rhythm to give the necessary variety. With an actual total of about sixty notes from the innocent bird-call, this sophisticated chorus becomes literally "all cuckoo."

PACK UP YOUR SINS

In more serious music this popular combination is equally common. Beethoven has it in his Pastoral Symphony, with the frank intention of suggesting the cuckoo himself, and an old French composer, Daquin, wrote a piano piece, Le Coucou, glorifying the bird in the shape of a finger exercise. Haydn makes it an important feature of his Children's Symphony, as it offers an instrument and a part in which the interpreter can hardly go wrong.

There seems to be some sort of relationship also between the cuckoo call and the traditional lullaby. Many of the cradle songs of the world address their refractory infants largely in these two tones, the classic example being the German "Schlafe, Kindlein." Brahms, in his famous Wiegenlied, turns the notes upside down, using the lower one first, but gets a similar effect.

THE TRIPLE THREAT IN MUSIC

The best way to find out the possible combinations of three tones in music is to study the familiar bugle-calls. The ordinary bugle really achieves all its results with only three tones as a basis, and these three tones are probably the most important in the whole musical scale. You can hear them in Reveille (listen for it in Berlin's "Oh, how I hate to get up in the Morning"), and it is a simple matter to pick them out on the piano.

REVEILLE

In the second half of the rising call, following "I can't get 'em up," etc., the bugle strikes a high note, but this is the same as the opening tone, only one octave higher. So the entire call is actually limited to three tones.

"Taps," the bugle tune for bed-time, uses the same three tones, in a slightly different pattern, and slowly, with the opening note again duplicated high up, but only once.

TAPS

While the army bugle can actually produce other tones after a fashion, they are practically never used. All the stock calls and marching melodies are three-tone combinations. Nothing more is required than the simple rhythmic accompaniment of the drums to give the soldiers or the Boy Scouts plenty of music for miles of marching.

MARCHING MELODY

The three fundamental tones of the bugle play an important part in some of the most significant melodies of the world. They seem to have set the pattern for all the great national anthems, and this coincidence must be something more than merely accidental. Our own Star Spangled Banner starts right in with the notes of the bugle, and announces its most important phrase in six notes derived from the three universal tones:

STAR SPANGLED BANNER

The German Wacht am Rhein did the same thing in its opening phrase of eight notes, and the arrangement is so similar that one can forgive the spectators at Yale football games who have invariably come to their feet during Bright College Years (to the tune of the German anthem) under the impression that they were hearing the Star Spangled Banner.

DIE WACHT AM RHEIN

The French Marseillaise derives its character from the universal figure of three tones, starting at the top, but only after two of them have served as an introduction, with an outsider to point the way to the climax:

LA MARSEILLAISE

Similarly the old Russian anthem, still sung in America as a hymn tune, and as the collegiate

"Hail, Pennsylvania," switches off after the first note, only to come back immediately to the fundamental three-tone figure that seems to give solidity to every one of these great melodies:

RUSSIAN NATIONAL ANTHEM

"Dixie" starts with the same combination, runs up the scale, and then works its way back in a series of jumps, landing always on a bugle note:

Classic examples of the three-tone figure are in the start of the Tannhäuser March, as well as the Pilgrims' Chorus, the prayer in Weber's Freischütz, the "thanks" theme in Beethoven's Pastoral Symphony, and (with the middle note omitted) the call of the Flying Dutchman in Wagner's famous overture:

The same composer lets Siegfried build up his horn melody from the bugle basis, and of course there are plenty of actual horn imitations, concentrating on the same three tones.

SIEGFRIED'S HORN

Three well-known hymn tunes start with bugle tones: "Come, Thou Almighty King" at the top, "Holy, Holy, Holy" at the bottom, and "True-hearted, Whole-hearted" in the middle. The Long, Long Trail rests on the same foundation.

"Over There" is, of course, obviously and intentionally a bugle tune.

When you can do so much with two or three tones, it is easy to believe that four were formerly enough for an entire scale. If you listen to a clock chiming the quarter-hours, as for instance in the Metropolitan Tower of New York, you will hear a four-tone combination that is very old and very popular. It varies the pattern for each quarter, but the tones are always the same. Here is a typical clock-tune in four tones (the Westminster chime):

WESTMINSTER CHIME

Then the clock strikes a low, booming note, and it is probably "Three o'clock in the Morning." The second melody of that popular waltz, incidentally, was taken directly from the third quarter of the Westminster chime:

THREE O'CLOCK

In their original order, these four notes made a tune that was once widely sung, and still finds a wistful echo here and there:

HOW DRY I AM!

Musically its chief interest is in the way Franz Lehar used it for the start of his Merry Widow Waltz:

MERRY WIDOW WALTZ

The same four tones, in a different order, give the opening of Sweet Adeline, the idol of all barber-shop "close harmony":

SWEET ADELINE

It is almost the same in the old "Say Au Revoir, but not Good-bye." Beethoven and Brahms both used the combination frequently, and it is closely related to the simpler and still more fundamental three-tone figure of the bugle.

THIS IS ANCIENT HISTORY

Inserting one extra note gives us the old five-tone scale, which was used most effectively in the modern tune of Stumbling. The composer worked his trick with rhythm rather than melody, simply shifting his accent from one note to another, as he repeated the five-tone formula three times in succession:

This suggests the possibilities of a merely superficial analysis of the music that you may hear at any time. You will find constant relationships of this sort, running through all kinds of melodies, and often you will be surprised at the close kinship between a so-called "classic" and the most obvious of jazz tunes.

THAT PATTERNIZING HABIT

You will find also that the fundamental patterns of music possess an extraordinary similarity, the same combinations appearing again and again, just as they do in carpets and wall-paper and lamp-shades.

There are actually only twelve different tones in the accepted scale, as you play it on the piano. The rest are mere repetitions on different levels of pitch. Mathematics can easily work out the possible permutations and combinations of twelve tones, carried through seven octaves, and the total is a big one. But experience seems to show that only a limited number of these patterns and arrangements can be credited with a universal significance.

To remember a tune, we have to have certain landmarks on which the mind or the musical sense rests easily. It must not be absolutely commonplace, for then we should soon tire of it. But we demand certain labels of familiarity, to act as guides to our memories.

Do you realize that Rachmaninoff's famous Prelude is really a study on three tones? If you listen for them, the whole piece becomes quite simple.

We remember the Wagner operas by their so-called "motives," the little scraps of melody by which the composer identifies his characters and episodes. If we think of a symphony, we do so in terms of the "themes," which are simply the tunes. There is no way of reminding anyone of a particular piece of music

PATTERN OF RACHMANINOFF PRELUDE C♯ MINOR

except through the tune. We may whistle a bit of it, or play it with one finger on the piano, or hum it in uncertain fashion. But it is our one means of identification.

Never let anyone tell you that great music exists that is absolutely without melody. That is the fallacy of some of our modernists, who think that they can string along a lot of notes without any connection, and that somehow the result will make sense.

TUNE UP, COMPOSERS!

Every great composer was first and foremost an inventor of tunes. When he failed to think up an absolutely original combination, and only a few succeeded in doing that, he gave his melodic idea a new twist, or he developed it in such a way, by harmony and form and instrumentation, that he made it essentially his own.

The mere fact that you may not recognize a melody at a first hearing does not mean that it is not there. Perhaps the fault is yours rather than the composer's. Even a fairly obvious composition may require several hearings before you grasp the essentials of its tune.

Listen to all music in the same spirit. Give it all an equal chance. Don't force yourself to hear the things you are sure you don't like, but don't go on listening to cheap stuff after it has begun to bore you.

If you like a tune, don't be ashamed to say so. If you change your mind later, that is your privilege.

YOU ARE THE MASTER OF YOUR TASTE

In the same way, resist the temptation to express an insincere opinion merely for the sake of agreeing with someone who may be considered an authority. The standards of musical taste are by no means fixed, and what is condemned to-day may be rapturously applauded to-morrow.

When, however, a piece has become well established as a "classic," by the unanimous approval of thousands of open-minded listeners, don't be in a hurry to disagree with the conventional point of view. Give yourself at least the opportunity to find out what you honestly think, after a fair number of hearings.

Don't worry about your musical taste. It will develop normally if you hear enough music, both good and bad. Form your own opinions and use your own ears.

CHAPTER II

OLD TUNES FOR NEW

Somebody once made this distinction between popular and "classical" music: "Popular music has tunes, and classical music has not."

That is a pretty hard saying, but it actually represents an idea that still lingers in the consciousness of too many people: the idea that good music is something difficult, something over our heads, something usually summed up in the blanket condemnation of the word "highbrow."

This popular attitude has been fostered and definitely encouraged by the critics and scholars of music, most of whom insist on placing it on a pedestal and emphasizing the exclusive quality of its appreciation. Yet it is possible to appreciate music without knowing a great deal about it, and there are those who know it well from a technical angle who nevertheless fail to appreciate it properly.

The snobbish treatment of music, the ignoring of popular taste, or the contemptuous dismissal of obvious facts as of slight importance, these are factors in the surprisingly slow development of the Common Sense of Music in America. Our well-intentioned guides have tried to pour music into the people from the top, instead of letting it grow normally from the ground up. They have impatiently dismissed every sincere expression of a limited or utterly mistaken appreciation, and by insisting upon "the best or nothing," they have thrown the average listener on the defensive, and he has sullenly decided that "that classical stuff is over his head." He does not pretend to know anything about music, but he "knows what he likes," and this is usually little more than jazz and melody ballads.

WHAT ARE YOU AFRAID OF?

The very word "classic" strikes terror to the heart of many a listener. Yet, after all, a classic is merely a composition that has proved its permanent value, by a consensus of approval covering an adequate period of years. It would be far better to call the classics "permanent music," as contrasted with the transient material that often wins a more immediate popularity.

Actually the popular tunes of the day represent the line of least resistance in music. They are the easiest things for the memory to assimilate, and while they do not last long, they are with us heart and soul during their brief span of life.

It is impossible to ignore this tremendous factor in modern musical taste, and it cannot be dismissed with a mere gesture of contempt. Rather may the popular music be utilized as a means toward the end of appreciating the classics themselves.

PUTTING JAZZ TO WORK

To say that our popular composers have discovered the classics and adapted them to their own use is no longer news. It is now admitted that practically every popular hit of the day is based upon some really fine music of the past, the invention of a great composer, or perhaps an immortal folk-song.

Some of this imitation is accidental, for the whole melodic material of music has already repeated itself many times over, and unconscious plagiarism is almost inevitable. But in most cases the borrowing has been deliberate, and often the title or the words of a song have given a shamefaced credit to the original composer.

This is not to be interpreted as an argument against second-hand composition. If the great melodies of the world get a hearing even in a cheapened and garbled form, it is better than keeping them buried altogether, and an obvious popular version may often be the only means of drawing average attention to the beauty of the original. If writers use the same plots, characters and literary forms over and over again, why should not the composers of music have the same privilege?

This is therefore intended merely as an analysis of a condition which is now generally recognized, the literal utilization to-day of "Old Tunes for New," a consistent melodic exchange which is gradually producing a jazz literature running parallel to the whole repertoire of great composition of the past.

CREDIT WHERE CREDIT IS DUE

There was a time, when popular song-writers were just entering the paradise of genius, and discovering how easy it was to pluck the fruit from the trees of knowledge, that they took pains to draw attention to the source of their melodic inspiration. Do you remember years ago That Mesmerizing Mendelssohn Tune, which of course was the familiar Spring Song in a slight rag-time disguise? It was perhaps the first song of its kind to achieve marked popularity, and it led the way for a number of others, each glorifying some classic, Rubinstein's Melody in F, the Wedding March from Lohengrin, and its companion from the pen of Mendelssohn, Schubert's Moment Musical (how many classic dancers, armed with double flutes, have skipped to its melody?), Rachmaninoff's Prelude, and what not. You may remember also My Cousin Carus', which quoted a strain from Pagliacci inseparably associated with the great tenor.

THEY DO IT BETTER NOW

These were early and comparatively naïve efforts. To-day they have their parallel in Blossom Time, an entire operetta based on the life and compositions of Franz Schubert. The Song of Love, which is the waltz hit of this highly successful musical comedy, makes clever use of the chief melody in the first movement of Schubert's Unfinished Symphony. It is a really good tune, and the whole success of Blossom Time has been a legitimately musical phenomenon. The fact that Schubert himself is the hero of the piece may be considered as giving due credit to the composer, who certainly is to-day a more vital figure for the American public than he was before Blossom Time appeared.

We have had also in the not very distant past the Blue Danube Blues from Good Morning,

Dearie, a fox-trot rendering of the immortal Strauss waltz, and the Song of India, a literal jazz transcription of the appealing oriental melody of Rimsky-Korsakoff. The very name of that composer would frighten many people away from his music, but after they have danced to the Song of India, even Snegourotschka becomes a possibility.

THE MUSICIAN IN THE WOODPILE

Modern kings of jazz, such as Paul Whiteman and Vincent Lopez, have, with the help of skilled composers like Savino and Lampe, made dance versions of every kind of "classical music," from Beethoven's Moonlight Sonata to MacDowell's To a Wild Rose. They have borrowed with equal success from the Funeral March of Chopin and the Hungarian Rhapsodies of Liszt. Theirs, however, is a purely orchestral music, a mere question of arrangement and transcription. They have introduced a new rhythm and a new instrumental coloring, but they have not tampered appreciably with the original melodies.

One of the first great popular hits to make a quiet and unobtrusive raid upon the classics was I'm Always Chasing Rainbows, that frankly quixotic song that spread itself over the country just as the World War drew to a close.

It was Harrison Fisher, the illustrator, a great lover of Chopin's music, who brought the tune to the attention of Harry Carroll, of Tinpan Alley. He played for the rag-time connoisseur a piano record of Chopin's Fantasie Impromptu, and pointed out the beauty of the slow melody in the middle. Mr. Carroll saw the point and produced I'm Always Chasing Rainbows, with an almost literal transcription of Chopin's tune for his chorus.

I'M ALWAYS CHASING RAINBOWS

(All these tones duplicated in Chopin's Fantasie Impromptu)

The words to that song-hit were written by a certain Joe McCarthy, who was later engaged to do the lyrics for the musical comedy Irene. He passed on the tip to Harry Tierney, who was responsible for the music to that show, and Mr. Tierney also saw the point. They decided that this fellow Chopin probably had some more good tunes up his sleeve, and they went systematically through his piano pieces to find out. In the middle part of the Minute Waltz they found the melody they wanted. By putting it into fox-trot time, they secured the chorus of Castle of Dreams, the hit of Irene, and note for note Chopin's music.

MINUTE WALTZ (Middle)

CASTLE OF DREAMS

This was flagrant plagiarism, if you will, but it certainly brought Chopin into the American home.

The thing became a habit after that. There were whole cycles of songs based upon the same original melody, and when a phrase had once proved its popularity, it was likely to be used again and again. Beethoven's little Minuet in G (played on the violin quite as much as on the piano) was one of the general sources of inspiration. The characteristic portions of this tune are in the opening phrase and its answer:

BEETHOVEN'S MINUET

ANSWER (Imitation)

The first was quite definitely imitated in a popular war-song, Rose of No Man's Land, and the second may have suggested the chorus of Apple Blossom Time in Normandy, of an earlier vintage. There was also a song about the ukuleles calling, which did not attain great popularity, although it used the entire melody of the Minuet.

ROSE OF NO MAN'S LAND

APPLE BLOSSOM TIME

For a time the aria, One Fine Day, from Puccini's Madame Butterfly, influenced much of the popular music. Thinly disguised, it provided the basis of The Vamp, and it came out boldly in every detail as Cio-Cio San, a frank and perhaps legitimate borrowing.

The Hippodrome song, Poor Butterfly, took toll of the story, but not of Puccini's melody. Rather did it suggest the familiar "Then You'll Remember Me," from The Bohemian Girl:

When Avalon appeared, however, it was discovered that the tenor aria, "E lucevan le Stelle," from La Tosca, had been completely appropriated, and Puccini's publishers, Ricordi & Co., brought suit.* There was a heated debate, in which Archer Gibson, the private organist of Charles M. Schwab, was called as a witness, and tried to argue that Avalon might just as easily be traced to thirty or forty different classics. But the Ricordis won their point, and the matter was settled with damages quoted as high as $25,000,

*Recently Puccini won another suit in defense of his Butterfly, and incidentally sold the entire jazz rights of Tosca to an American publisher.

while Avalon abruptly disappeared from the market.

The parallel between the two melodies is interesting. Mario Cavaradossi, hero of Puccini's opera, sings his big aria in the third act, just before they shoot him. (Opera composers generally manage to give their tenors and sopranos their best music just before they kill them off.) The real melody of the aria starts in minor key:

E LUCEVAN LE STELLE

This does not sound much like Avalon, but turn it into major and see what you get:

SAME IN MAJOR

Now put this into fox-trot time, with simplified harmony, and it is only a step to Avalon itself:

SAME IN FOX-TROT TIME

Further examples could be multiplied by the hundreds. "My Baby's Arms" copied the Cavatina of Raff. "Crooning" was merely a variation of Liszt's Liebestraum, which has also appeared in waltz form. "Sweetheart" called on Tannhäuser's Evening Star for its inspiration.

There was a tune taken from Tschaikowsky's Romance, and another from the same composer's string quartet, the slow movement (Andante Cantabile). Lou Hirsch found his Love Nest in the chorus of Anona, plus a strain from an unfamiliar song of Oscar Straus, incidentally contributing a remarkable study in compact musical form to the popular literature.

ANONA

Jerome Kern turns instinctively to folk-music and admits a Bohemian ancestry. His "Till the Clouds Roll by" is from a Bohemian original, and has also figured as a closely related hymn-tune. When Mr. Kern modernized "Kingdom Come" he did something that bespoke honest musicianship.

Geoffrey O'Hara made his first killing with the stuttering song, K-k-k-katy, a great war-time favorite, which is originally a folk-tune, also in use as a college air out on the Pacific

Coast. When he set to music the words "Give a Man a Horse he can Ride" he looked for a fittingly vigorous melody, and he seems to have found it in the old waltz song popularized by Blanche Ring, Yip I Yaddy, I Yay, or whatever the spelling was. O'Hara's more serious "There is no Death" is reminiscent of The Lost Chord in its climax.

When popular composers have run short of classics, they have borrowed from each other, or from themselves. Injunctions and suits crop up from time to time when the raiding grows a little too bold. Four bars are legally the limit to borrowing from copyright music.

If a song makes a hit, the imitations are likely to follow thick and fast. This includes the words as well as the music.

Sometimes one melody is not enough to create a popular song. That riot of Græco-Americanism, "Yes, we have no Bananas," contains three melodic germs. Its opening strain is a shock. If you have ever listened to Handel's Messiah, the oratorio that is sung every Christmas in Carnegie Hall, and even more often elsewhere, you may remember the solemn moment when the chorus rises (and the audience rises too, by a fixed tradition) for the famous "Hallelujah Chorus." The first four notes uttered by the mixed voices are intended to convey the word "Hallelujah."

Hereafter they will inevitably suggest their modern offspring, "Yes, we have no," and jazzinine listeners will unconsciously add their mental "bananas." There is no escaping the exact parallel.

YES, WE HAVE NO BANANAS

But this is only the beginning. The Bohemian Girl contains a fine melody, "I Dreamt that I dwelt in Marble Halls." Its middle section is literally transcribed in the corresponding portion of "Yes, we have no," etc. Next comes (by

I DREAMT THAT I DWELT (Middle section)

"WE HAVE," etc.

way of "An Old-Fashioned Garden") a complete phrase from that good old American song, "Aunt Dinah's Quilting Party," also known by the words of its chorus, "I was seeing Nellie Home," and at the end the Hallelujah of Handel once more resounds triumphantly, an everlasting reminder of our unconsciously good taste.

AUNT DINAH'S QUILTING PARTY
(Copied by "An Old Fashioned Garden")

"WE HAVE," etc.

("Oh, bring back my Bonnie to me" may be recognized in the closing line, but as this is a conventional ending, the parallel is probably accidental.)

But even such absurdities need not make us ashamed. We like better things than we realize. Often we would be surprised at the revelations of our inner preference.

A luncheon chairman in the far South, insistently "lowbrow" in his reactions to music, commented upon a really serious composition to which his club had listened with a sincere and uniform attention. "That may be all very well," he remarked at the close, "but give me 'Hail, Hail! the Gang's all here' and 'We won't go Home until Morning.'" As it happened, he had testified to an inherently good taste, for those are both great tunes. "Hail, Hail! the Gang's all here" is merely the American version of Sir Arthur Sullivan's clever parody of Verdi's Anvil

"HAIL, HAIL!" (Pirates of Penzance) | ANVIL CHORUS (Il Trovatore)

Chorus from Il Trovatore. The composer of The Mikado, Pinafore, The Lost Chord and "Onward, Christian Soldiers" wrote that rollicking tune as a chorus in The Pirates of Penzance.

As for "We won't go Home until Morning," better known in England by its second stanza, "For he's a jolly good Fellow," it is one of the oldest and best of the French soldier-tunes, "Malbrough s'en va-t-en Guerre," a satire on the Duke of Marlborough, recently revived by the Chauve-Souris in America. Marie Antoinette sang it as a lullaby, and Beethoven used it in one of his symphonies to represent the French army. What a demon for culture that club chairman was, after all!

"HONESTY IS THE BEST POLICY"

Once more, in all sincerity: Don't worry about your musical taste. Just stop being a hypocrite and say honestly what you like and what you don't. Eventually you may find a reason for your choice.

There are people who are ashamed of liking so good an American tune as Turkey in the Straw, also known as Zip, Coon. There is an irresistible dance-rhythm in that piece, and it has established its immortality in every barn of the country. David Guion, a young Texas composer, made a concert arrangement of Turkey in the Straw, and now many of the great pianists have it in their repertoire. There is nothing the matter with that tune, nor with the man who likes it.

Dixie, Maryland (from a German Christmas song, "O Tannenbaum"), Old Folks at Home, My Old Kentucky Home, Old Black Joe, "Massa's in de cold, cold Ground," "Carry me back to Old Virginny,"—these are all great melodies, alive with the spark of genius. Stephen Foster was by nature the greatest of all American composers. But his rare gift of melody could not produce the symphonies of a Beethoven, for it remained practically undeveloped.

THE MUSIC-LOVER'S PROGRESS

The love of a good tune is the surest starting-point on the road to musical appreciation. Let your taste grow in a logical and normal fashion.

You will follow the line of least resistance at first, for that is human nature. But gradually you will tire of the cheap and obvious things in music. You will find that some pieces grow tiresome very quickly, whereas others become more fascinating every time you listen to them.

If you own a phonograph or a player-piano, your library of records will improve in an inevitable upward curve.

You may discover some immortal composition quite by accident, but this very accident will make its acquisition all the more satisfying.

PERSONALLY CONDUCTED

By the time you have progressed by natural steps through the melodious trifles of Nevin, Chaminade, Delibes, Moszkowski and Godard, past the successive stages of Grieg-mania, Tschaikowsky-madness and Puccini-worship, to the heights of Schubert, Schumann, Wagner, Chopin, and finally Bach, Beethoven and Brahms, you will be a music-lover in the true sense of the word.

Not one of these composers is exclusive. There is room for all of them in a growing appreciation of music, and it would be a serious mistake to eliminate a single link from the endless chain of melodic inspiration.

Echoes and imitations are also by no means unforgivable sins. The invention of one mind may be glorified in the adaptation of another. Liszt opened the treasure of Hungarian music to the world in his Rhapsodies, all built from borrowed material. He transcribed the songs of Schubert and the operatic airs of Verdi for the piano, of which he was perhaps the greatest master of all time.

"FINDINGS, KEEPINGS"

Brahms saved much good folk-music from oblivion, as did Haydn, Schubert and Beethoven. Wagner drew copiously on the melodic inventiveness of his friend and father-in-law, Liszt, and did not hesitate to imitate Weber and other earlier composers.

In our own day Fritz Kreisler has proved himself a gifted transcriber of Viennese melodies, indefatigable in his search for old material that would sound well in a new violinistic garb. But he has put the stamp of his own personality on all his work, and, like the paraphrases of Liszt, it has become truly his own.

Plagiarism is not the greatest sin of art, least of all of music. The unforgivable crimes are dullness, ugliness and insincerity, and the greatest of these is insincerity.

CHAPTER III

THE ANATOMY OF LISTENING

How do people listen to music? Any bright little boy would probably answer, "with their ears"; but nine times out of ten he would be wrong.

Admitting that music must be audible before it can affect a human being, the real art of listening does not begin until after those antennæ that we call ears have picked out of the air some sounds sufficiently interesting to create a physical or emotional or intellectual response.

Many people do not listen to music at all. Their eyes are so much stronger than their ears that they allow visible things to command their attention to the exclusion of everything else. That is a principle well known to performers and managers.

A big proportion of those who attended Paderewski's recent concerts went to see him rather than to hear him. They asked anxiously about the length of his famous chrysanthemum hair. They were disappointed when he had the stage lights turned low. They were chiefly interested in Paderewski as a world figure, a musical statesman, a genius who could do many things well, and who still played the piano in a compelling fashion. But his music was really a secondary matter.

I have heard Jascha Heifetz criticized because he did not smile when he played the violin. Farrar, Chaliapin, Jeritza and other great artists appeal to the eye as well as to the ear. Our most successful orchestral conductors are those who "swing a mean baton." They conquer by their gestures, their motions, the quivering messages of shapely backs and eloquent arms. One does not have to listen to orchestral music if the conductor acts it with sufficient realism.

Even piano-playing leans on the eye for support. We credit a pianist with a "sympathetic" or "caressing" touch, with wonderful power and "temperament." Actually we may mean that he moves his hands caressingly, or swings them powerfully, or shakes his head temperamentally.

A pianist without these visible evidences of his feelings is considered "cold." Once the eye has assured us that we are to hear a crashing chord, or a tender melody, we often take the rest for granted. Hence also our hesitation to accept the recording of a pianist's playing as his actual performance. Our ears are too lazy to do the whole job, and with no one at the keyboard our eyes wander away to other things.

PHYSIOLOGICALLY CONSIDERED

The anatomy of listening deals chiefly with three parts of the body, the feet, the heart and the head; and to one or more of these the great mass of all the world's music has been addressed. Granting that people listen to music at all, which is not necessarily true, the great majority listen primarily with their feet.

The almost universal habit of foot-listening has created the huge mass of foot-music, the music which we whistle, to which we dance, and which inserts itself most easily into our consciousness.

The sense of rhythm is evidently a physical matter, a physical response to a physical stimulus. We can't help keeping time to good rhythm. When the band goes by, or the orchestra strikes up a teasing fox-trot, we "just can't make our feet behave."

THE PHYSICAL SENSE OF TIME

There is very little credit in having this universal response to rhythm. When people brag about it, it is very much like boasting that whenever they are hungry they eat. But the purely physical response to rhythm does not indicate by any means that everyone is able to beat time for a band, or count off a certain number of measures correctly. There is all the difference in the world between creating rhythm and responding to it.

The universality of rhythm is shown by the number of dance forms in music. We have marches, waltzes, minuets, mazurkas, polonaises, polkas, one-steps, two-steps, gavottes and plain old-fashioned jigs, reels, clogs and hoe-downs.

Popular composers found out long ago that human nature responds to a tickling of the feet. They wrote Green Sleeves and The Irish Washerwoman in the olden time. Nowadays they write fox-trots and one-steps. Turkey in the Straw is a wonderful piece of foot-music. So is Dixie. So is The Girl I Left behind Me.

THIS ONE DIED HARD

The case of Dardanella was an interesting study in the significance of rhythm. The man

DARDANELLA

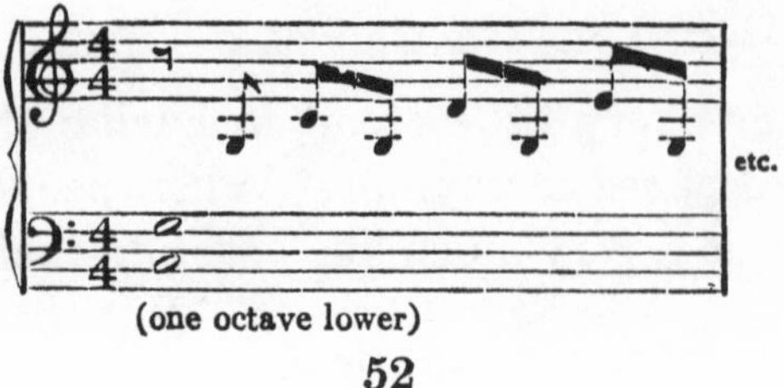

who wrote that tune started by simply establishing a rhythmic figure, which he repeated over and over until he was sure that all the feet were moving.

Then he put a line of notes over this rhythmic figure, merely going up the scale by half-tones, "chromatically," as musicians would say, but always keeping up the insistent beat of the time:

CHROMATIC AIR

(rhythmic accompaniment continues)

After a little of that, he was able to bring in any kind of a melody for a chorus, and it would necessarily sound fine. Few people remember that chorus now. But play them the little hammering phrase of eight notes and watch their feet grow restless!

Keeping time to music is no disgrace. The best of musicians do it, in their minds if not with actual shoe-leather. It is a wonderful starting-point for enthusiasm, this normal, physical foot-response, but, after all, it does not prove much about the appreciation of music.

Bill Simmons summed it up in a popular chorus of some years ago:

Mister, let me tell you, when the music starts (boom, boom) I can't keep still,
Got a feeling in my feet just like St. Vitus's dance, although it is against my will.
Trying mighty hard-a for to concentrate (boom, boom), what shall I do?
The music sets me going like a jumping-jack, I gotta dance till the band gets through.

That chorus might well be taken as a motto by some of our modern jazz-hounds. They are foot-listeners, pure and simple, and the emphasis is on the second adjective.

Thousands never progress beyond the foot-listening stage. They go through life quivering with repressed rhythm, and all they need is a good, active trap-drummer to get them under way.

LO, THE POOR WHITE-MAN

The Indians got the same effect with a mere tom-tom, and probably the first savage musician satisfied his soul with simply beating on a hollow log with a club. When a child runs a stick over fence-palings, or romps around the nursery, clapping or shouting in time with its jumps, it is doing the same thing that appealed to its parents at their last dance: indulging a sense of rhythm; and both are closely akin to the savage, with the exception that he made much less fuss about it.

Not that people in general dance in time. Far from it. But it is the orchestra playing in time that stimulates their rhythmic centers, and even though these respond in very clumsy fashion, the music has done its work.

THIS COMES FROM JOHNS HOPKINS

It is said that when you make a pun you are really not using your brain at all, just your medulla oblongata, or whatever it is. The similarity in sounds causes what is practically a reflex action, and out pops the pun, without any mental effort at all.

That is about the way the sense of rhythm works with most of us. We don't stop to think or analyze. We just go ahead and keep time the best we can. We are all foot-listeners by nature, and some of us take a long time to develop beyond that primitive stage.

At that, much good music has been written whose appeal was primarily to the feet. Turkey in the Straw has already been sufficiently eulogized. There is nothing wrong with the Sousa marches, Sambre et Meuse, or the Marche Lorraine. The waltzes of Johann Strauss are great melodies, but their appeal is still largely one of rhythm.

Don't be ashamed of the things your feet do under musical stimulus, but don't be satisfied with this purely physical response, for it is only a beginning.

MUSICAL HEART-DISEASE

Those who listen with their hearts may be a little higher up, but this would be hard to prove. Many foot-listeners are also to a certain extent heart-listeners, and most people are absolutely satisfied with the naïvely emotional response to music.

Heart-music is again all very well in its way, but it also hardly goes far enough. There are some who seem to think that the joy of listening to music is destroyed if one knows too much about it. They prefer to succumb to their emotions, and let it go at that.

The great drawback to this kind of listening is that it is affected by so much outside of the music itself. Try over any of the so-called "Heart-Songs" of the world. You will find that their appeal depends not only on the melody, but the words, the title, and the inevitable associations brought up by them.

Our own mothers and our own homes deserve most of the credit for the success of the great mass of home and mother songs. Their tunes are easy and appealing, but we are predisposed in their favor because we immediately create our own sentimental picture of what the composer wants his music to suggest.

Melody, as already indicated, is a most important factor in music. But it can get along with very little real substance if it has the support of an attractive title and appealing words. Mother Machree and Little Grey Home in the West are merely reminders of our own mothers and our own homes. Any "Dream of Love" will call up sentimental images, from childhood to the grave. The melody may be a great one, but how accurately can we gauge its total responsibility?

Stevenson called the tune of Home, Sweet Home a case of "wallowing naked in the pathetic"; but to what extent was he influenced by the words? That is the weakness of heart-music. It has too much else to lean upon.

VISIBLE MEANS OF SUPPORT

Some concert-singers seem to make it a rule to give their hearers everything but music, particularly in their encores. They talk baby-talk, tell jokes and do a pantomime, all with a tonal background. But the music is negligible.

That is also the fundamental weakness of "grand opera," which is heart-music *par excellence*. The story, the words, the action, the costumes, the scenery, and perhaps the social glamour as well, create an illusion so strong that an emotional response is almost inevitable, and the music itself may have very little to do with it.

THE WAGNERIAN EMINENCE

About the only operatic music that consistently stands on its own feet is that of Richard Wagner. That is why we hear excerpts from his operas played in the concert halls, an honor seldom given to any other operatic composer.

It is all very well to listen to music with our hearts, but let us not be overwhelmed by sentiment, or, worse yet, sentimentality. An honestly emotional melody may affect us directly and strongly, even though no program has been announced, no title suggested. It may even be argued that melody is the logical messenger of emotion in music. But it takes a very great composer to deliver such a message directly, without help of words, program, or previous association.

This matter of association, tradition, habit, is

a most important factor in music. We all know the stories of murders that were stopped, friendships that were patched up, marriages renewed and burglaries uncommitted, through the sudden intervention of some familiar melody. Here is heart-music rampant, the ultimate in the psychology of association! The tune itself may have been utterly worthless. But because a mother sang it at a cradle, or a sweetheart at the turn of the stairs, it becomes suddenly an irresistible influence.

When the soldiers sang Tipperary or The Long, Long Trail, they glorified the music by association. It was as significant to them as the symphony of a Brahms or a Beethoven to a confirmed music-lover.

MELODY'S HEART-INTEREST

There is, however, great heart-music in the world, and much of it can be honestly appreciated without moving one inch from the seat of the emotions. Most of the finer folk-songs have a distinct heart-interest. They appeal by a genuinely moving melody, which often fits several sets of words equally well.

An old German folk-song, "Innsbruck ich muss dich lassen," became one of the most solemn of Lenten hymns, and the tune of our own Star

Spangled Banner originally belonged to a ribald tavern song, To Anacreon in Heaven.

Compare the associations called up by the different sets of words used to the tune generally known as John Brown's Body. As the Battle Hymn of the Republic it is a most inspiring anthem. As a college football song it quickly develops a banal streak. Kiwanis clubs sing it as an exhortation to "S-m-i-l-e," and there are plenty of other versions, including one which eventually agrees that "They were only playing leapfrog."

ART AND UTILITY

Actually such a tune does not belong in the realm of heart-music. It is a purely utilitarian article, adaptable to any purpose, for the simple reason that it is easy to sing, and that everybody knows it. Julia Ward Howe happened to write great words which fit it after considerable shoehorn gymnastics, but that does not make it a solemn or an essentially patriotic tune.

The old Russian national anthem has been used with equal success as an inspiration to the students of the University of Pennsylvania and an opening hymn for rural congregations. America is merely the republican version of God Save the King, and it serves equally well to express the aspirations of a dozen other countries.

Our hearts are interesting little companions, and we like to listen to their prattle. But they are frightfully changeable. They flutter with every breeze, and do the silliest things without any real reason behind them.

"HEARTS AND FLOWERS"

That is why heart-music is not entirely dependable. It falls too easily under the spell of non-essentials. It enlists the coöperation of word-slingers, scene-shifters, caption-writers, costumers and valentine poets, and it is more than likely to lose its integrity in the process.

But much real heart-music has adhered to a single purpose and accomplished it. Stephen Foster's fine melodies are almost unthinkable divorced from their own original words. Old Folks at Home means something quite apart from the negroes of the South. So do My Old Kentucky Home and Old Black Joe.

Call to mind also such songs as Annie Laurie, Comin' thro' the Rye, Auld Lang Syne, etc. They have a permanent heart-quality which no change of words could alter. They are purely melodic in their appeal, and hence purely emotional. No "rhythmic kick" is needed here, and no depths of intellectual analysis. It is heart-music at its best and simplest.

A FORGOTTEN ART?

Popular composers of modern times have seldom struck the same note of inevitability. The "melody ballads" of the day are mostly quite obvious tunes set to words of unmistakable intention but no real distinction. Ernest Ball has been perhaps the most successful in striking the popular note, and Carrie Jacobs-Bond, in such a song as A Perfect Day, shows the value of the simple melody from Faust which was her unconscious model.

Victor Herbert, Cadman, Ethelbert Nevin and Reginald De Koven have shown a similar gift at times, and in England Sir Arthur Sullivan has shared the winning of hearts with Elgar, Liza Lehmann and Amy Woodforde-Finden. Grieg scores strongly with "I Love You" and other short heart-pieces. Tschaikowsky is overflowing with the same kind of music. Liszt secures honorable mention for his Liebestraum, with Rubinstein's Melody in F and Dvorak's Humoresque running neck and neck.

The greatest composers have not dabbled much in conventional heart-music, but Mendelssohn, Schubert and Schumann took an occasional fling at everyday emotions, while Chaminade, Godard, Moszkowski, Drigo, and various obscure members of the Czecho-Slovak fraternity ran wild over the same rich field.

When Bach, Beethoven, Brahms or Wagner had an emotion to express, they did it, of course, but with a supreme command of materials that required far more than an accelerated heart-action for either their creation or their interpretation.

So much for heart-music. It has its place in the world, but it is not enough. While the emotional response enters into practically all appreciative listening, it cannot begin to do the whole work.

THE MENTAL ABERRATION

But to argue that music is entirely a matter for the intellect is equally wrong. Those who think they can listen to music with their heads alone are just as much at fault as those who try to get along with no more than a foot or a heart response.

Actually very little good music has been written as an appeal to pure reason. Some scholars insist upon emphasizing the intellectual quality, but they find no material of lasting value that has not also an emotional or a physical appeal.

Bach is credited with writing the most brainy music in history, but his permanent popularity depends upon his dramatic sense and his ability to create memorable melodies. He used his head constantly, but for the complete expression of instincts that were essentially human.

DRAMATIZING INTELLECT

To Bach the adventures of his tunes through an "invention" or a fugue were actually exciting, and he can make them exciting also to a listener who has taken the trouble to find out what it is all about. In his St. Matthew Passion the materials of the New Testament became a huge drama, the most significant in all history.

Intellect alone may be the excuse for a composition, but it cannot possibly become the ground of its permanence. Even finger-exercises may be made melodically beautiful, and such composers as Chopin and Liszt put some of their finest inspirations into pieces that they called simply Etudes or Studies.

All such head-music has a legitimate place in art, far beyond that of its intellectual significance. To listen to it with the brain alone would be a fatal mistake. Brahms gave his piano pieces such non-committal titles as Capriccio, Intermezzo and Rhapsody. But in each he established a definite mood, which after a few hearings becomes unmistakable. Even his waltzes have individual characteristics which make them thoroughly human.

GET YOUR BODY INTO IT

Head-listening is not enough, just as foot-listening and heart-listening are not enough. The true appreciation of music comes through all three channels simultaneously, and every truly great composition has this triple appeal. It might be summed up as the appeal of rhythm, of melody and of technique, although all three are so interlocked that an accurate dissection is practically impossible.

In its sum total, however, the combined physical-emotional-intellectual appeal may be termed "æsthetic" in the highest sense of the word. For æsthetic appreciation is nothing if it does not partake of all three factors. It has no independent existence.

We cannot be "æsthetic" by simply making up our minds to it. If our response to music means anything at all, it must make honest confession of its physical and emotional elements, and often one or both of these may exclude the intellectual altogether.

Every listener is entitled to his personal

response, and in his own experience the balance of power is sure to vary. It will vary even as regards the same composition, heard at different times and under different circumstances. The performance of a symphony by a great orchestra may overwhelm him with incoherent emotion, after which he may pick out the themes and technical details on his piano with nothing more than an intellectual interest.

IT ALL DEPENDS

Schumann and Beethoven may deliver an essentially rhythmic message when their music is danced by a Pavlowa or an Isadora Duncan. The same composers can suggest the fun of a cross-word puzzle or the fascination of a laboratory experiment when submitted to practical study by an amateur string quartet.

In either case an æsthetic enjoyment is produced, and none shall say just what the component parts of that enjoyment are to be. There is no discredit in the animal response of feet to rhythm, or the human reaction of hearts to melody. Neither can the mysterious activity of the spirit be analyzed independently. The three hang together, and the result is not only æsthetic but ethical as well.

HOW A COMPOSER WORKS

Composers, however, seldom have definite intentions, ethical or otherwise, when starting out to write a piece. They put down the thoughts that come to them, and develop them musically with the aid of such scholarship as they possess. If the original inspiration was worthless, all the technique in the world will not avail. Conversely, if their technical equipment is inadequate, a splendid musical idea may be almost wasted, perhaps obliterated entirely.

Every really great composer has in his masterpieces shown the ability to command a physical, an emotional and an intellectual response; and every really appreciative listener ultimately reaches the goal of grasping the composer's threefold intention, even though he may never succeed in sounding music to its uttermost depths. It is better that it should be so, for great art cannot afford the weary satiety that follows so quickly in the trail of the obvious.

TRY SOME OF THESE

There are hundreds of compositions in the smaller forms that will serve to illustrate the complete æsthetic appeal of great music. Rachmaninoff's two best known Preludes are good examples. Kreisler's little pieces for the violin, also transcribed for the piano, are an easy introduction to bigger things, with all the elements of musical appeal clearly emphasized.

Mendelssohn, Chopin, Schubert and Schumann point the way toward Beethoven, Mozart and finally Bach and Brahms, and all of them offer music with the triple appeal to feet, heart and head, without unduly straining the attention of even the average listener.

APOLOGIES IN ADVANCE

A poet, writing about an orchestra, began his poem thus:

> A noise arose from the orchestra, as the leader drew across
> The intestines of the agile cat the tail of the noble hoss.

He was one of those people who see the things in a concert-hall, but do not hear the music.

> A fiddle by the footlights' rim
> Catgut and horse-hair was to him,
> And it was nothing more.

Listen to music, not merely with your feet, or with your hearts, but with your whole being. Use your own ears, instead of taking someone's opinion and slavishly parroting it. Find out what you like and why you like it, if possible; and if your pleasure has in it the intellectual quality as well as the physical and the emotional, you may be pretty sure you are listening to good music.

This has been a rather serious little sermon, perhaps the most serious part of this whole book. Let's have something lighter for a change.

CHAPTER IV

MUSIC À LA CARTE

Food and music seem to have much in common. To many people the one is a necessary accompaniment to the other.

Lots of us go to restaurants "where there is good music," not because we want to listen to it, but to be sure of a harmonious background to our conversation and mastication.

Some people do their best talking while music is going on. In fact, they fail to get a good start until the music begins. On the other hand, it has never been proved that conversation, or even clinking teacups, helped the quality of a musical performance.

One of the stock stories of food and music is that of the young thing in a café who was asked, "What are they playing now?" The menu-card was one of those practical ones, with the food on one side and the musical numbers on the other, and a hasty consultation brought the reply, "Filet Mignon, by Champignons."

The hostess who invites musicians to her table, on the assumption that they will pay their way with music, is familiar enough. Her arch afterthought, "By the way, bring along your violin," cannot always be dismissed with the answer, "My violin never dines." Unfortunately also, the singing voice invariably dines, and often all too well.

Pianists have been known to object to playing on a piece of furniture which was in no sense a musical instrument, but in general they are powerless, once the coffee-cups are cleared away.

TO-DAY'S SHORT STORY

Here is one they tell of a violinist who was invited to a house-party with the definite understanding that he was to play for everything he received in the way of hospitality. His hostess presented him at set intervals with itemized statements of the music which he owed for his bed (a Berceuse), his bath (an unaccompanied Bach Gavotte), valet service (Poet and Peasant) and every article of food that passed his lips.

By the end of a long Sunday the violinist was close to exhaustion. But he played resolutely through the program representing his final meal, just eaten. His last number was Dvorak's Humoresque, for the coffee. He went through with it up to the point where those sweet, cloying strains begin, and then suddenly stopped.

The hostess bustled up in a dudgeon of considerable height. "What do you mean by stopping?" she asked fiercely. "Why don't you finish?"

"Madame," replied the violinist, "you may not have realized it, but I took my coffee *without sugar.*" *

THIS IS EVEN WORSE

Have you ever known anyone who could not listen to music without keeping time to it in whatever he was doing? You may have noticed that when someone is playing the piano and you ask him a question, he has to answer rhythmically. Similarly people who stutter can often help themselves out by simply singing the words, or perhaps whistling between phrases. (There is an analogy also in the rhythmical gum-chewing of a vaudeville or movie audience.)

I knew of one man who was such a slave to rhythm that he had to eat his meals at a restaurant where he knew that the orchestra always played in a good, even time, thus encouraging a healthy Fletcherism.

*I wrote this originally for the Associated Sunday Magazines. It is not a true story. S. S.

Eventually, however, he was double-crossed. It happened on an evening when he was eating a peculiarly indigestible lobster-salad, but with mastication progressing quite satisfactorily. Suddenly, and without warning, the orchestra broke into the jazziest of jazz tunes.

He tried to follow the syncopated rhythm, but it was impossible. His jaws worked desperately. His face turned purple, and he began to choke. In a few moments he had fallen to the floor unconscious.

Fortunately this was one of those New York restaurants where it is customary for the orchestra to break into Chopin's Funeral March the moment a patron drops apparently lifeless from his seat. The slow, regular strains had the effect of a pulmotor, and respiration was soon restored. Before further damage could be done, his friends had dragged him outside, under the elevated, where no music of any kind could be heard.*

MAKING MUSIC PALATABLE

Seriously, however, music may be consumed à la carte or even table-d'hôte, by following the formula of a well-planned meal. If concert-pro-

*This was written for Life. It is entirely my own invention. S. S.

grams only took a hint from successful dinner-parties, how much more interesting they would be!

Imagine a hostess starting right in by offering her guests a solid, nourishing roast! Imagine her following this with another roast course, and then another and still another! It would be a gloomy party from the outset.

Solid nourishment is entirely proper in its place, but it is not the sole object of an attractive dinner. One heavy course is usually considered sufficient. The wise hostess leads up to it with appetizers, a light soup, fish, perhaps an entrée, and then tapers off her program with a salad, dessert and coffee.

That is best for the digestion and most considerate of the appetite. It makes a real climax of the plain but useful meat and vegetables, and stages that substantial course so that all else leads up to it or away from it.

ROAST, ROAST AND ROAST

A concert-program might well adopt a similar system. Why is it necessary for a concert-pianist to start always with Bach, and proceed through Beethoven and Schumann to Brahms and Debussy, with Chopin and Liszt as his lightest fare?

That is all splendid musical food, but it is far too much of a meal for one sitting. It is a dinner of solid roast and nothing else.

Let concert-artists begin to arrange their programs along the lines of good housekeeping, and watch their audiences grow. Why should not Beethoven appear about the middle of a program instead of always at or near the beginning?

Are Chaminade, Godard and Moszkowski entirely unworthy of a place with the elect of the recital hall? May they not at least have the honor of ushering supreme genius into the presence of a critical audience and, after the climactic performance, bowing out their betters again?

WHY ARE DATES, ANYWAY?

Chronology has played havoc with concert-programs. Just because Bach lived long before Debussy, he is always placed far ahead of him in the list of musical events. Actually the two composers would furnish most interesting contrasts and analogies if placed side by side on a program.

Is the music of Mendelssohn more advanced than that of Beethoven just because he lived later? And why the eternal distinctions between the classic and the romantic, with the modern still regarded as an intruder?

The one and only object of a concert-program is to interest its hearers. If they are prejudiced in favor of the historic, biographical and chronological method of presenting music, then by all means let them have it so. But the most common prejudice in a concert-audience to-day is merely that against music in general. The constant problem of the concert-giver is to find some way of forcing people to listen to music as such, without resorting to tricks of sensationalism, personality-mania, or circus gymnastics.

What, after all, do people listen for at a concert, even the well-developed enthusiasts? Mostly it is a combination of tonal beauty and technical dexterity. They are emotionally soothed or excited by sensuous beauty, as it floats into their consciousness from a voice, a violin or a piano. They are amazed, dazzled, hypnotized, when an instrumentalist executes passages of incredible rapidity or complexity, when a singer strikes an apparently impossible high or low tone, or sustains the breath long enough to turn purple.

VARIETIES OF EXCITEMENT

But what has all this to do with a composer's intentions? The response to a sensuous tonal appeal is much the same as the pleasurable sensation resulting from the enjoyment of food or drink; and excitement over the technique of Heifetz or Galli-Curci is not so different from excitement over a Dempsey-Firpo fight, a Ruth home run, or a Bobby Jones approach.

It is human nature to enjoy stimulants of all kinds, from coffee to jazz. With this prevalent taste for excitement goes the inevitable sweet tooth, the demand for a cloying, saccharine soothing-syrup, whose effects are in their own way almost alcoholic.

PERHAPS YOU WERE ABOVE THIS

There is a lesson to be learned from the bread and jam of our extreme youth. We all remember a time when we thought it the limit of bliss to eat jam with a spoon, and we made ourselves sick in the process of discovering our mistake.

If we had a wise mother, she gave us our jam between two layers of solid, nourishing bread, and the sticky sweetness was all the more agreeable after its protecting walls had been bitten through. We may have resented the first intrusion of prosaic bread upon the poetry of the jam-pot, but in the end we came to like the combination.

In music we have the jam of incessant melody, of the obvious, the line of least resistance. We think we would like to listen to nothing but "linkéd sweetness long drawn out." We would like to devour a continuous tonal dessert, just as we once thought we would like to eat jam with a spoon. And we are likely to become sick in just about the same way.

Our common sense of music can stand just so much of mere melody, then it balks and refuses to go further. So the wise composer, like the wise mother, encases his melodic jam in the substantial bread of musicianship, developing his material with an honest mastery of technique, and reminding his hearers of the fundamental sweetness of his tune just often enough to make each reminiscence a fresh pleasure.

NOT TOO MANY SWEETS

That is the secret of a great symphony or sonata. Every repetition of a theme, or even the snatch of a theme, pierces through the enclosure of formal workmanship as does the jam through the bread of a sandwich. But if the piece were all theme, all melody, all sweetness, we would soon sicken of it, as we sicken of the obvious in all forms of art.

So also with the complete meal of a concert-program. A succession of sweets would be fatal, even to a childish taste. We have our periods of wanting to eat nothing but dessert, to live on candy or pie. But the laws of health gradually correct our taste until we come to appreciate the merits of a wholesome dinner, well arranged and attractively served.

THE GOLDEN MENU

Our musical meal should not be all roast, and let us hope that it need not be mere bread and water. But to make it a succession of sweet trivialities would be even worse. The ideal is a well-balanced combination of the palatable and the nourishing, with perhaps an indigestible trifle thrown in here and there by way of experiment.

Such a musical feast may be served in the home as well as on the concert-stage. But how many actual dinners follow the laws of good taste and good hygiene alike? And how many musicians and potential music-lovers are prepared to follow the suggestions of this epicurean chapter?

Now that the damage is done, however, we might as well be a little more explicit. Here, then, are your appetizers, some fairly stimulating, some merely designed to tickle the musical palate.

Godard, Chaminade and Moszkowski have already been mentioned. They have all expressed themselves in dainty, whimsical pieces, a whole platter of hors-d'œuvres, colorful, often highly spiced, always charming. Fritz Kreisler has done for the violin what these and others have done for the piano. There are also Raff, Svendsen, Sinding, Rubinstein, Delibes, Bohm, and the Americans, De Koven, Nevin, Gottschalk, not forgetting Victor Herbert, Friml and the foreign waltz-kings.

THIS GIVES YOU THE ENTRÉE

The lighter works of Mendelssohn, Grieg and Tschaikowsky belong in the early stages of music à la carte. They are akin to our own MacDowell, but all of them occasionally produced a really nourishing dish.

Schubert, Schumann and Chopin are already close to the climax of a musical meal, and the variety of their creations permits a wide range of adaptability. Similarly Weber, Gluck, Haydn, Handel and Mozart offer melodic food of all kinds, suitable at times for an entrée, and at times for a whole quick lunch. In the field of song, Robert Franz belongs in this group, and in orchestral music we have Spohr, Berlioz and Goldmark.

Rossini, Donizetti, Mascagni, and Leoncavallo are operatic precursors of the better Verdi and Puccini, with Wagner the eventual climax. Bizet and Gounod are best saved for dessert, with Rimsky-Korsakoff a Russian dressing to the salad of Moussorgsky.

HERE IS FOOD FOR THOUGHT

Bach, Beethoven and Brahms remain the staples of every musical larder, yet even these may be approached through their own lighter inspirations. There is a relish in a two-part invention, a minuet or a waltz, as treated by such masters.

Just as these have their less serious moments, so may almost any one of their minor colleagues be caught at times on a level of sublimity. It is not a question of the composer, but rather of the composition. To say that the three B's are always overwhelming would be as absurd as to deny greatness to any one of a dozen other masters of music.

After the climax, we still have the possibility of Liszt in a variety of moods, many of them reminiscent. We have the tang of modernism from Debussy to Stravinsky, not to mention the strong cheese of Schoenberg. There are the sweets of Elgar, Drdla, Drigo, Offenbach, the stimulants of Sibelius and the Spanish composers, finally the downright normalcy of a Sousa march.

Take your pick, ladies and gentlemen! Step up to the counter and help yourselves, or sit down and be served according to your choice. Order à la carte if you wish, or take a chance on the day's table-d'hôte, as arranged by an experienced musical chef.

HOW IS YOUR APPETITE?

It is all music in any case, and in the long run you will be able to make your own selections with good taste and judgment, satisfying your palate and your digestion alike. Try everything, not once but several times, until you have permanently separated the parsnips from the cauliflower, and know the difference between roast beef medium and a Roman punch. You will be surprised to find how well your appetite for nourishing music keeps up, even when the stuff is extraordinarily plentiful.

Our main difficulty is the unwillingness to adopt any system or follow any set rules, either in our diet or in our music. We prefer to take our sensations blindly, to gobble absent-mindedly whatever is set before us, looking for neither reason nor definite intention.

THIS GIRL ATE UP FOOTBALL

Young man, did you ever sit with a girl at a football game and try to explain the rules to her?

Did you hear her tell you how she loved football, how she was crazy about it, and then rave about the way they kicked the ball high up in the air? You couldn't stop to tell her that it was not so good to kick it high as to get some distance and direction. You couldn't explain that she was missing something by not knowing when her side had scored a touchdown and when it was only a field-goal.

She loved football, but she didn't know the rules.

In the same way I have had friends with me at concerts or the opera. They loved music. They were crazy about it. But they didn't know the rules. They loved to hear Caruso sing loud and high, and they grew excited when the brass instruments played in the orchestra. But they had no idea of what was going on, beyond their purely physical or emotional reactions. They were getting some fun out of music, but they were missing as much as the girl at the football game.

Everybody is not able to play football, but show me the boy who would watch a game from the side-lines without knowing anything about the rules. Similarly only a few can take an active part in the performance of music. But everybody can be on the side-lines, showing an intelligent interest in the proceedings.

The rules of a musical diet are simple enough, and æsthetic health is just as easily maintained as physical well-being. A little knowledge may be a dangerous thing, but a lot of music was never yet known to hurt anyone. You are far more likely to starve yourself than to overeat, musically.

Systematize your musical diet if you can. Learn the rules by experience, if in no other way. But above all, don't hesitate to help yourself when the dinner-bell rings.

CHAPTER V

"OFFICIAL PROGRAM HERE!"

Now that you are aware of the close relationship between music and food, not to speak of music and football, you are ready to dig a little deeper into the whys and wherefores of what you are likely to meet in the average program.

You will hear people speak occasionally of "program music" and of its opposite, "absolute music." They do not mean music that is suitable for a program, but music which, by its title, or a descriptive analysis, or its words, action, scenery or accompanying pictures, tells a story, indicates a definite episode, hence follows a distinct program.

Most of the music of the world is "program music" in this sense. Every time a composer gives you even a hint of his intentions, by an explanatory note, a subtitle, the reference to a poem or story that was his inspiration, still more when he weds his music to words, and perhaps action as well, he is writing "program music."

To this great class belong all operas, all the

song literature of the world, cantatas, oratorios, ballets and pantomimes. It includes even those pieces that have a definite descriptive title, which may have been supplied by the public rather than the composer himself. This is program music in the broadest sense, and for the sake of the argument let it be considered official here.

"Absolute music," on the other hand, is music that depends entirely on its own material to establish a mood or create directly an emotional or intellectual response. It has no descriptive title, nor does it lean on any other extraneous factors for support. It is music, pure and simple, with nothing but tones and time to carry its message.

THIS IS ABSOLUTE MUSIC

Most of the symphonies, the sonatas, the string quartets, trios, etc., the concertos, études, preludes, even the shorter dance forms, may be classed as "absolute music." Their titles or playing directions may give a hint as to the gayety or somberness of their mood, but beyond this their message is absolute, an abstract proposition, entirely removed from the concrete, except as it exists in the materials of music itself and the physical qualities of the interpreting instruments.

The absolute music of the world is not overwhelming in its volume, but it contains most of the truly great thoughts of the master composers. In fact, the best of the "program" music may become "absolute" in the sense that it will stand the test of performance quite apart from its narrative or realistic factors, and still deliver its message with inevitable effect. If a song or a piece of operatic music is still beautiful and appealing when divorced from its text or its action, then it has an absolute value, and should be promoted beyond its class.

Wagner's Prelude to Tristan und Isolde and the Liebestod are great expressions of human love, quite aside from the opera, and similarly the Lohengrin Prelude and the Good Friday music from Parsifal express a sublimity of religious feeling that needs no words or stage-setting.

TOO MUCH MUSICAL CODDLING

The great weakness of program music in general is that it has so much to lean upon. The man who walks always with crutches may eventually lose all the power in his legs, and constant automobile-riding is certainly no help to strenuous mountain-climbing on foot.

It is sometimes argued that no piece of music is interesting unless it tells a story or paints a picture, and some people even claim that every composition in the world has some such significance. That seems rather absurd, in view of the confessions of the composers themselves.

DESCRIPTIVE LABELS

The real value of a program, however, lies in drawing immediate attention to a piece, even when such a program is artificially aided by an admiring outsider.* We are not all capable of grasping immediately the exact intentions of a composer of absolute music, and most of us find it difficult even after a number of hearings. Therefore some extra suggestion as to a possible program is quite legitimate as a means of arousing a preliminary interest. If the piece is worth while for itself alone, it will eventually push this artificial significance into the background and continue to hold its place quite independently in our affections.

COMES A PIECE IN THE MOVIES

The motion pictures make the most primitive use of a program to draw attention to good music.

*In this connection it should be noted that a legitimate literature of "program notes" has developed in America, with Philip Hale and Lawrence Gilman as its High Priests. A preliminary reading of such annotations will often stimulate the hearer's interest in a composition, and their statements as to literary, pictorial or biographical backgrounds are consistently authoritative.

Here the story and the picture are always more important than the music itself, and the latter is most commonly used as a mere background to the sensations aroused by the screen.

Further flaws in program music are indicated by the ability of a clever movie organist to improvise at will to fit any situation, and often he uses practically the same material for a variety of effects. Agitated chords, known in the movie orchestra as "agits," may hold tense the emotions of an audience, while a pursuit, a strike, a fire or a murder is taking place.

Traditionally, such a tune as "Hearts and Flowers," played tremolo, quite softly, celebrates the reunion of the estranged pair, as their little blond offspring, simply clad in a nightie, draws their hands together again. It does equally well for the death of the grandmother, or the close-up of two young things appraising their first kiss.

But the motion picture theater nowadays offers its patrons in most cases a musical program quite aside from its films, and in this it is doing the public a real service. Those who come to see Mary Pickford or Charlie Chaplin may remain to listen to Nicolai's Merry Wives of Windsor overture, or even a Richard Strauss tone poem.

In some cases they will hear good music with a background of artistic lighting, perhaps a fairly elaborate pantomime, and this also is a legitimate use of the program feature. Even while the pictures are on the screen, some of the accompanying music must find its way into the subconscious life of the confirmed patrons, and thus many a soul has been involuntarily stimulated by strains of Grieg, Tschaikowsky, Liszt, even Wagner and Beethoven. (The use of music for mood and "tempo" in actual movie photography is now well established.)

CO-OPERATIVE ASSOCIATION

It is almost impossible to analyze human sensations so closely as to fix the exact value of the music in a piece which has a program of any kind. We find it difficult even in the concert-hall, and in our own homes.

Association, tradition and habit again enter into the question, and, as has already been said of "heart-music" in general (all of which is program music), it is impossible to tell how much credit the music itself deserves, and how much should go elsewhere.

Singers are in the habit of selecting their songs largely on the strength of the words, and a cute little sentiment, delivered in captivating style by a well-dressed prima donna, often passes as an actual inspiration.

Such songs as Danny Deever and The Road to Mandalay are fortunate in possessing words that would carry almost any tune that was rhythmically fitting. Minor composers frequently set the texts of Shakespeare and other great poets to music, because they know that the words will do the work if the musical background is merely adequate. But the greater composers usually fight shy of any too familiar text.

THE OPERATIC COMPLEX

Grand opera is program music in its most elaborate form. Here the music may be comparatively insignificant and yet give the impression of real value through the help of the words, the costumes, the scenery, the action, not to speak of the librettos, and the conversation between and sometimes during the acts.

Fundamentally, opera is an artificial proposition, for its characters are supposed to be talking, when everybody knows they are really singing. That is what makes opera in English so difficult to accomplish. So long as we don't understand the words, we can create the necessary mental illusion. But as soon as an everyday phrase leaps across the footlights, a prosaic intruder in the realm of music, our dream is violently interrupted.

Italian librettos are full of similarly commonplace expressions, but we do not recognize them in the foreign language, and the Italians themselves have too good imaginations to be bothered. To them it is all real and beautiful, with the simplest phrase glorified to poetic sublimity.

BE YOURSELF, AMERICAN!

We Anglo-Saxons may well envy this faculty of complete illusion that is characteristic of the Latin races, for we are still a self-conscious people, and literalness is our curse.

We even insist on different vocabularies for the prose and the poetry of our language. "Hair" becomes "tresses" or "locks." Our clothes are translated into "raiment." We resent the intrusion of everyday words into our dogged communion with the æsthetic.

To the Italian words make no difference. He is listening to beautiful music, believing a beautiful story. Opera is to him both a triumph of technique and a ravishing reality. He is satisfied if the heroine sings well, even though she may not look the part. He is quite ready to call back the hero for an encore, or at least a bow, even though his pursuers may have to step aside to permit his return to the stage; and if a death scene has been beautifully done, he will revive the corpse enthusiastically with his applause.

Some scholars may object to this rather broad definition of "program music," for they have used the term in a much more limited fashion, as applying only to instrumental music for which the composer announces a definite program. But strictly speaking any music that tells a story or paints a clear picture, with or without the aid of words, is program music.

It runs all the way from the faintest suggestion to the absolute literalness of realism. Often it calls in instruments that are not really musical at all. Thus Richard Strauss uses a wind-machine in his Don Quixote for the battle with the windmills. But in the same composition he imitates the bleating of sheep most amazingly by an entirely legitimate use of brass instruments, and characterizes the knight and his faithful squire by truly beautiful melodies, each personal and distinctive.

WHEN REALISM RULES

Strauss has always liked to experiment with the literal in music. His opera, Electra, contained the realistic blows of a hatchet, while his Rosenkavalier translated actual silver into musical tones. The limit was reached when he included a family squabble and a baby's bath in his Domestic Symphony.

All this was merely the climax of what had often been attempted before. Bach wrote a descriptive piece on the departure of a beloved brother. Beethoven made a Rondo of the Excitement over a Lost Penny, which, it is said, De Pachmann used to act in detail, looking for the penny under the piano.

FAMOUS PROGRAMS

Beethoven's great contribution to program music, however, and the first masterpiece of its kind, was the Pastoral Symphony, in which he described a whole country scene, with a storm and subsequent calm. Beethoven called another symphony Eroica, and originally intended it as a tribute to Napoleon. He admitted that the opening notes of his famous Fifth Symphony were analogous to Fate knocking at the door.

FATE MOTIF

Mendelssohn wrote an overture descriptive of Fingal's Cave, in the Hebrides, with the swirling water clearly heard. His fairy music is of course completely programmatic.

MacDowell's Scotch Poem is a popular example of true program music, with verses by Heine telling the complete story. Similarly Debussy composed his Afternoon of a Faun after a poem by Mallarmé. Tschaikowsky called his sixth symphony "Pathétique," but gave out a much fuller program for the fourth. Berlioz, Liszt and Strauss all loved to write program music, and all had a command of realistic effects.

CHOOSE YOUR OWN NAME

Many popular titles, however, have been artificially added after a piece was written, as in the case of Beethoven's Moonlight Sonata. It is well that this is so, for we would never remember such pieces by their opus numbers, which have a mere cataloguing convenience.*

Chopin's Waltz, opus 64, number 1, in D flat, is far better known as the Minute Waltz, and perhaps best as the "waltz of the little dog chasing his tail." The composer is said to have written it after watching the whirligig of a little pet, which he imitates at the very start with a rapid, twisting figure. Thus understood, the waltz has a significance for the most casual listener.

*Opus, Latin for work, is the word generally used (in its abbreviation op.) to indicate the place of a piece in its composer's history. One opus may contain several numbers.

Rachmaninoff's Prelude in C sharp minor has been supplied with lots of programs, although the composer himself denies any such significance. The three tones on which it is built up are generally considered representative of the bells of the Kremlin.

PATTERN OF RACHMANINOFF PRELUDE C♯ MINOR

Then the story goes on to say that Napoleon's army is attacking Moscow, and the Kremlin is set on fire, so that the stores will not fall into his hands. (This is the lively middle part.) Finally we hear the bells again in triumph as the French army begins its retreat. Sometimes the story is of exiles going into Siberia, and it fits equally well.

A teacher tells an interesting experience in this connection. She played the Prelude for her class, and then emphasized the three tones as its pattern, and asked the children what it meant to them, and if they could put the three tones into words. One boy got up and said, "That piece sounds like a prayer to me, and I think the three tones mean 'Hear us, Lord.' "

That was an entirely legitimate interpretation.

Another child said, quite as logically, "I know that piece was written by a Russian, and I know that the Russians are starving. It sounds to me like a cry for help, and the three tones mean, 'Give us bread.' "

Everyone has a right to listen to music in his own way, and even if a composer announces a definite program, we are by no means obliged to accept it slavishly. One man's tragedy may be another man's joke.

SO FAR AND NO FURTHER

Program music has a practical significance, if only in drawing the attention of those who might not otherwise be interested. It gives its inherent beauty a chance to assert itself gradually, after a hearing has been secured by the perhaps meretricious aid of things that have nothing to do with the music as such. But all is fair in creating music-lovers, and if you can invent a story or imagine a picture that will make listening easier, by all means go ahead and do it.

The more music you hear, however, the more you will lean in the direction of the absolute type. As you advance in direct appreciation, you will find moods more important than stories or pictures. You will realize that the great composers are those who have produced a constant effect upon all their hearers, with a certain degree of inevitability.

YOU WILL RECOGNIZE THIS

The thrill of a direct response, identical with that of thousands of others, is something indescribable. It is one of the joys of life that cannot be denied the poorest of us, nor can it be supplied if the receptive spirit is not there.

Such a thrill is not limited to music, for it is a part of all true appreciation of beauty. But it comes most easily through music, for the stimulus of music is more direct and unmistakable than that of any other kind of beauty.

It is the direct and involuntary response to beauty that places man above the so-called "lower animals," who, incidentally, possess most of the virtues that we treasure as our own: loyalty, self-sacrifice, ambition (another word for self-preservation, or survival of the fittest), even love. Whatever man does with supreme success must have in it some element of beauty.

THE ARTIST'S IDEAL

That is why artists for all time have set themselves the task of expressing the abstract in concrete terms, for thus does one realize beauty most directly and inevitably. It has been practically a hopeless task for all but the musicians. A painter, a sculptor, a writer must deal with definite things. He may give his work an abstract title: courage, love, hate, fear, calmness, ecstasy. But we see only a concrete figure, or group of figures, endowed with such qualities.

The musician is more fortunate. Through the medium of absolute music he comes closest to the ideal of abstract expression. He can make you feel joy or sorrow, courage or despair, calmness or excitement, by the direct transfer of his own emotions, and if he is a genius he needs no program to tell you his intentions.

The truly great music of the world has eventually affected every listener in approximately the same way. The Greeks believed that the thing could be brought down to an absolute science, and argued that certain tones, certain scales and certain harmonies had a constant and inevitable effect. They thought that the Doric mode would invariably stimulate high courage and brave resolution, while others had a leaning toward effeminacy and a weakening of the character. What we now know of their music makes us believe that they were merely guessing.

But the idea has persisted that music could

directly affect human emotions and human character, and the history of the world seems to bear this out. How much of it may be due to association and tradition it is impossible to say. The fact remains that certain pieces by the greatest composers, as well as certain pieces of folk-music, have created in many hearts a thrill of response that is practically identical, and to this extent they have actually expressed the abstract in concrete terms.

BE PHILOSOPHICAL ABOUT THIS

The final answer lies not with futurism, nor any of the other wild experiments made in the name of art. It depends upon the ability of a great creator to express himself in universal terms, and then to find a receptive spirit sufficiently aware of those terms to accept them as his own. Musically this can be achieved without the aid of a program, whenever the creator, the interpreter and the listener reach a common level of understanding.

Are we growing too philosophical? Let's ring the bell! Time!

CHAPTER VI

TIME

All music is basically a series of tones in time. Time and tune are the real elements of music, and they wait for no man.

Just as language is merely one little word after another, so music is just one tone after another, supported by other tones in harmony, and all strung upon an endless thread of time.

Everything in the world partakes of the time element. If you can think independently of time, you can explain eternity, immortality, and all other mysteries.

Children are fond of asking, "And what happened before that?" or "What will happen after that?" The questions are endless, and there is no final answer. For we can think only in terms of time.

THE VIRTUE OF REGULARITY

Since we think always in time, it is quite natural to divide time into equal sections, and in this way we get rhythmic time, which is the basis of all music.

Listen to the ticking of your watch, or to water dripping from a faucet. Take your pulse, or feel your heart beating after you have stirred up a little circulation. Notice the regularity of your breathing, or, better still, that of a sleeping child. Listen to the panting of a dog, or the purring of a cat. Keep tab on your footsteps, as you walk briskly to a definite goal.

These are all examples of rhythmic time in nature. Similarly the rush of Niagara Falls, the flow of a babbling brook, the surf on the edge of the ocean, all have a certain rhythmic regularity. It is a normal and logical thing for time to divide itself into equal parts.

MUSIC SPEAKS WITH AN ACCENT

This natural grouping leads directly to an equally natural accent or emphasis. Wherever the beats of time assert themselves, they also emphasize a definite accent, which falls usually upon the first beat of a group.

In walking we are quite likely to come down harder on one foot than on the other, and this is especially true of marching, where the accent is always on the "left." Our indrawn breath is actually more important than the blowing out, and our heart-beats seem to follow a system of regular accents, a strong beat being paired with a weaker one.

TWINS AND TRIPLETS OF TIME

Even a brief examination will show that all time divides itself naturally into groups of two and three, with one accent to each group. A group of four is really only two pairs, and a group of six consists of two sets of three beats each. Even the irregular five-beat time is merely an alternation of three and two.

A few lines of verse, which the voice recites rhythmically almost by instinct, will make the matter of musical time entirely clear. For example:

/ / / /
When the days are dark and dreary,
/ / / /
Then my heart is sad and weary.

Each of these lines contains eight syllables, and each syllable is a beat. But the accent necessarily falls on the first of each pair of syllables or beats. You cannot logically read the lines any other way. Rhythmically, therefore, they contain four accents apiece.

A musician would divide such a line into four groups, each consisting of two beats, and he would separate the groups by bars for the sake of convenience. Then he would indicate at the start that each bar represented two beats of the music.

Suppose the lines were changed thus:

/ / / /
When the days are not so drear,
/ / / /
Then I know that Spring is near.

There are still four accents to the line, but one syllable has been dropped off the end of each. The eighth beat is still there, however, to the imagination. If you read the lines aloud, you will find that you unconsciously pause for a beat at the end of each, thus keeping the time even. That is the simple principle of the "rest" in music.

MUSIC HAS NO VACUUM

Nature abhors any irregularity, and even though the music may stop the beats are mentally registered, and the time continues without a break. A jazz orchestra will often give you just the first note of each bar of music, knowing perfectly well that you will involuntarily count the rest, with your feet keeping time and coming in exactly on the accent of the next bar. There is a similar effect when people sing "John Brown's Body" in trick fashion, dropping off one word at a time from the end of each line.

In other words, music runs right along in regular fashion, even though tones are not sounded on every beat of the time. You may have noticed how people do not always wait long enough at the end of a line in such a song as Old Folks at Home, but go right ahead to the start of the next line. That is because they are not mentally beating time. They do not realize that on the word "stay," for instance ("there's where the old folks stay"), there is only one tone, but four beats of time, and that these must all be filled in, either by resting or hanging on to the tone, until the next line starts with its proper accent.

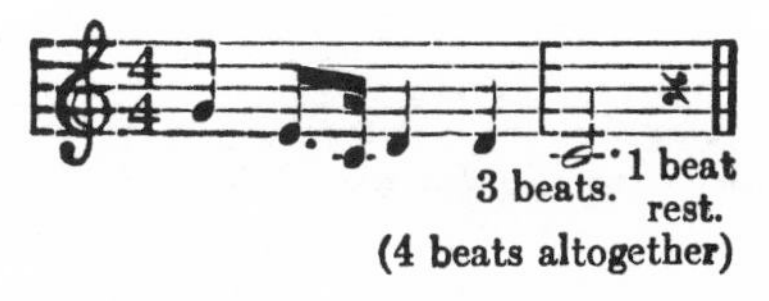

If you examine the verse lines above, you will notice that while the accents can come only on certain words, the number of beats may vary according to the length of time that you sustain the accented words. Try singing the first line to the tune of the Merry Widow Waltz. You will find that the accented syllables, "when," "days," "dark," and "drear-," now require two beats apiece, and the unaccented syllables only one beat each. You have therefore discovered that waltz time in music has three beats to the bar, with the main accent on the first beat:

Tune: MERRY WIDOW WALTZ

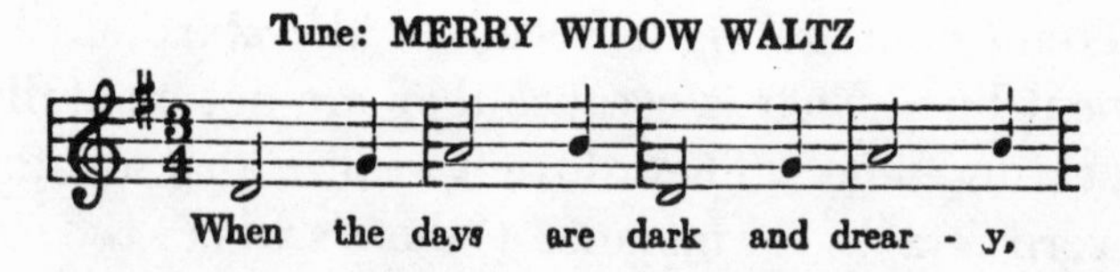

You can go beyond this, and string out the important words to three beats apiece, which, with the added syllable, will give you musically four beats to a bar:

IN FOUR-FOUR TIME

You can also group the syllables four at a time, giving the first in each group the main accent:

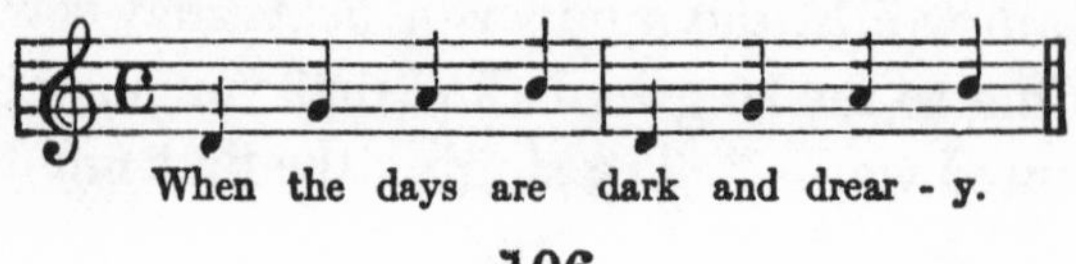

In either case you have achieved a four-beat time, which is very frequent in music, and therefore often called "common time." Actually it is merely a combination of two pairs, for convenience, and proves again that all time divides itself normally into groups of two or three beats.

It becomes obvious that the slower you beat the time, the more syllables or notes you can bring in on each beat.

Theoretically, there is no limit to the number that can be included on one swing of the pendulum. Actually you seldom find more than eight, and sixteen is about all that musical notation figures as a probability.

HOW IS YOUR ARITHMETIC?

Mathematically time is a very simple proposition. Suppose you are counting in groups of two beats, each lasting one full second. Recite the two lines about the dreary days with one syllable to a beat, and at this rate you will find it is pretty slow work.

Now take two syllables to a beat, and you will get through each line in exactly half the time, four seconds instead of eight. Double up again, taking four syllables to a beat, and your line is finished in two seconds.

With eight syllables to a beat, you do a whole line in one second, and you may find it possible to recite both lines complete in the same space of time; in other words, at the rate of sixteen syllables to the beat. If there were four lines, you might still be able to gabble them off in one second, that is, with thirty-two syllables to the beat, but better not try it.

COMFORTABLE QUARTERS

Since the grouping of two and four is so common, and so easy, it has become traditional to count time chiefly by quarters, each quarter carrying one beat. Four beats make a normal group, which may be considered a complete unit.

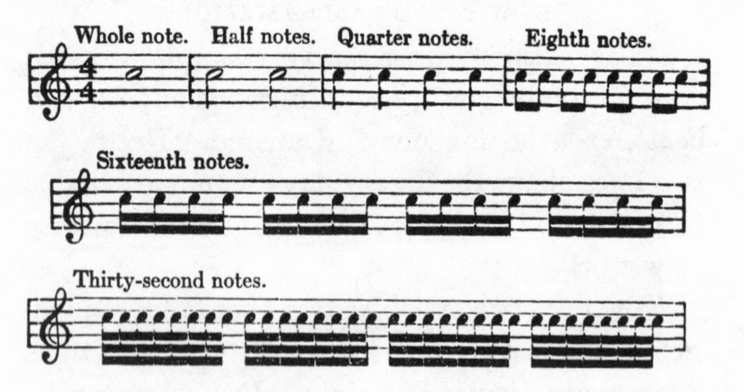

If you happen to sound four notes in this common time, one to each beat, they are naturally quarter-notes, as it takes all four to make a unit. If there are only two notes, each sustained for two beats, they have the value of half a note apiece, and if there is only one note for the entire four beats, it is a "whole" note.

If you are beating a quick march-time and want to group your beats in twos instead of fours, each beat is still considered equivalent to a quarter-note, and thus the mathematical system remains undisturbed. Similarly in waltz-time there are three beats to each group, and these also count as a quarter-note apiece.

It is easy enough to indicate at the start of a piece of music what the grouping of beats is to be:

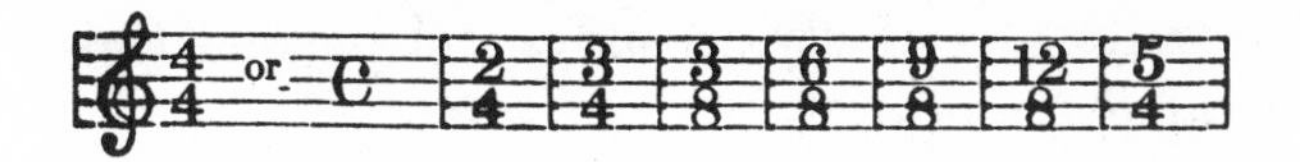

The performer himself generally decides just how fast the time is to be counted, although a composer may give quite accurate instructions in this respect also. (His wishes are usually disregarded in any case, so it doesn't much matter.) With dance-music, of course, the speed is regulated by custom, and an orchestra must follow the wishes of the dancers if it wants to be successful.

Now if the time-grouping has been fixed by a

definite number at the start, and the speed is also settled in your own mind, it is easy enough to figure how long each note must be sustained. As the quarter-note is generally the basis of your count, you may be sure that each quarter-note will represent one beat. A half-note will necessarily be sustained for two beats, and a whole note for four beats.

If a composer wants a note sustained for three beats, he can indicate this by a dot after a half-note, which makes it worth one beat more. If he wants to get two notes on one beat, he writes them as eighth-notes. (See page 108.) If he needs four notes to a beat, they mathematically become sixteenths. Eight notes to a beat would be written as thirty-seconds, and beyond this it is difficult to go.

(Dividing a quarter in half makes it two eighths, by the rule of fractions. Similarly a quarter equals four sixteenths, eight thirty-seconds, etc.)

A DOT IN TIME

Just as a dot after a half-note increases its length by one full beat, i.e., to three quarters, so the same useful little punctuation mark may be applied to any of the notes of smaller dimension. In every case the following dot lengthens the preceding note by one-half its original value. A quarter-note plus a dot becomes three eighths, i.e., one quarter plus one eighth. An eighth-note plus a dot becomes three sixteenths, i.e., one eighth plus one sixteenth, etc.

If the voice or instrument is to be silent for any number of beats, or even part of a beat, this is easily indicated by a system of rests, corresponding exactly with the notation itself. In counting musical time, don't overlook the rests. They are just as important as the notes, and sometimes even more expressive.

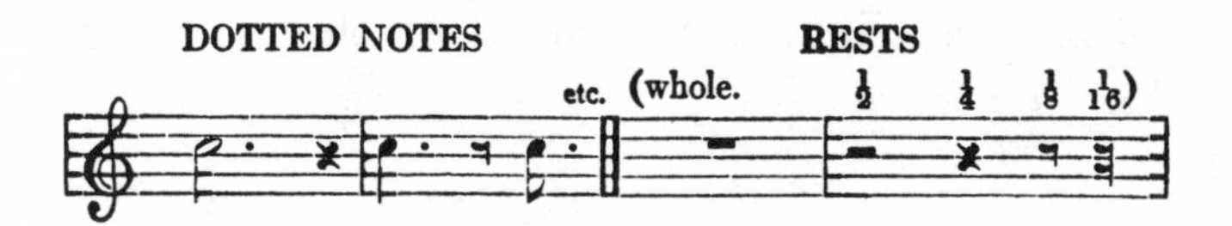

(If you happen to play triangle or tambourine in an orchestra, you may have a part that is mostly rests. Don't worry. The conductor is supposed to give you a good, clear signal when it is your turn to play. If you miss it, he will glare at you for the rest of the piece.)

INCREASING THE PACE

Sometimes you will find it necessary to group notes in threes all through a piece, but faster than in the conventional three-quarter waltz-time.

For example, read the following revision of the lines that have so cheerfully supplied us with rhythm thus far:

/ / / /
Back in the days of the darkness and dreariness,
/ / / /
Then was my heart overcome with its weariness.

This could be sung in waltz-time, with one syllable on each beat. But if you wanted to take it at a rather fast pace, you could indicate it musically by giving each beat the value of an eighth-note instead of a quarter. Then your tune will be in three-eight time instead of three-quarter.

THREE-EIGHT TIME

You can conveniently take these short beats six at a time, if you wish, thus dividing each line in half, with two accents in each group of six beats. (You may notice that even though these lines are in triple time, they fall naturally into four accents.) Musically such time would be indicated as six-eighths. It is possible also to have a nine-eighths grouping, and even one of twelve-eighths:

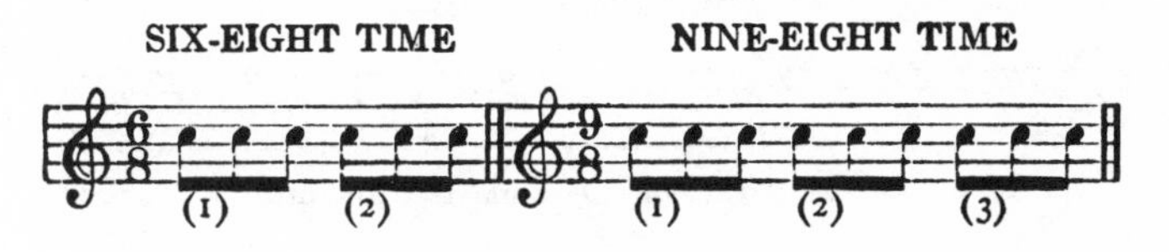

(Here again you are simply stating the total number of beats to a group, but the accents actually give you an underlying rhythm of two, three or four, as the case may be. Six-eighths time can be beaten as two-quarters, and it is quite frequent in marches, such as Sousa's Washington Post. Similarly nine-eighths would contain three accents, and could therefore be beaten as three slow quarters, and twelve-eighths as four-quarters.)

MORE EXPERIMENTS

Examine those tinkling lines above once more. They can be turned from threes into fours by the simple process of giving each accented syllable an extra beat. This does not in any way upset their rhythm as verse, and yet produces musically an entirely different effect:

FOUR-FOUR TIME

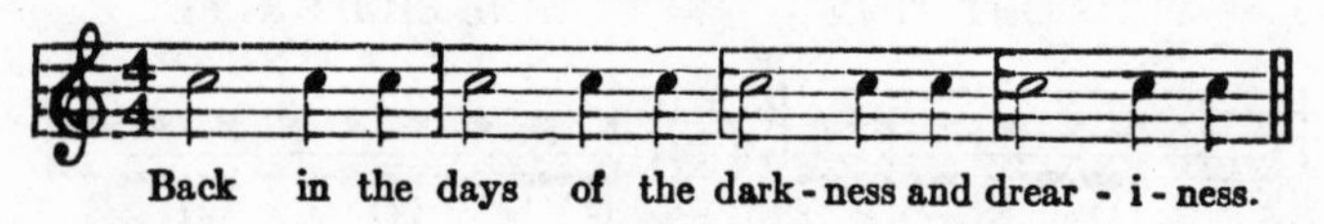

Now try this experiment. Instead of giving the extra beat to the accented syllable (back, days, dark-, drear-), give it to the second of each group of three (in, of, ness, etc.) Thus does one arrive at syncopation, which, under the name of "rag-time" has long delighted our rhythmic souls:

SYNCOPATION

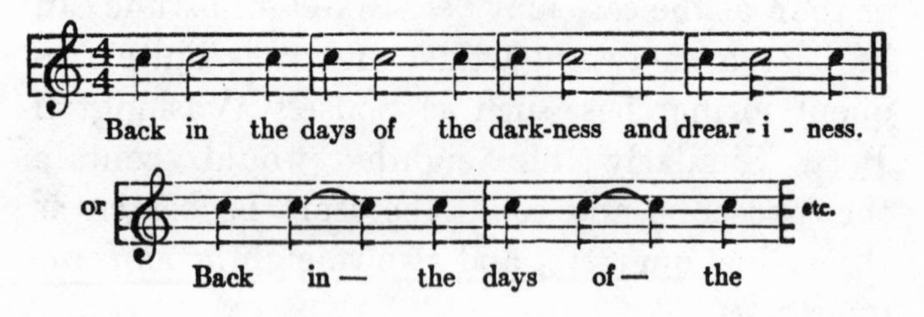

A "syncopated melody" is simply a tune in which some of the naturally unaccented notes are given an artificial prominence by being started before or sustained beyond their original beat. A good jazz band can find more ways of introducing false accents than most scholarly musicians ever dreamed of.

INTRODUCING RAG-TIME

In our sample lines, syncopation may be introduced in several ways. The lengthening of the second syllable in each group is the simplest. But you can also bring the accented syllables forward a whole beat, and thus secure a very insidious rag-time. In this way "days" comes on the fourth beat of the first group, and carries on through the first beat of the next, with "dark-" and "drear-" moving forward in similar fashion, and securing an extra emphasis by the very fact that they start on an "off-beat."

MORE SYNCOPATION

Rag-time of this sort is just about as old as music itself. It appears in all kinds of folk-music, and the American Indians and the negroes were equally fond of it. You can hear it in Annie Laurie, Comin' thro' the Rye and most of Stephen Foster's melodies.

We show our fundamental savagery in our fondness for rag-time. It is a game in which the basic rhythm goes relentlessly on, while every effort is made by the musicians literally to tear it in pieces.

Debussy wrote a good rag-time piece in his Golliwogs' Cake-walk, and every other great composer has used syncopation to good effect. The old Smoky Mokes, Maple Leaf Rag, and Georgia Camp-Meeting were fine examples of American rag-time, and more recently we have had Alexander's Rag-Time Band, The Robert E. Lee and No, No, Nora. Casey Jones was a classic of the premature, in the way of syncopation, while Stumbling and Berlin's Pack up your Sins presented a shifting of accents that was positively bewildering.

INTERNAL COMPLICATIONS

The conclusion to be reached about time, therefore, is that, while it marches steadily on, with an absolute regularity of beat, it may be subjected to all kinds of internal arrangement and disarrangement, with an almost unlimited confusion of false and true accents.

If you are a poor mathematician, the details of musical time may baffle you, but if you leave the whole matter to your feet, you are not likely to go wrong. There is a certain indescribable pleasure in coming down, bang, on the real accent, even when the jazz musicians have started their note a whole beat ahead of time.

To dance in time is really no more difficult than to walk in time. But most good dancers feel a rhythm that is more significant than the actual beats, and they follow its dictates rather than the absolute count of two, three, or four.

THE LITTLE THINGS THAT COUNT

It is said that a good bridge-player is one who can count thirteen. Musical time seldom requires ability to count beyond four at the most, and if you follow your dancing instincts, you may not have to count at all.

A fox-trot, taken slowly, is about the same as the old-fashioned two-step, and its beats run necessarily in twos or fours. When it is played fast, it becomes practically a one-step, and this is nothing more than a march.

You can make a fox-trot out of a waltz and vice-versa. Witness Marcheta, a so-called Mexican tune that has had much popularity. It was written as a waltz, but is danced chiefly as a fox-trot. The Song of India, originally in triple time, became famous in America as a fox-trot, and Castle of Dreams, also a two-beater, came right out of the Minute Waltz of Chopin.

Conversely Home, Sweet Home, Auld Lang

Syne and Good-night, Ladies can be and are all played as waltzes when the orchestra begins to feel that it has earned its evening's pay.

When you have heard Rubinstein's Melody in F and a few of the older classics played in waltz-time, you will believe that rhythmically all things are possible.

The more you beat time, with your feet, or mentally, or out loud, the more you will realize that musically it all comes down to groups of two and three.

With this simple grouping as a basis, all kinds of elaboration are possible. The tango is a slow four-beat rhythm, full of syncopation, and with several notes to each beat. The old-fashioned Schottische and Gavotte are similar, and their poor relation is the humble barn-dance, which returned for a while to the ballroom not so many years ago.

Similar in rhythm are such "square dances" as the Virginia Reel, whose most effective tune was Pop goes the Weasel. Anyone who ever saw Pavlowa in her yellow Directoire, dancing the Gavotte, will not forget the music of Linke's Glow-Worm, which accompanied it.

The Polka of olden time belongs in the same class, and there was also a fast dance in even time called the Gallop. Back in Colonial days they danced the Minuet, which was in triple time, slow and graceful. Many a Spanish dance is really a waltz, with a strong accent on the first beat.

WALTZES VS. MAZURKAS

In our own old-fashioned waltz, the three beats are of almost equal value, although the first is the strongest. The second beat is always more important in a waltz than the third. In the Polish Mazurka, the third beat has a quite decided accent of its own, and this is what chiefly distinguishes it from the waltz.

The Polish waltzes are faster than ours, while the Viennese style demands a curious stressing of the second beat, which Victor Herbert has adapted somewhat to his American waltzes.

The Polonaise is really a march in triple time. It has all the effect of a stately walk, and never suggests the more trivial waltz forms. Such a composer as Chopin could take the waltz, mazurka and polonaise and turn them into wonderful concert-pieces, without any necessity of strict time in their interpretation.

HERE IS A STARTING-POINT

Rhythm is the first thing anyone discovers in music. It is the primitive stimulus to a physical response, which savages and children alike express by the simple method of beating on something. It is a fundamental part of music, because it is a universal factor in life itself.

Folk-song began with the common sense of rhythm. It was found early in the history of the world that manual labor was easier when done to a rhythmic accompaniment. Even to-day you will hear a workman swing his sledge-hammer to a rhythmic chant, just as the sailors will sing rhythmically while pulling on a rope.

Soldiers march much better to music, and if no melody is to be had the rhythmic beat of the drums is sufficient. Singing on the march has been found helpful in eating up the miles.

RHYTHM CREATES FOLK-MUSIC

The primitive peasant sang his rhythmic accompaniment to the pounding of his flail on the threshing-floor, or the swish of his scythe in the fields. From this simple individual expression of fundamental music, there grew the communal folk-song, in which all joined at least in a refrain or a burden, while individuals made up verses as they went along.

The age of machinery has practically eliminated such folk-song. It is no longer necessary to sing at work, for true manual labor has almost ceased. Even the song at the spinning-wheel has given way to the whir of machinery in the mills. But the mother still sings her lullaby over a rocking cradle, and time goes on, in music and in life, as inexorably as ever.

CAN YOU BEAT TIME?

If you can count time and beat time to music, you are expressing a universal truth, and this is quite different from merely keeping time to the beat of someone else. A true sense of rhythm practically creates the patterns within the endless flow of sand from Father Time's own hourglass, while the ordinary sense of time, which is a physical instinct, merely adapts its response to these patterns.

Your skilled leader of an orchestra or band knows exactly how to impress the rhythmic pattern of a piece of music upon the men who are following him. If you watch his beat, you will notice that he concentrates always upon groups of two or three.

WATCH A FEW TIME-BEATERS

There are no absolute rules of beating time. Generally, however, you will see the stick come down on the accent, and go up or sidewise on the unaccented beats.

When Sousa is beating march time, he swings his baton down and up, in regular, lively fashion, and occasionally he drops both hands at his sides in a full, emphatic swing. When he gives the signal to a particular instrument for its entry, he points his stick or his free hand, as if he were aiming at one of his pet clay pigeons. His gestures are few, but they tell their story.

(Many orchestral conductors make unnecessary motions because the gallery likes them.)

If the time is counted in groups of four, it is customary to beat down on the first of the group, which has the chief accent, then to make a slight motion to the left, and one to the right, finishing with an up-beat, so that the baton is ready to come down again on the opening accent of the next group.

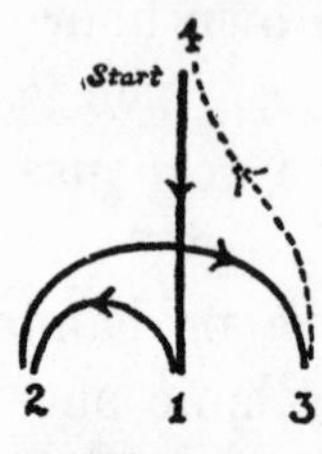

Three-quarter time is beaten similarly, the baton coming down on the first beat (which again has the accent), going across, usually to the right, and then up for the finish of the group. All other time-beating is simply an elaboration of these fundamental types.

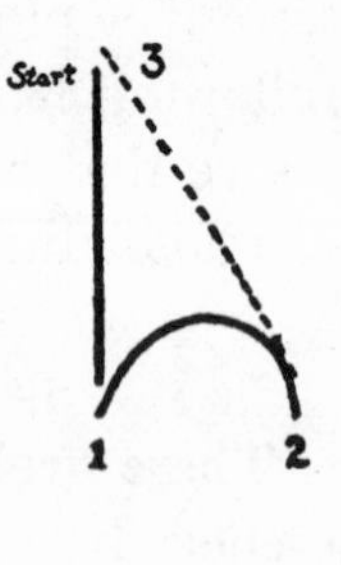

If you try to beat time yourself, you will find that it is fairly easy to find the accents, but that you will not always come down inevitably on those beats. That is largely a matter of experience.* But anyone with a good sense of rhythm can keep a crowd together, at least in singing, for he will instinctively emphasize the accents in such a way that his intention cannot be mistaken.

You might as well grow accustomed to keeping time, for the universe is doing it right before your eyes every minute of the day. Time was not invented by some scholarly musician, to impose upon students. It has always been a part of our very selves, and needs only to be analyzed for its practical possibilities. It is yours for the taking. Time!

*You can beat time at its own game by using phonograph or piano records and going through all the motions, as though an orchestra were actually before you. Try it some rainy evening.

CHAPTER VII

LUCID INTERVALS

Sɪᴛ down in front of a piano, preferably your own. (If you haven't one handy, better skip this chapter and spend the time looking for a bargain. Your eyes and nose can't do the work cut out for your ears.)

Now count the total number of keys, both black and white. You will probably find eighty-eight altogether, but for practical purposes you needn't bother with more than about four dozen, stretching both ways from the middle.

If you examine the keyboard carefully, you will immediately notice a regular pattern formed by the black keys. They run in groups of two and three, and are easily assembled by the eye, five at a time.

Now concentrate on the group of five black keys right in front of you, as you face the middle of the piano. Select the group so that the pair is on the left, with the three of a kind on the right.

Arrange your right hand so that the thumb and forefinger rest over the pair of black keys, and the remaining three fingers over the other three within reach. If you play the five in succession, starting with your thumb and working up

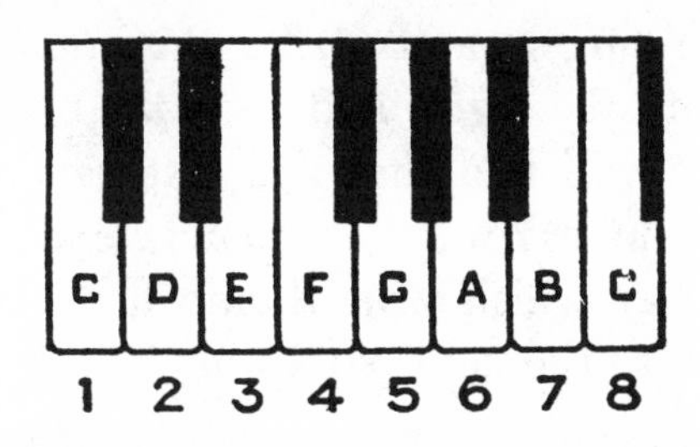

to your little finger, you will hear the tune of Stumbling (see p. 26), which is the same as the old five-tone scale. (Some people think they can play the piano on the black keys alone, but they are wrong.)

As soon as you have satisfied your musical soul with the black five-tone scale, you are ready for a real discovery.

Put your thumb on the white key just to the left of the black one where it rested a moment ago. Drop each finger in place on the white keys stretching to the right of your thumb, and strike each in turn. You will hear another five-tone pattern, rather more solid and satisfying than that of the black keys.

Run your thumb and fingers over this group of five white keys, up and down, until the sounds are clearly outlined to your ear. (You may recognize the most familiar of all "five-finger exercises.")

Now proceed to the white key just beyond your little finger, and strike this and the one beyond it to the right, and even the one beyond that. You will find that this last key, which is the eighth in a row, corresponds exactly with the white key which your thumb first struck, in its relation to the next group of five black keys.

DISCOVERY OF THE OCTAVE

If you sound the first and the last of this row of eight white keys simultaneously (and you can easily do it by striking the lower one with your right thumb, and the upper one with your little finger), you will notice a curious blending, giving the impression of a single tone, but re-inforced, as it were, by its own double.

You are now in possession of one of the great secrets of music, namely that there are actually only twelve tones altogether, represented on the piano by seven white keys and five black keys, which simply repeat themselves in the same pattern over and over again.

The average keyboard can be divided into

seven such sections, with one key left over at the top and three at the bottom. But theoretically the system could go on endlessly, for every eighth white key (which is the thirteenth tone in succession, if you include the black ones), starts a new group, exactly like that which has just been completed.

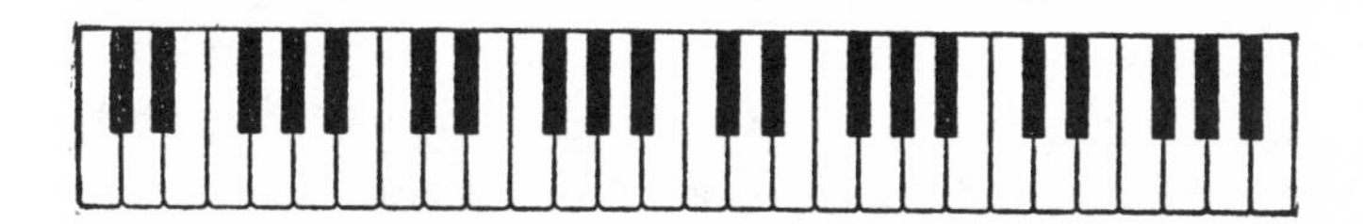

The piano is the practical instrument by which all music may be analyzed, and actually it includes far more tones than are needed for general use. So far as the human voice is concerned, it rarely covers a range of more than two of the twelve-tone sections, lying right in the middle of the keyboard. Whatever tones it adds below the average are balanced by an equal loss at the top, which explains the difference between sopranos and altos among the women, and tenors and basses among the men.

If you try to think of music in terms of the whole piano, or even the whole range of the human voice, it becomes a difficult and complicated matter. If you think of it simply as a structure in which the same pattern is repeated over and over again, and if you think of this constant pattern first as a seven-tone combination, and then as a twelve-tone combination (including the black keys) the whole thing becomes quite obvious and logical.

START BUILDING OPERATIONS

Take this matter of structure literally, and imagine a building several stories in height. Each floor is the ceiling of the floor below, and according to Mr. Woolworth you can keep adding new stories indefinitely. Even the ground floor may have a basement below it, for which it acts as a ceiling.

Now make a cross-section of your musical building, with each floor clearly doing its double duty for the stories above and below it, a starting-point for the one, and a finishing-point for the other. It would look something like this:

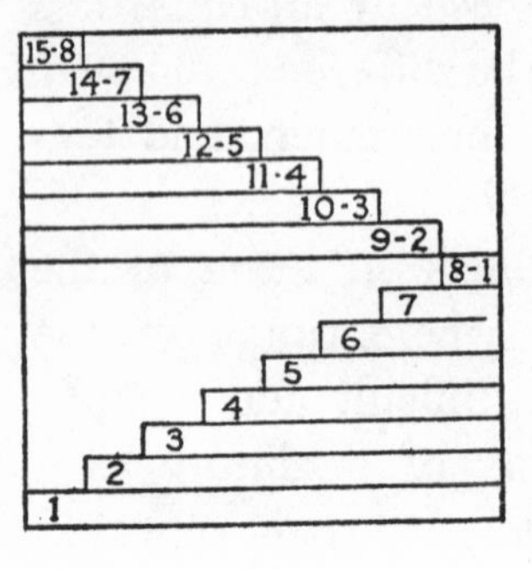

Suppose you have a staircase leading from the ground floor to the one above. If you let the steps correspond to the white keys in one typical section of the piano, and count your ground floor as number one, you will find that number eight forms the ceiling of your first story and at the same time the floor of your second story.

This eighth tone is our old friend of the curious blending (which musicians call the octave), and practically duplicates its relative of the floor below, except that it is one story higher. If you can remember these eight steps, both by ear and by sight, on the keyboard of the piano, you will have a firm basis for your musical education.

ARE YOU REALLY DOING THIS?

Take a look at the white keys again, starting with any one just to the left of a group of two black keys. Sound the eight white keys in a row, going to the right, one at a time, and remind yourself of the close relationship between number one and number eight, the floor and the ceiling of a complete story.

You can make a tremendous amount of good music with just that one little row of eight tones, duplicating themselves in successive stories up and down the keyboard. The black keys may be left out in the cold altogether, for the time being.

After you have thoroughly accustomed yourself to the sounds of those eight tones, number them mentally, and by ear, and stick to the numbering: one, two, three, four, five, six, seven, eight. Each is a constant tone in the constant pattern of music.

Now let the black sheep into the fold, if you wish. You will find that they fit snugly enough among the white steps already laid out. Each represents a half-step only, and must not be allowed to upset the numerical system already established.

But by making use of the black keys as well as the white ones, you secure thirteen tones to a complete pattern, where before you had only eight. (Strictly speaking there are only twelve different tones, since the last of one section is also the first of the next.)

HERE IS ANOTHER STORY

Suppose your building has two stories, with steps running all the way to the roof. You can number the steps all the way up, in relation to the ground floor, which is your real starting-point. In that case you have steps number nine, ten, eleven, etc., all the way up to fifteen, which in this case is the roof. But you can also call step number eight "number one" of the second story, which it is (being simultaneously a ceiling to what is below, and a floor to what is above), and with this fresh start your steps from the second floor to the roof will again be numbered from one to eight.

This reveals another dark secret of music, namely that every tone may be numbered as within its own octave-pattern, and also in its relation to the pattern just below its own. Step number two of your second story is number nine of your building as a whole; number three of the top section is number ten in its relation to the ground floor, etc. But still further revelations are in store for you if you will just keep your eyes on that keyboard, your ears on its tones, and your mind on architecture.

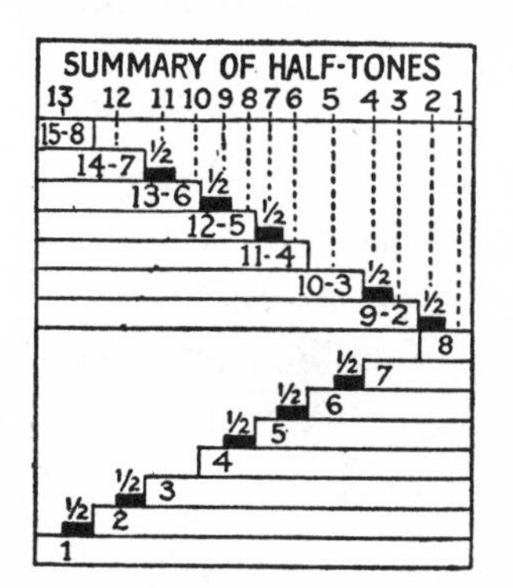

HALF-TONES CLOSE-UP

If you sound white key number one, then white key number two, and then the black key between them, your ear will tell you that the division is mathematically as correct as possible. Since the second white key is one step, or one tone, higher than the first white key, the black key between them is half a step, or half a tone, higher than the first, and the same distance below the second.

You can hardly imagine any tone between that of the black key and either of its next-door neighbors. In fact, if you did not have the piano to help you, it might be difficult for you to sing or whistle even the half-steps.

Accustom your ears to the difference between a half-step and a whole step by playing these first two white keys and their black go-between, in every possible order and combination. (Do these tones remind you in any way of the old Maxixe?)

A LITTLE JOURNEY BY HALF-STEPS

Now play right on up the keyboard, including every key, black or white, as you come to it. After you have passed the first two black keys, you will discover something startling. From white key number three to white key number four is only half a step. There is no black key between them, and you would probably find it impossible to make a tone higher than number three and yet lower than number four.

After that everything progresses regularly, with alternating black and white keys, up to white key number seven. Here again there is no black key to follow, and you find that white key number eight is only half a step higher in its tone than number seven.

You can now safely say, "Come out of there, music, we know you." For you have analyzed the make-up of a cross-section as necessarily consisting of twelve half-steps, or half-tones, after which the same process begins all over again. **These twelve half-steps, endlessly repeated in the same pattern, are the whole tonal material of music.** Arranged in various combinations, on a time basis, they will supply you with every possible melody and harmony.

(The Chinese are credited with a command of quarter-tones, and some of our ultra-modern composers are trying for similar effects, but this has nothing to do with the Common Sense of Music.)

To musicians the steps represented by the keys of the piano are known as degrees or intervals, and it is through its lucid intervals that music becomes intelligible.

DON'T LOSE YOUR BREATH OVER THIS

You can now revise your plan of a musical building, so as to make your entire staircase run in half-steps. You will find also that you can start anywhere at all and count thirteen half-steps up or down, and thus reach, in the next section above or below, the same interval from which you started. Convince yourself of this by experiments at the keyboard, and get yourself accustomed to the sound of this half-step progression.*

Here is another experiment, a little more difficult but well worth trying. Play once more your original pattern of eight white keys, omitting the group of five black ones. Notice again that you have whole steps from one to two, two to three, four to five, five to six, and six to seven, but only half-steps from three to four and seven to eight. Try now to work out this same tonal pattern in other parts of the keyboard, starting

*Musicians call this half-tone progression the "chromatic scale," probably because it has more possible "colors" than the regular "diatonic" scale, which simply goes through the normal tones or steps, from number one to its equivalent, number eight. (This relationship of the "octave" is constant in all scales.) When you hear a siren whistle, going up and down, you are listening to a progression which includes all the chromatic intervals, and even closer ones. Any scale formed of smaller intervals than half-tones is called "enharmonic," but don't bother about that, as comparatively few ears really make such distinctions.

anywhere you please. (You will find that it is necessary to use some of the black keys in every case except that of the original and its higher and lower duplicates.)

THIS MUST BE AT THE PIANO

For instance, take the lowest black key in a group of five as your starting-point, or step number one. Step number two will be the next black key above, for it must be a whole tone (or two half-tones) higher than number one. Number three will again be a whole tone (two half-tones) higher, falling in this case on the white key just below the black group of three. Number four will be the lowest of this black trio, for it is only half a tone higher than number three. Steps five and six will land on the remaining black keys of the group, and number seven will be the white key just below the next black pair. With only a half-step between seven and eight, you finish on the black key corresponding exactly to that on which you began.

Once you get the hang of this, you will find it a most fascinating occupation to start anywhere on the keyboard and run a correct progression from one tone to its equivalent above, and back again. That is exactly what a child is made to do when practicing "scales." But it is much more fun to find the scales for yourself than to have them drilled into you by rote.

GETTING TUNES BY INTERVALS

Now that you have your working materials well in hand, you are ready to pick out some tunes, for all tunes are simply successions of lucid intervals. Just playing a pattern of eight or thirteen tones does not give you a real tune, although you may remember "Ragging the Scale," which went right up and down the regular eight-step progression.

One of the simplest tunes in the world is that which is usually sung to the words, "Over the

OVER THE FENCE IS OUT. SEE?

Fence is Out." The succession of intervals is 1, 2, 3, 2, 3, 1, and you can add 8 (which is the equivalent of 1, an octave higher) to give it a saucy finish.

Children sometimes pick out a tune on the

black keys alone, filling in with a little two-finger harmony.

BLACK KEY TUNE

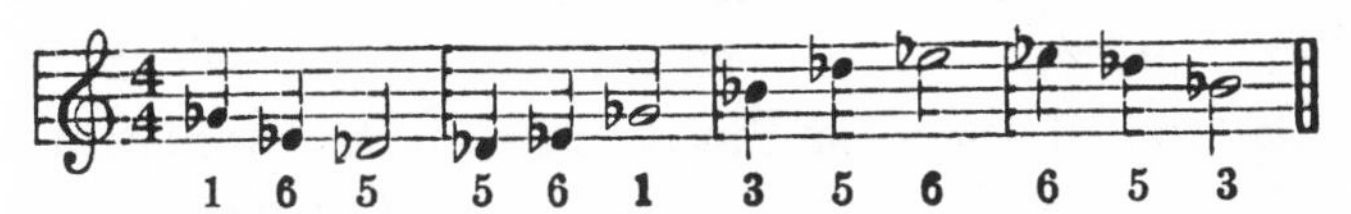

In Chapter I you discovered some of the commonest intervals and patterns in music, including the two tones of the cuckoo call (5, 3), the three used by the bugler (1, 3, 5, with the 5 repeated below), and the four-tone combination of the Westminster Chime (1, 2, 3 and the 5 below).

CUCKOO BUGLE

WESTMINSTER CHIME

Now apply these universal facts to the plan of your musical building. You will soon find that the steps numbered one, three and five are the most important in music.

Therefore, in thinking of your musical structure hereafter, suppose you consider number one as the floor, number three as a convenient landing, and number five as another convenient landing, on the way up to number eight, which is the top of the first flight, and at the same time the beginning of the second flight (or, as we had it before, the ceiling of the first story, and the floor of the second).

Now comes an amazing fact. Although a melody may start on any step or even half-step of the scale, actually there are almost no tunes of universal significance that start anywhere except on the intervals of one, three and five. The division seems to be about equal among these three favorites. Number eight is an occasional starting-point, but does not deserve much attention, as it is really the equivalent of number one.

Number six and number seven have a few supporters, but number four is very rarely used as a jumping-off place, and number two practically never.

The reason for this curious predominance of steps one, three and five may be found partly in the habit of the human memory, which sticks to these familiar intervals, and hence remembers the tunes that feature them. But probably there is more to the mystery than this, for the universal laws of harmony and melody seem inevitably to bring us back to these three milestones of music, and many a philosopher has argued that everything in the world is built up on a similar system.

It is impossible here to examine even superficially the entire list of well-known melodies originating in the universal landing-places of the scale. A few examples of various types should make the point sufficiently clear.

Do not forget also that we are now dealing with melody in universal terms. Each tune is considered not as it is played, in its own key, but as an absolute reality in the constant pattern already explained. You can start your tunes anywhere on the keyboard, and by working out the necessary scale-pattern in the background, quickly decide the number of every interval from first to last.

Think of your tunes, therefore, as quite independent of any particular section of the piano. They may have a certain fairly obvious place in the keyboard because of your vocal range, but musically they amount to the same thing, no matter where you start them.

For the sake of convenience, however, the following examples will be considered in a uniform position, in the natural key of C major.

You will find that more than one complete

flight of thirteen steps and half-steps is needed for practically every tune ever written. Therefore keep in mind your two-story building, or, better still, think of it as a one-story building with a basement, for many a tune starts below the level of the real number one step.

Your cross-section will now look like this, with either one of the two floors available as a starting-point, so that you can work up or down, from above or below your main level:

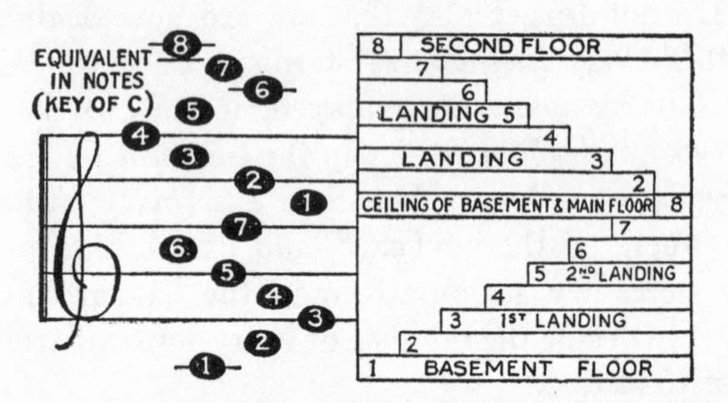

Remind yourself once more of the surprising fact that practically all tunes start on one of three steps, 1, 3 or 5. Consider first those which rise from the solid ground of number one.

America is perhaps the best known example, and the Star Spangled Banner, in its original and correct version, does the same thing, although it is now sung almost altogether in the more convenient arrangement which starts on number five, and works down to number one by way of number three. Other ground-floor starters of the national type are our own Yankee

Doodle, and "Rally round the Flag," Hail Columbia, the once notorious Deutschland über Alles, which is really Haydn's Austrian Hymn, Ireland's Wearin' of the Green, and the Welsh Men of Harlech, which, by the way, opens exactly like the utterly unmartial and beautifully lyric "All through the Night" of the same people.

The hymn-book contributes plenty of tunes that are satisfied with the bottom step for a

starting-place. Most familiar are the Doxology (known as Old Hundredth or, more loosely, Old Hundred) and Holy, Holy, Holy. Sullivan's Lost Chord really belongs with the sacred school

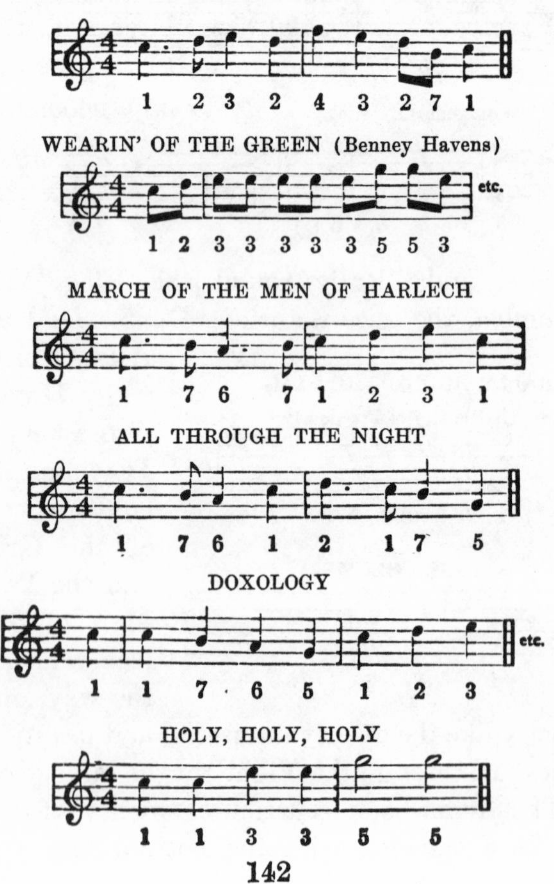

of the ground floor, and Handel opens his Hallelujah Chorus on number one for the orchestra, and the same step, an octave higher, for the voices (where its 1923 offspring, "Yes, we have no Bananas," also jumps off).

Folk-music and its imitators show that Home, Sweet Home finds the ground a good place to start from, as do Old Black Joe, The Banks of

the Wabash, The Last Rose of Summer, Gaudeamus Igitur, Integer Vitæ, the verse part of Love's Old Sweet Song, an old German ABC song, known to most children, another children's game-tune, "Here we go round the Mulberry Bush," or whatever the words may be, "Ninety-nine Bottles a-hangin' on the Wall," and other such nonsense songs, the famous French Malbrough, known to us as "For he's a jolly good Fellow," and "We won't go Home until Morning," another French folk-song, Au Clair de la Lune, and the exquisite Minuet of Exaudet (included in the Weckerlin Bergerettes) the Levee Song ("I've been workin' on the Railroad"), Yale's Bingo, and Cornell's Alma Mater song, "Far above Cayuga's Waters."

Among the more conscious tunes, by recog-

nized composers, starting on the first interval, are Handel's Largo (the introduction, not the chief melody) Mozart's delightful La ci Darem, from Don Giovanni, the best known tune from Haydn's Surprise Symphony, the theme from Schubert's Unfinished Symphony which created the Song of Love in Blossom Time, the Soldiers' Chorus from Gounod's Faust, Wagner's Song

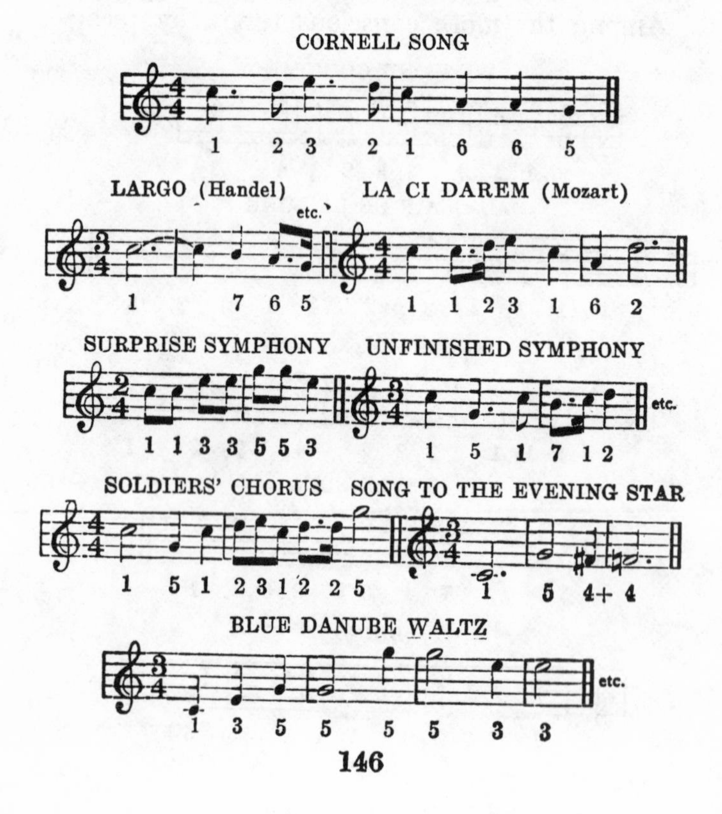

to the Evening Star, from Tannhäuser, the Strauss Blue Danube waltz, Dvorak's Humoresque, and the first part of the Intermezzo from Cavalleria Rusticana.

If this seems a strong array, landing number three can do just as well, or even better. National tunes starting on the interval of the third include "Tramp, tramp, tramp, the Boys are Marching," Marching through Georgia, the Canadian Soldiers of the King (adopted by Haverford College as an Alma Mater song),

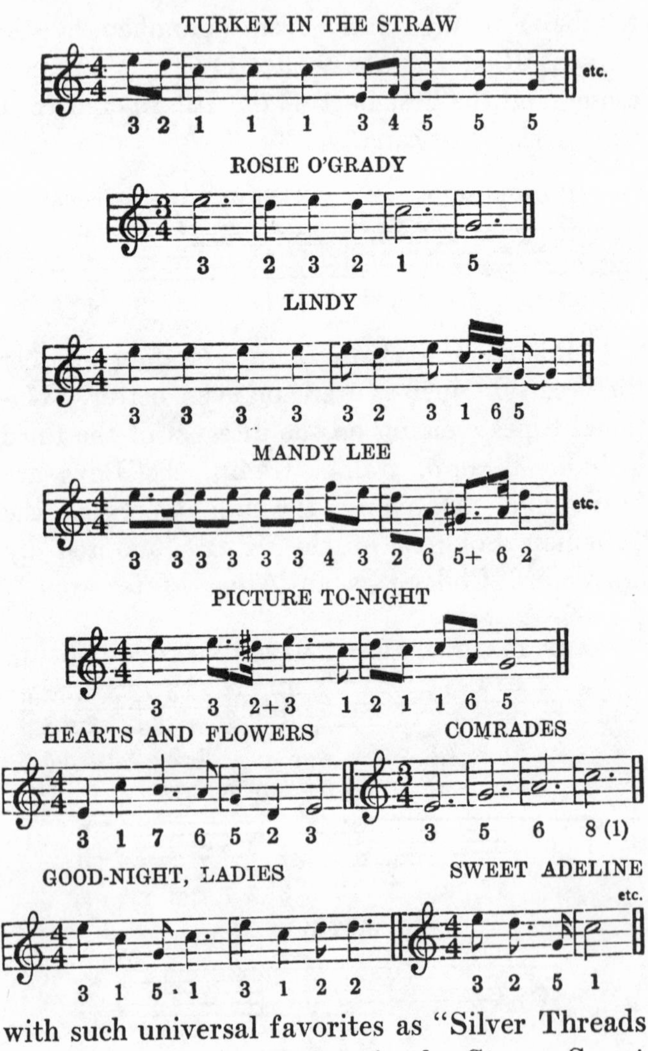

with such universal favorites as "Silver Threads among the Gold," Turkey in the Straw, Sweet

Rosie O'Grady, Lindy, Mandy Lee, Picture To-night, Hearts and Flowers, Comrades, Good-night, Ladies, Sweet Adeline, and "Hail, hail! the Gang's all here" (appearing, you will remember, as a chorus in The Pirates of Penzance).

There is real folk-music in "Believe me, if all those endearing young Charms" (the same as Fair Harvard), Old Folks at Home (or Swanee

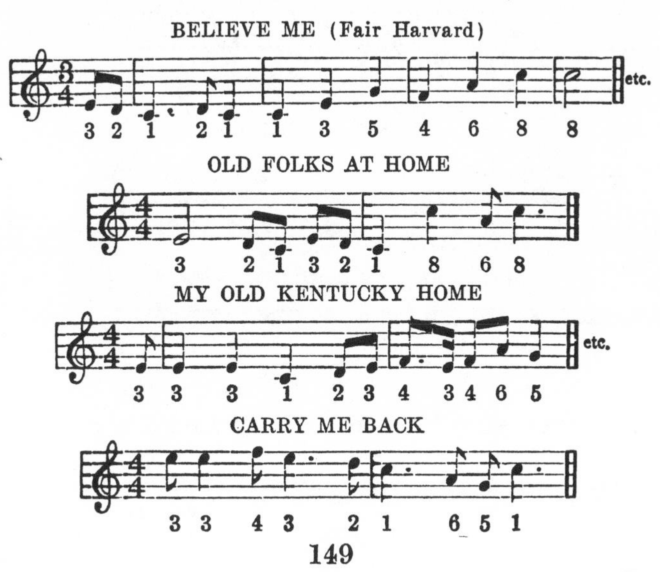

River), My Old Kentucky Home, "Carry me back to Old Virginny," "Drink to me only with thine Eyes," Ben Bolt, and Annie Laurie, all beginning on step number three. Close to the same standard, and of the same third-step origin, are Aunt Dinah's Quilting Party, "The Shade of the old Apple Tree," Mother Machree, My Hero (the chorus only), Liza Jane, "Keep the

Home Fires burning," "Till we meet again," the chorus of Casey Jones and that of Juanita, the verse of the Stein Song, The Bowery, the Eton Boating Song, the second waltz in Three o'clock

in the Morning, Sing Me to Sleep, Barnby's Sweet and Low, Herbert's Kiss Me Again, School Days, Yale's Boolah refrain, Elgar's Salut d'Amour and its parallel, Violets, and Ethelbert Nevin's Rosary and Narcissus.

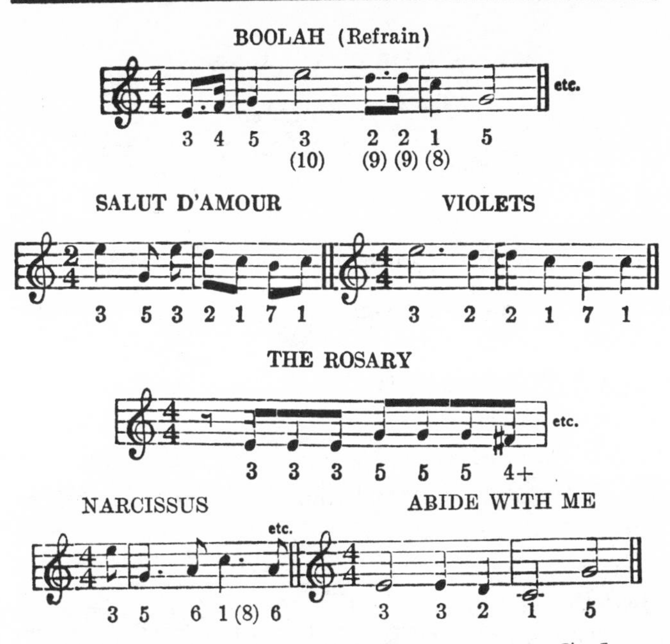

Abide with Me and "Nearer, my God, to Thee," are the strongholds of the third interval in hymnology, and the field of great secular composition contributes

Bach's Air on the G string, Beethoven's Minuet in G, Gluck's Gavotte, arranged by Brahms, Verdi's Anvil Chorus from Il Trovatore, Schubert's Who is Sylvia? Mendelssohn's Spring Song and Consolation, Chaminade's Scarf Dance, the second part of the Cavalleria Inter-

BACH'S AIR ON THE G STRING

BEETHOVEN'S MINUET GLUCK'S GAVOTTE

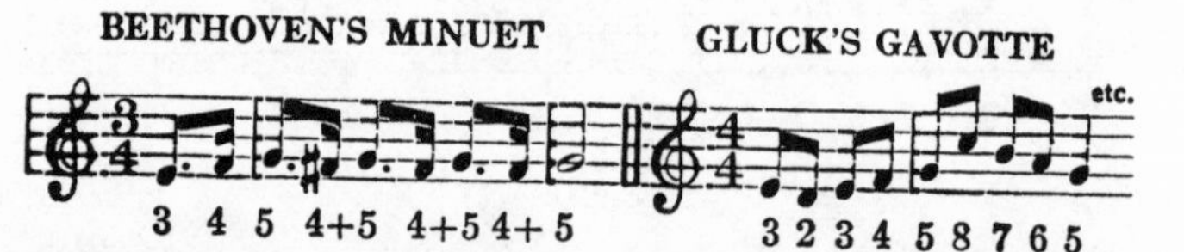

mezzo, the Meditation from Thaïs, Cadman's At Dawning, Charpentier's Depuis le Jour, from Louise, and the Brahms Wiegenlied and Waltz in A flat.

SCARF DANCE

ANVIL CHORUS WHO IS SYLVIA?

SPRING SONG CONSOLATION

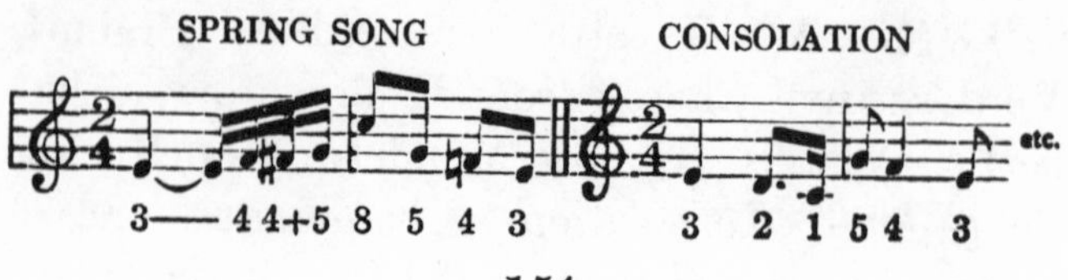

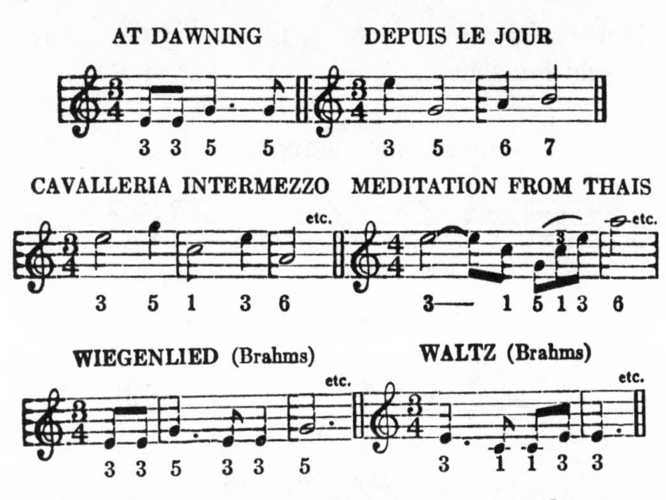

But interval number five presents perhaps an even more imposing array in its capacity of guide to tunes that satisfy. It has the advantage of working equally well in two directions, for you can start a melody effectively on the fifth above the level, or on the same interval below. Consider first those tunes which work down from landing number five toward the ground floor.

As already indicated, the Star Spangled Banner is generally sung this way by preference, and it has its patriotic parallels in the Battle Hymn of the Republic (John Brown's Body), the old Russian Hymn (duplicated in Hail, Pennsylvania and our own hymn-books), Belgium's Brabançonne, America the Beautiful (really "O

Mother dear Jerusalem"), Dixie and Germany's Wacht am Rhein.

RUSSIAN HYMN (Hail, Pennsylvania)

LA BRABANÇONNE

AMERICA THE BEAUTIFUL

DIXIE

You will also find step number five the starting-point of Chopsticks, "O du lieber Augustin," "O where, O where has my little Dog gone?"

"Massa's in de cold, cold Ground," Annie Rooney, "East Side, West Side," "London Bridge is falling down," Soldier's Farewell, the Good Old Summer Time, Daisy, the verse of

Juanita, Onward, Christian Soldiers, Rock of Ages, Come, Thou Almighty King, the verse of O Sole Mio, and the chief melody of Handel's

Largo, not to speak of The Palms and the major tune in the Miserere from Il Trovatore.

SOLDIER'S FAREWELL

GOOD OLD SUMMER TIME

DAISY

JUANITA (Verse)

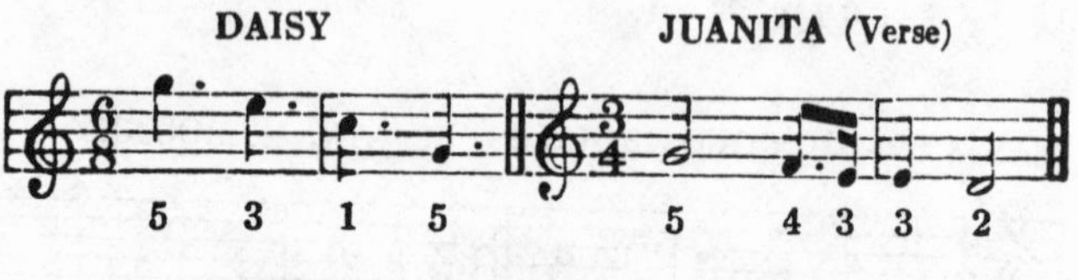

ONWARD, CHRISTIAN SOLDIERS

ROCK OF AGES

COME, THOU ALMIGHTY

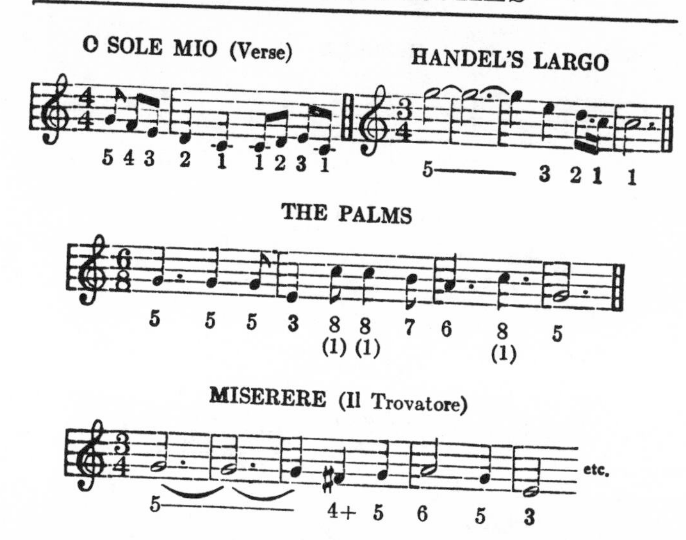

Starting below the main level, the fifth interval is still more common. The Red, White and Blue ("Columbia, the Gem of the Ocean") begins this way, as does the French Marseillaise, Italy's Garibaldi Hymn, Hawaii's Aloha Oe, Maryland, my Maryland (whose original is the German O Tannenbaum), Rule, Britannia, Tenting on the Old Camp Ground, and most of the bugle calls.

LA MARSEILLAISE

GARIBALDI HYMN

ALOHA OE

MARYLAND (O Tannenbaum) RULE BRITANNIA

TENTING ON THE OLD CAMP GROUND

There is a shocking parallel between Lead, Kindly Light, How Dry I Am, and Beethoven's symphonic melody, listed among hymn tunes as Berlin. Brahms uses the same succession in his Sandman and a sonata, and its significance in the Merry Widow Waltz has already been pointed out. (See page 25.)

The step up from five to one (or eight) is exemplified also in Blue Bells of Scotland, Auld Lang Syne, Forsaken, the start of the Yale Boolah, "In the evening by the Moonlight," The Long, Long Trail, Old Nassau, Lord Jeffrey Amherst, the choruses of "Love me and the

World is mine" and The Holy City, the Lohengrin Wedding March, the Pilgrims' Chorus, Schumann's Träumerei and Happy Farmer, and Weber's Invitation to the Dance.

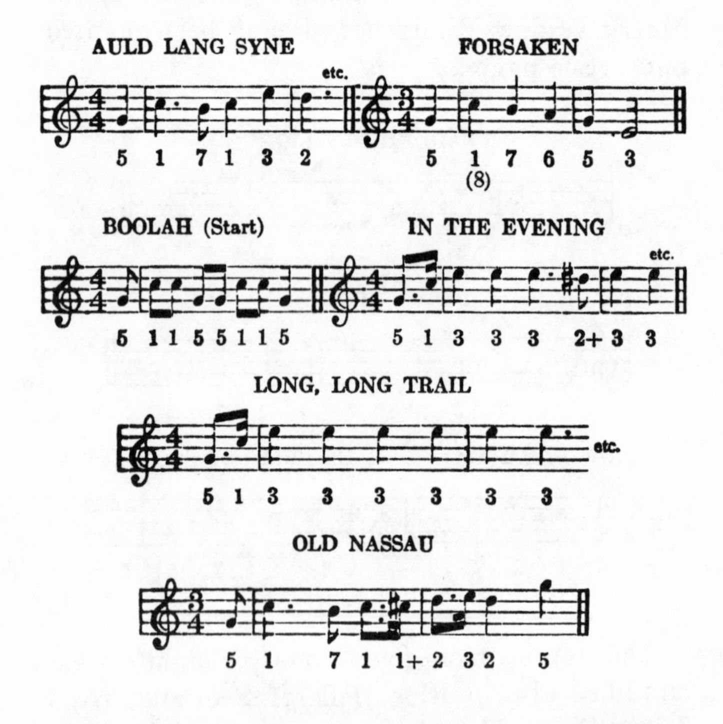

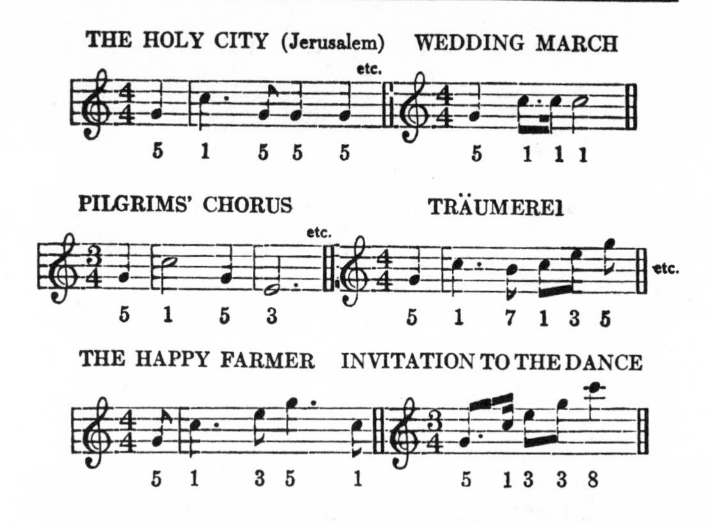

The fifth below jumps to the third above in The Old Oaken Bucket, Liszt's Liebestraum, Schumann's Nachtstück (also known as a hymn-tune), "My Bonnie lies over the Ocean," and a Prelude of Chopin.

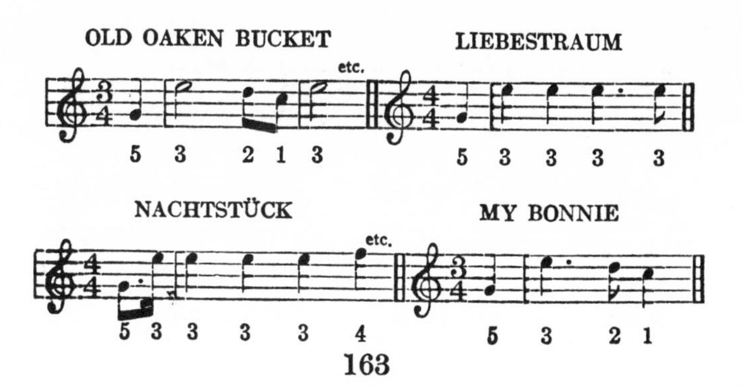

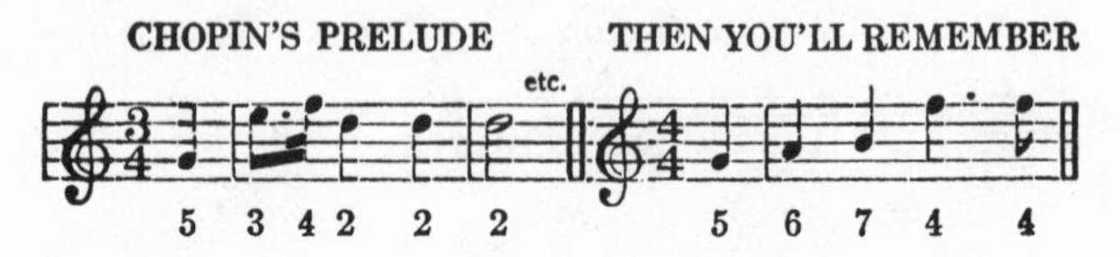

It moves only one step upward in such tunes as "Then you'll remember Me" (from The Bohemian Girl), Teasing, the chorus of Love's Old Sweet Song, Smiles, My Evaline, and "I hear you calling me"; and the lower fifth repeats itself in "I dreamt that I dwelt in marble Halls," Comin' thro' the Rye, Santa Lucia, A Perfect Day, the Rigoletto Quartet, and the Lucia Sextet. A lucid interval indeed!

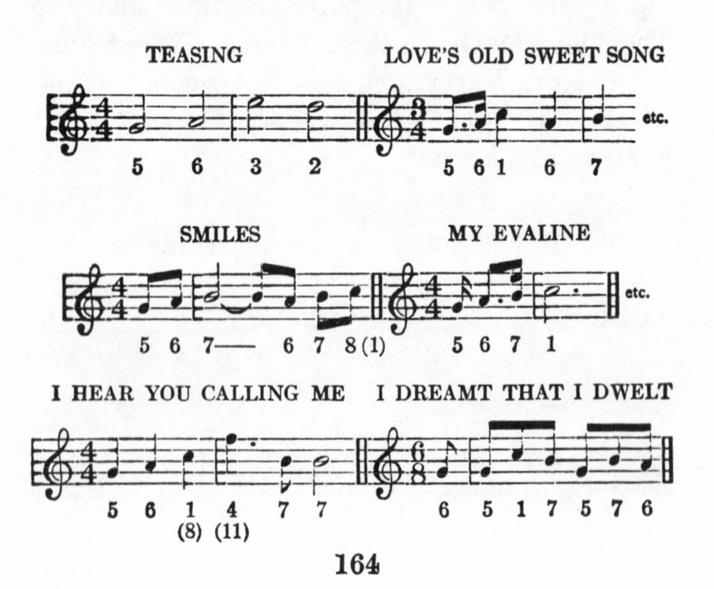

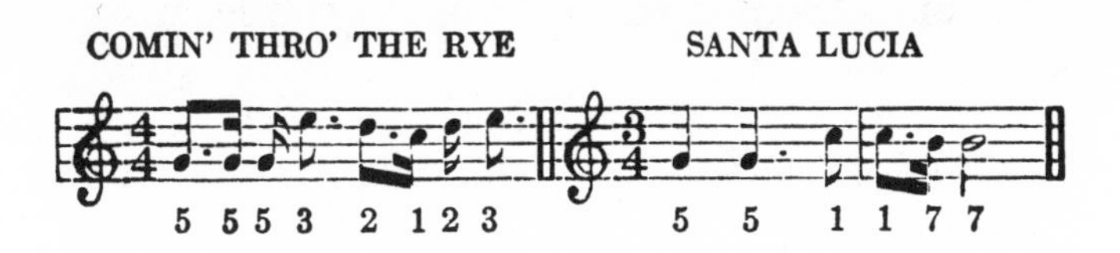

The other steps of the scale are almost barren, as compared with these riches. It is possible to figure a few tunes as starting on the eighth, although this deserves no independent consideration, as it is the equivalent of number one below. A legitimate start on eight is made by that great fife-tune, "The Girl I left behind me," and other possible examples are the chorus of O Sole Mio, the beginning of Casey Jones, Luther's Ein' Feste Burg ("A mighty Fortress is our God"), Puccini's One Fine Day (from Madame Butterfly) and a Song without Words by Tschaikowsky.

The Neapolitan Funiculi Funicula starts its chorus squarely on the seventh interval, and is almost unique in this respect, although a recent

popular tune called Dearest achieved a similar distinction.

On the sixth you may find the starting-point

WILD FLOWER

of such popular numbers as "No, no, Nora," Wildflower, Roses of Picardy, and an old-timer,

Moon Dear. Victor Herbert's Toyland also belongs in this group.

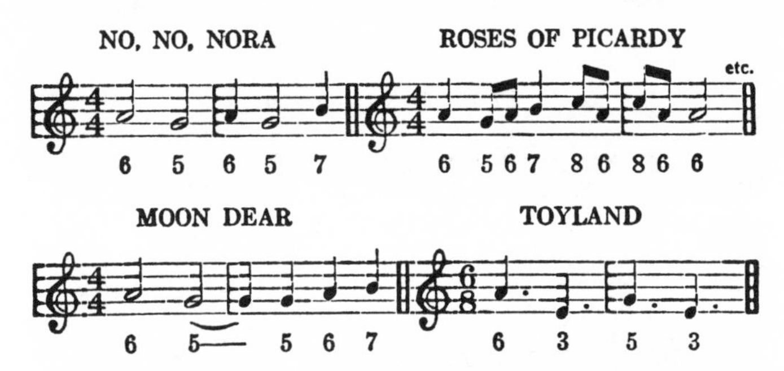

The fourth has almost nothing to offer, although some of you may remember a chorus that began on this interval: "You're here and I'm here." There was an old song, "Shine on, harvest Moon," which, after an introductory third, really started its tune on the fourth.

Similarly the familiar Stein Song approaches its chorus on the words "For it's always fair Weather," and, with two tones considered as introductory, the actual start is on the interval of the second. This is true also of that one-step hit from Shuffle Along, "I'm just wild about Harry," which, after an introductory third, came down hard on number two for its real beginning of the chorus.

Clearly, however, the honor of starting something in the world of melody can be shared only by the intervals numbered one, three and five, in the musical scale. Musicians call them affectionately the Tonic, the Mediant and the Dominant (it sounds like a whole barber-shop), and you will hear more about them in the approaching discussion of close harmony. But, like football players, they are best recognized by their numbers. So if you ever decide to compose a tune, write down or play the intervals one, three and five, in any convenient part of the keyboard, start on one of them, and keep working in their neighborhood. They are the safest of all musical bets.

Now that you know how tunes begin, you may as well look into their endings and possibly their middles. Actually all melodies end on the same interval, the tonic, number one. If this is not literally at the top of the row of notes forming the closing chord, it is sure to be somewhere on the way down. Generally it is both at the top and at the bottom, for tunes have a habit of ending solidly on their key-note.

Examine any number of familiar melodies, and you will find this absolute consistency of endings. Occasionally a singer is permitted to go up an octave for the sake of a high note, or perhaps to end on the third or the fifth. But the tone that remains in your memory when any piece is finished is interval number one, the ground floor.

THOSE GENTLE CADENCES

Study the various ways in which "Amen" is sung in church. You will find that its final tone can be approached from almost any interval, but will itself always be one of the three guardsmen of the scale, Tonic, Dominant or Mediant. And the basic tone, whether it is in the treble or the bass, will be the key-note, number one, in a word, Do.*

Here are several varieties of Amens, all illustrating this principle:

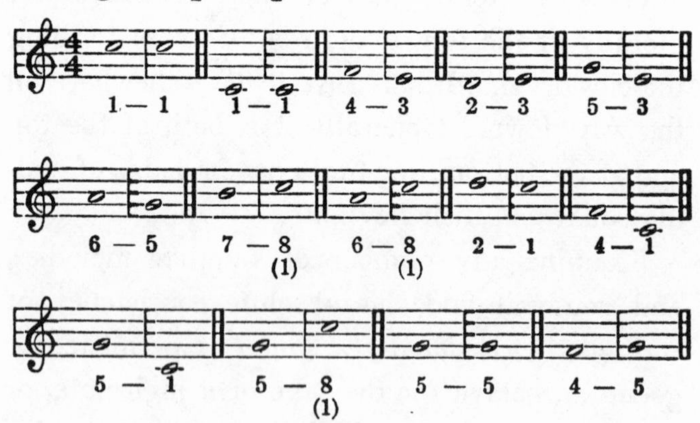

Between the beginning and the end of a melody much may happen. It seems impossible to formulate any set rules for the making of successful tunes. All kinds have won popularity. In some cases it seems to be an obvious progression of tones that wins favor. In others it is a distinct twist of originality.

Clearly, however, a tune should not be too difficult, if it is to gain wide acceptance. It must not jump around to unexpected intervals, nor should it demand too great a range of voice from the average singer.

*So-called in the "tonic sol-fa" system. See Glossary.

Ernest Ball did a very clever thing when he wrote the chorus of "Love me and the World is mine." The actual range of that tune is only seven intervals, really less than six full tones, for its top note is only eleven half-tones higher than its bottom note. But the composer gives the impression of a tremendous range by saving the jump to the top note until quite near the end, meanwhile making a very gradual ascent, and returning each time almost to where he started.

LOVE ME AND THE WORLD IS MINE

There is a great satisfaction in singing that chorus, quite aside from the close harmony that it invites. You can easily persuade yourself that you are a great singer as you rise lustily to its climax, although you are actually covering less than one octave in the scale.

A few tunes like Abide with Me and Lead, Kindly Light, have an even smaller range than this, being limited to six intervals and only ten half-tones. America and The Old Oaken

Bucket have the same range as "Love me and the World is mine," seven intervals.

The range of the Doxology, My Old Kentucky Home, "Carry me back to Old Virginny," and "Massa's in de cold, cold Ground" is one octave, eight intervals.

Nine intervals are enough for Old Black Joe, Old Folks at Home, and Love's Old, Sweet Song. The chorus of My Hero, generally considered as having quite a range, shares with Dixie and Annie Laurie the possession of ten intervals. Auld Lang Syne (with its top note) and Handel's Largo require eleven, and The Star Spangled Banner frightens the best of patriots with its range of twelve.

Thirteen seems to be about the limit for tunes that attain any real vogue. Victor Herbert risked this unlucky number in "Kiss me again," and you find it also in Turkey in the Straw, and the first waltz of Three o'clock in the Morning.

If you made a chart of the chorus of "Love me and the World is mine," like a fever-chart, or sales statistics, it would look something like this, with gradually rising intervals:

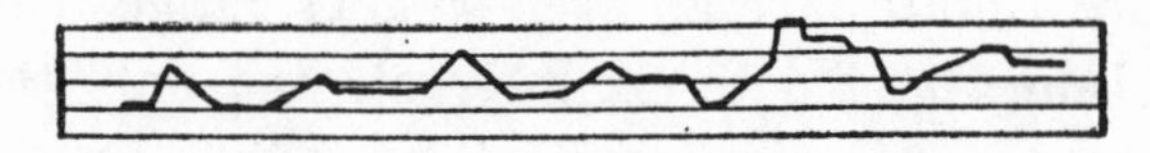

Some successful tunes follow the progression of the scale itself quite closely, and there seems a certain satisfaction in this. Handel's Largo is a good example. It really consists of two tunes, one the introduction, the other the vocal or instrumental solo. The first moves always along the line of the scale, with an occasional jump for a fresh start. The second has more variety, but also inclines toward the regular progression from one interval to its next-door neighbor.

Old Black Joe shows a chart of greater variability, and Old Folks at Home jumps from chills to fever without a qualm.

OLD BLACK JOE

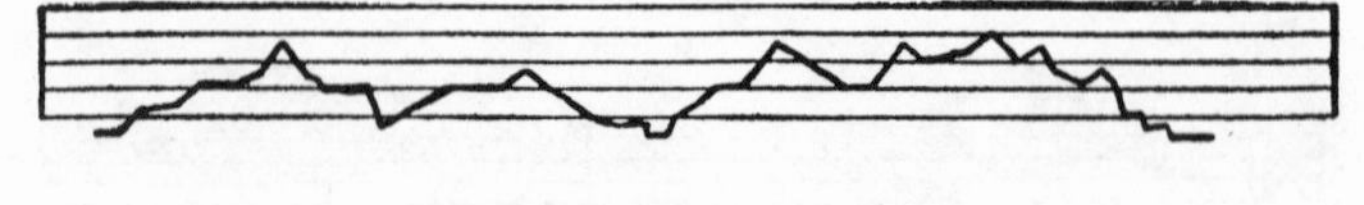

OLD FOLKS AT HOME

If you are learning to read notes, the chart system is a good one to adopt. In fact many a choir or glee club singer supposedly fulfilling the condition of "reading at sight" actually follows a rather hazy mental diagram of higher and lower intervals, without ever being quite sure of where they are, until the director sounds them on the piano, or the singer alongside, proudly confident, blares them out with an accuracy perhaps far in advance of the vocal quality.

Really good sight-readers are rare, and if you develop the faculty of picking up vocal parts largely by ear, and at the same time succeed in bringing out whatever natural beauty your voice may possess, you will probably be welcomed in any amateur chorus. You can train yourself also to look at a page of music and hear it mentally, without the help of a single tone actually sounded.*

TRY THESE NUMBERS OFTEN

If you glance again at the charts above, you will realize more than ever how melodies come

*This book does not pretend to teach note-reading, although you should have a fair idea of its fundamentals by the time you have finished. Karl W. Gehrkens handles the subject clearly and interestingly in his new book, "The Fundamentals of Music," which begins the course of study adopted by the National Federation of Music Clubs, and you will find lots of other helpful guides to this and the greater musical mysteries, once your interest is aroused. See also Appendix A.

home to roost on those comfortable perches numbered one, three and five. They are worth remembering, by ear and by sight, for they have supported a vast brood of musical offspring.

There are no hard and fast rules of melody-making, and some of the finest tunes in the world are equally effective in several variations. But those three steps, one, three and five, seem to keep a constant significance. They are truly the lucid intervals of music.

Great composers do not seem to have worried very much about the originality of their tunes. They went ahead and wrote down sincerely what they felt. Perhaps some of our modern writers of music are too anxious to be original at all costs.

Melody in music is something more than a haphazard leaping from interval to interval. There is a universal law of some sort which demands that we do not wander too far from the paths of tradition. The quality of reminiscence is not strained, provided a composer finds some way of dropping the gentle rain of individuality somewhere into his work.

HONEST MASTERS OF MELODY

Franz Schubert wrote over six hundred songs, many of which are admittedly rather commonplace. But more than a hundred of them are permanently enshrined as masterpieces, and for their sake all of the obviousness and self-repetition in the rest may well be forgotten.

Beethoven, Brahms and Wagner were all inclined to repeat themselves, but their intense honesty gave a tremendous power to every shot that hit the bull's-eye. They did not stop to inquire whether every note that came from their pens was absolutely original. They simply trusted their musical instincts and let it go at that; and their listeners have found it fairly easy to separate the immortal inspirations from the mere space-fillers.

SCHOLARS WOULD A-WOOING GO

Our popular composers of to-day make originality the least of their worries. They echo whatever has a quick appeal, consciously or unconsciously, and the public glories in the reminiscence. More than one serious musician has been heard to say, with melancholy envy, "I wish I could write a popular hit," and perhaps it is self-consciousness alone that keeps him from doing it.

There is a story that Brahms wrote of the Strauss Blue Danube Waltz, "Alas, not by Brahms." Rachmaninoff, Levitzki and Heifetz are fascinated by American jazz, and the well-constructed melodies of Victor Herbert win the honest admiration of his most scholarly colleagues.

The lucid intervals of music find their way eventually to every composer and in turn to every listener.

Do not be discouraged if some of the foregoing has seemed a little difficult. Remember the milestones of melody, one, three and five, and proceed blithely to apply them in the discovery of "close harmony."

CHAPTER VIII

CLOSE HARMONY

HAVE you ever listened with envy to people who can sing "close harmony" by ear, especially the first bass part in a male quartet, or can sit down at a piano and pick out chords that sound just grand, and maybe "fake" an accompaniment to any tune you whistle?

A natural musician can do all that without half trying, or even thinking about it. Perhaps you can already do a little of it yourself, but not enough to satisfy you.

Every child, if given the opportunity, will go to a piano and pretend to play, and after a certain age it will try to pick out tunes with one finger. Later it may look for some easy harmonies, and if it is blessed with any talent at all, this quickly leads to a fair command of "playing by ear." Most popular music is played in that way, and much of it is composed by the same process.

If you have not some special musical gift, you will never go very far as a "natural" player or singer. But whatever instinct may be yours can easily be developed to a stage at which you at least will get some fun out of it, no matter how other people may be affected.

MAKING THE BEST OF IT

Take a good look at this subject of harmony, as your fingers pick it out of the keyboard, or your voice hauls it down from the air. (It is always "close harmony" to the novice, although musicians limit the term to tones which actually lie close together in the scale.)

Find again those white keys of the piano that play the opening of the Star Spangled Banner. Go down from number five to three and one, or start right on the bottom step, whichever you wish. After you have played the tones of

"Oh, say can you see," strike them all four together. What you now hear is a perfect chord of C major (assuming that you are using the white keys only), and you can get the same effect in any other part of the keyboard by placing your fingers in the same relative positions.

Listen to this combination carefully and notice the intervals of which it is composed. You will recognize once more our old friends of the bugle-call, the natural landings between the first and second floors of our musical building, the three guardsmen of melody, Tonic, Mediant and Dominant, who now prove even more important in the court of harmony. Topping their pyramid is little old Octave, the same tone as number one, but a whole section higher up.

THE MAJOR CHORD

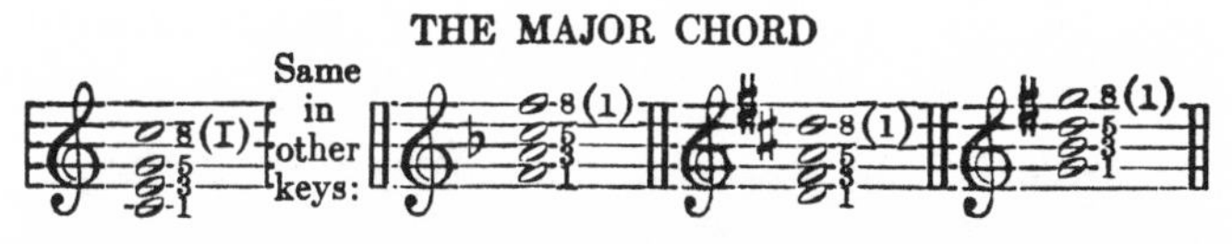

HARMONIOUS PERFECTION

You cannot add anything to that chord without spoiling the effect, or simply repeating tones already marked "present." It is complete in itself, even though you can take a whole left hand full of one-three-five-eight to give it more range and solidity. It is the chord that the minstrels play as the interlocutor says, "Gentlemen, be seated."

TA-DAH!

It marks the finish of the bareback riding act in the circus, when the beautiful lady leaps lightly to the tanbark from her well-upholstered steed; and it has introduced many a stump speaker or political candidate to a crowd far less harmonious than the band that stimulated its enthusiasm.

Keep that chord in your memory. It is the finish of every normal piece of music that ever existed in a major key. Four tones are enough for any harmony, and when it is a perfect major chord, one of the tones is sure to be doubled, just as here number eight doubles number one (*i.e.,* is its equivalent). If you drop interval number three half a tone, to the black key just to its left, you get a minor instead of a major chord.

Play the chord both ways, and let the difference sink into your ears. The minor chord sounds less robust and satisfying than the major. It has a suggestion of melancholy, an atmosphere of incompletion, mixed with regret.

That is the significance given to the minor harmonies by most composers. They are common in folk-music, much of which has a distinct strain of sadness. You can turn any major chord into a minor, and similarly you can take any major tune and play it in minor style. (Look up the case of Avalon, page 40, which was changed, vice-versa, from minor into major.)

Here is the way it would work with the Star Spangled Banner:

STAR SPANGLED BANNER WITH MINOR THIRDS

You already realize that nothing can be added to the perfect major chord except repetitions of the intervals already in it. You realize also that any other combination between a tone and its octave (one and eight) would sound incomplete, unsatisfactory, or even downright ugly.

EXPERIMENTS

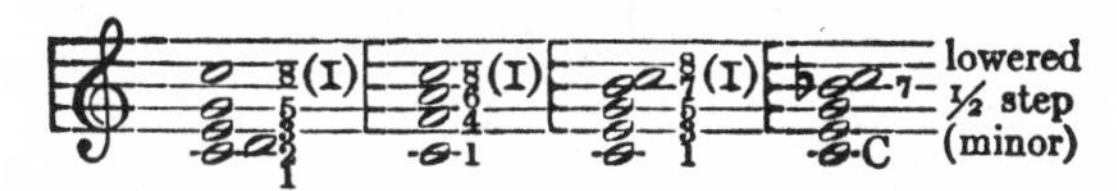

Try slipping in a number two step. Terrible! Take it away! Try a number four. O. K. if you substitute six for five and drop out three altogether. But then you have an entirely different chord, actually in a different key, one which merely suggests the beginning of an Amen, without any sense of completeness.

Mixing in the shy little half-step sister, number seven, is no better than the experiment with number two. No harmony there!

A SEVENTH HEAVEN?

Drop the seventh half a tone lower, keeping one, three, five and eight in the chord, and the effect is pleasing enough, but still absolutely incomplete. Much the same thing happens if you allow any of the other black keys to take up the white keys' burden.

Start therefore with the conviction that the perfect major chord is worthy of your lasting loyalty. It will give a satisfying finish to any piece, and it will act as a guidepost for all explorations you may wish to make into the more distant fields of harmony.

ALL VOICES DIVIDED INTO FOUR PARTS

As there are four intervals in the perfect chord (even though two of them may be the same), so there are four voices in every perfect combination for creating harmony. In a mixed quartet, or chorus of men and women, the voices are soprano, alto, tenor and bass. In a male quartet, or glee club, they are first tenor, second tenor, first bass and second bass. In a string quartet they are first violin, second violin, viola and 'cello. (In an orchestra the bass viols merely add extra depth and power to the 'cellos, without changing the essential line-up of the string quartet.)

SOMEONE GETS THE AIR

Now the easiest part to sing in any harmonizing crowd is of course the air, or the "lead," as some people call it. If you have a good lusty voice, able to keep in tune, with plenty of confidence (and particularly if you know the words of a lot of songs), sing the lead by all means. Then you can gaily say to the world, "Every man for himself, and the devil take the highest."

But if you find it easy to "moan" in harmony with the air, and if your imagination suggests ever new ways of filling out the "barber-shops," then you will leave the more prosaic work of melody-shouting to others (which is one reason why you so often hear a crowd that seems to be all tenor and very little air.)

BASS-SINGING SIMPLIFIED

Next to the melody, the easiest part to sing in either a mixed or a male quartet is the low bass. Some people have the illusion that the bass merely doubles the melody, "way down yonder." They are not intended for bass-singers.

Actually a bass needs only about three tones to do all the necessary damage in a quartet. They are the intervals one, four and five, an octave or more below the melody.

Usually the bass starts on the key-note, and he always ends on it, which may be one reason for the idea that he can simply follow the melody on the lower level in between times.

But if the bass gets the right start, which should not be difficult, he need only keep his ears open and shift to number four or five, as the case may be. He can sing these intervals either above or below his original key-note, depending partly on his low range. For example:

OLD BLACK JOE

MY OLD KENTUCKY HOME

For all practical purposes, in the kind of harmonizing that is likely to be done around the home or the club, these three tones are sufficient for the bass-singer. If he is ambitious, he may occasionally use a sixth with good effect, and now and then the number two step. The third and the seventh have almost no place in his vocabulary, and where they might seem to be used, it is really a change of key that takes place.

Notice, however, the possible variations of the

bass in the three pieces above, beyond the obvious intervals already suggested:

FANCY BASS (OLD FOLKS AT HOME)

SAME FOR OLD BLACK JOE

MY OLD KENTUCKY HOME

There are no absolute rules for singing bass, although it is generally bad business to double any part except the melody. You will find by experience, however, that the key-note (number one) will harmonize with the melody when it is itself on the keynote, the third or the fifth.

A fourth in the bass will harmonize with its double in the melody, or with a sixth, or, for that matter, with the key-note and its octave (one and eight). When the bass properly sings a fifth above or below the key-note, you will probably find the melody also on the fifth, or, more likely still, on the second, the fourth or the seventh.

There is about such combinations (based on the fifth) a feeling of secondary importance, as compared with the primary quality of the major chords on the key-note (tonic). In fact, you may conveniently speak of all ordinary harmonizing as being done on primary and secondary chords, with an occasional extra, based on the fourth interval.*

Just because he can get along with three tones, however, is no reason why a bass-singer should be satisfied with this limited equipment. He will find more and more beautiful effects, particularly as he develops the ability to read notes.

The half-tone steps will become gradually fa-

*Musicians call this secondary chord the chord of the "dominant seventh," because it has the dominant, or fifth interval, as its base, and builds up to the minor seventh above that tone.

miliar to him, and he will delight in changing the entire character of a chord by such a slight shifting of his part. Eventually he will be able to manage so difficult a bass as that of Sweet and Low, which is practically never sung correctly by ear, either by the bass or by the tenor, and which even the printed notes do not always clarify for the average reader.

TOUCHING EVERY BASS

The only possible advice to a would-be bass harmonist is to start with the two or three absolutely necessary intervals, the key-note, the fifth, and perhaps the fourth. In some pieces he may get along with a single change, from tonic to dominant (one to five) and back again. Then he may gradually branch out, experimenting with different intervals that seem to harmonize, working out new combinations at the piano, and, if possible, learning to read notes.

His progress may be slow, but it will be sure, and the thrill of sustaining a tone that is absolutely necessary for the character of a chord is something that can never be taken away from him. The second or low bass in a male quartet or glee club follows the same system as the bass in a mixed group (male and female voices) so no distinctions are necessary.

THE EVEN TENOR'S WAY

After the bass comes the tenor.

In a mixed quartet he sings a part very much like that of the first or high tenor of a male quartet. In each case the effect is that of singing above the melody.

With girls' voices to carry the air, a tenor and a bass will make sufficient harmony for general satisfaction, and similarly three parts are adequate for most of the masculine effects. (Sometimes the girls will try a tenor part, over a male melody, but this is not so good.)

For the ambitious tenor singer it is best to start out with pieces that allow him to travel most of the way just three steps above the melody (counting it as "one"). A good example is the familiar Good-night, Ladies:

GOOD-NIGHT, LADIES

Notice that the tenor stays three steps above the melody at all times except when it drops below the key-note, when the tenor simply hangs on to the third above the key-note, below which he need never go. Other examples, which prove the same point:

When the air stays solidly on the key-note, the tenor has a fine chance to lead the way through various "barber-shop chords," which really represent changes of key, with one tone remaining constant. Thus are the "close harmony endings" created. "Hold it!" is the silent command to the leader, or melody-singer, as the last notė is reached, and then the other two or three harmonizers "moan" their tentative modulations till breath departs:

BARBER-SHOP ENDINGS

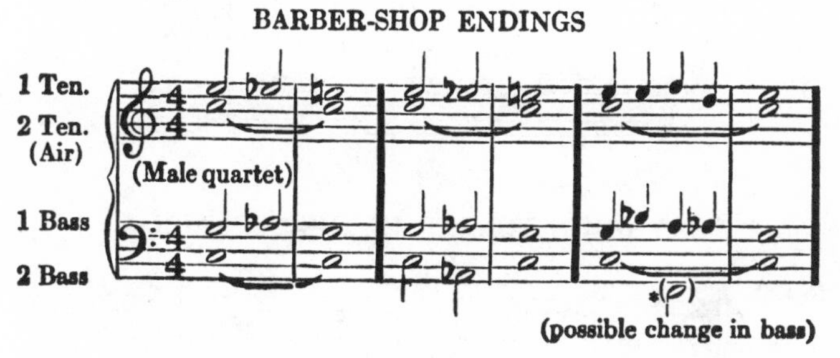

On tunes like Sweet Adeline and "Way down yonder in the Cornfield," these effects can be introduced all the way through, as the air repeatedly stops on a sustained tone:

SWEET ADELINE

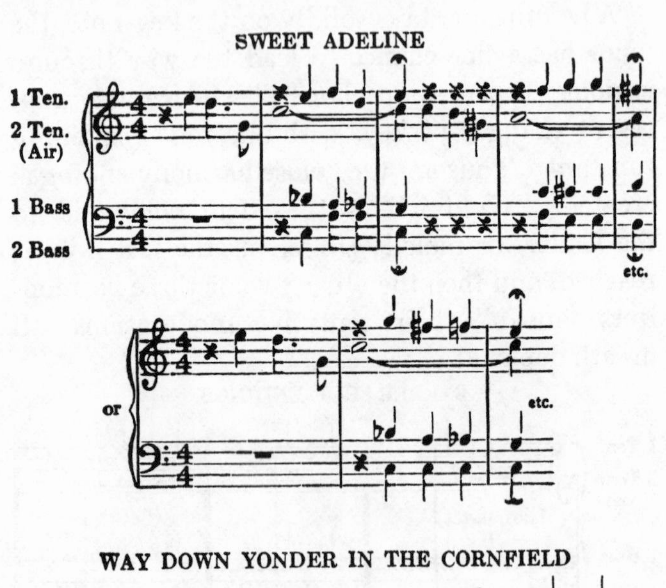

WAY DOWN YONDER IN THE CORNFIELD

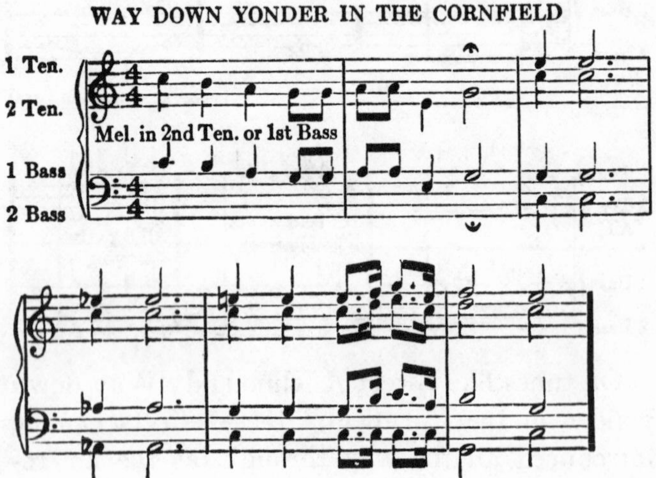

POSSIBLE VARIATIONS

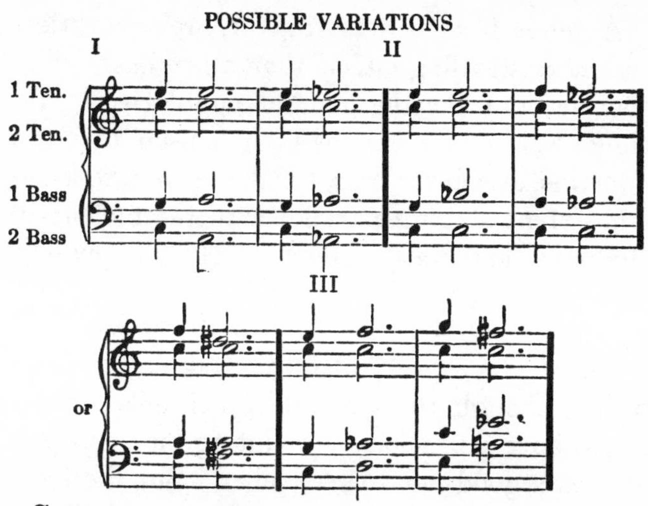

Some tenors like to soar to the heavens at every opportunity, but in doing this they are very likely stealing a tone from the first bass or alto, as the case may be, and simply forcing the singers of those parts to switch without warning to what should normally be the tenor notes.

FROM LINDY

A tenor has chances for far greater variety and more startling effects than a low bass, which may account for the general popularity of the higher voice. He cannot limit himself to a few intervals, as can the bass, for the tenor is to a certain extent singing parallel with the melody at all times, and must follow its changes closely.

ENDURANCE IS ABSOLUTELY NECESSARY

There are no set rules for "faking" a tenor part, although the general principle of "three steps above the melody" (counting the melody as one) is a good one to remember. But the more you sing tenor, the more possibilities you will find for new and original effects, and again it is advisable that you learn to read notes, and thus discover some real part-writing for yourself.

Tenor parts in mixed quartets are apt to be a little lower in range than the top tenor in a male quartet. They also lean a bit toward the first bass quality when the alto completes the harmony, and require therefore even greater accuracy and confidence.

ALTO AND FIRST BASS

This brings up the remaining links in the chain of "close harmony." The ability to sing by ear a correct first bass part in a male quartet is one of the best tests of instinctive musicianship. For such a voice must complete the four-part harmony in every case, and it practically never duplicates any of the other parts. In a mixed quartet, this responsibility falls mostly upon the alto, although the tenor has his share of it when the alto follows any simple course.

Some altos work on the theory that they cannot go wrong if they simply follow the melody three steps below its level. This is only partly true.

BATTLE HYMN OF THE REPUBLIC

In all except the simplest songs the alto is more than likely to have a fairly intricate and responsible part. Here again Barnby's Sweet and Low is an interesting model, and it is worth quoting in full, as a mixed quartet, to prove how difficult it would be for any of the singers except the soprano to "fake" their parts by ear.

SWEET AND LOW
TENNYSON
BARNBY
Larghetto.
Soprano
Alto.
pp
Sweet and low, Sweet and low, Wind of the west-ern
Tenor.
Bass.
sf
p
sea, Low, low, Breathe and blow, Wind of the west-ern
mf
sea, O - ver the roll - ing wa - ters go,
pp
Come from the dy - ing moon, and blow,

Once more let the advantage of reading notes be emphasized, for it is only thus that the energetic alto will find the fullest expression for the harmonies of her musical soul.

As for the first bass, or baritone, he is sometimes given the melody in glee clubs or male quartets, partly because of the range and partly because his type of voice is likely to have the richest quality. Strictly speaking, however, the second tenor is the melody part, and, as already suggested, with a first tenor and a low bass, the remaining part may be omitted altogether. (When the first tenor has the air, the second tenor becomes practically an alto, which is difficult.)

But a good first bass, filling out an interesting four-part harmony in male voices, is something not easily forgotten; and the satisfaction of singing such a part, whether by ear or by note, is almost indescribable.

The chief duty of the first bass is to find the missing link in the human foursome, and fill it in with confidence and in perfect tune. His part will practically never duplicate any other, for even if a chord contains only three real intervals, the duplication is almost sure to occur in the low bass.

Experiment first with the logical completion of such harmonies as the following:

1 Ten.
2 Ten.
1 Bass
2 Bass

See also the first bass parts in the "barber-shop chords" above.

A few general deductions may be drawn. For instance, in a perfect major chord, the first bass normally sings the interval of the fifth. This may be considered his home-base, from which he works in both directions, according to the needs of the harmony. He must remember that good part-singing demands a fair consistency in the harmonizing voices as well as in the melody. A tenor part should have something like a tune of its own, and even a low bass may occasionally suggest an actual independent melody. The first bass is the most difficult part to keep on a strict melodic basis, especially when the other singers, working by ear, force the baritone into strange and illogical jumps. But it can be done; and a truly melodious first bass part is a joy indeed, to the singer as well as the listener.

Let the ambitious exponent of this most musical and most difficult of all the four parts remember then that upon him devolves the responsibility of completing every chord. No matter what the other voices do, there is generally one tone left, which will fill out a satisfactory harmony. Let him stubbornly refuse to take refuge in the mere doubling of some other part. That is the province of the low bass, and of the "extras," who always add volume and sometimes quality to group-singing, but without contributing anything of musical leadership.

Finally, let the baritone, like the other singers, work up some knowledge of note-reading, so that the skilled composer may indicate to him, in the simplest of codes, how his voice will blend most beautifully with those around him. A natural first bass, able to harmonize anything by ear, is rare enough to be called practically extinct. But a baritone may be developed into both a good reader and a fairly consistent part-finder by the simple process of drilling correct music into his ears through the printed page, with perhaps the help of a leader at the piano.*

Through this brief excursion into the not so mysterious realm of part-singing, you have discovered some fundamentals of harmony in general. You now know that four parts are sufficient for any chord, and that beyond this you seldom find more than a duplication of the individual voices. You have found also that two or three chords will serve to harmonize most simple tunes, and that in these chords the intervals of tonic and dominant (number one and number five) are the most common, with occasional help

*The foregoing is merely to get singers' ears started in the right direction. Don't worry about the numbers of intervals, once your ear tells you you are right.

from the fourth (or subdominant) and other steps.

For purposes of harmonizing at the piano, the same principles may be applied, with a greater range over the keyboard, as contrasted with the limitations of the human voice.

One of the simplest lessons in piano harmony is the familiar Chopsticks, which is usually performed by two players. One uses two fingers (the forefinger of each hand) to play a tune, with variations, generally high up on the keyboard, and this tune consists merely of different combinations of the seven tones in the diatonic scale. (It is considered quite a trick to work in a "glissando," or sliding effect, trills, etc.)

Written out with its simplest accompaniment (played by the second performer, further down on the keyboard) Chopsticks looks something like this:

CHOPSTICKS

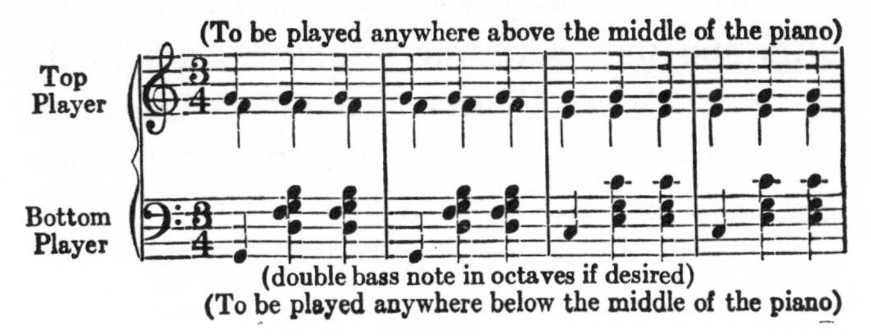

If you study this combination from the standpoint of vocal part-writing, you will discover that you are dealing once more with your old friends, the primary and secondary chords, otherwise known as the tonic major and the dominant seventh. But in this case the piece begins with the secondary chord, and leads from that into the perfect harmony on the key-note. Notice also that the melody, such as it is, begins on the fifth, and works by way of the seventh to the key-note above. The entire tune requires no more harmonizing than the alternation of tonic and dominant chords, and you will be surprised how far this naïve pattern of harmony will carry a number of quite respectable composers.

Now look for some more natural combinations. If you drop to the fourth instead of the fifth below (as the bass singer had to do at times) you will have to build up a new chord, filled out by the sixth and the key-note:

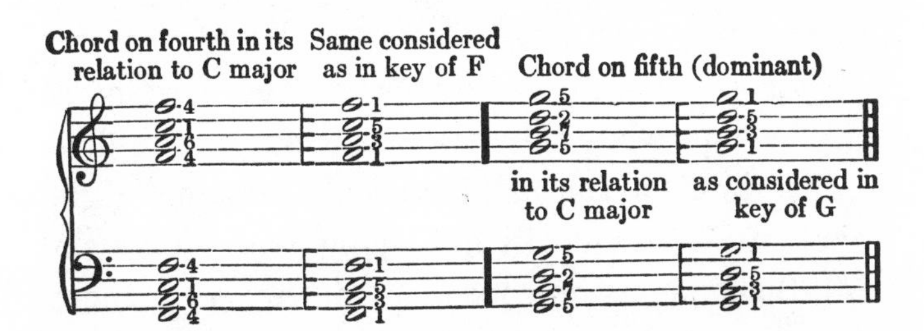

You are now discovering a whole family of harmony, all centering in the relationship between a key-note (in this case C) and its dominant and subdominant (fifth and fourth, or, in this case, G and F). You will find that you can move from the tonic chord of C major to that of G major or F major and back again, without any sensation of abruptness or artificial strain. (It is done constantly in the Amens already noted.)

If you are still game, try dropping your bass of C major to the sixth (A) below. You will have to change your G to an A above, but your E and your original key-note C can remain:

C MAJOR AND RELATIVE MINOR

C major A minor

MUSICAL FAMILY OF C MAJOR

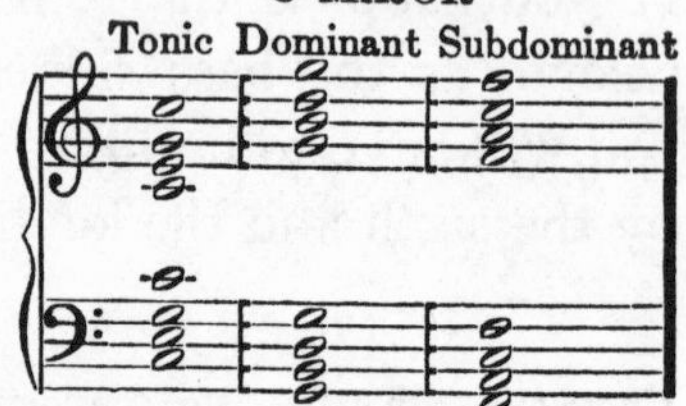

What you have now struck is the chord of A minor, and while the scale of A major would require three sharps (F, C and G) to sound right, that of A minor can get along without any at all, the same as its cousin, C major. It is therefore known by musicians as the "relative minor" of C major. All through music you will find that every major scale has a "relative minor," with the same "signature" (*i. e.* the number of sharps or flats indicated at the start, as holding good all the way).*

THE SCALES—A FABLE

THE Land of Music is peopled by a unique tribe known as The Scales, and sometimes The Keys. They are all inter-related, but some of them hate to admit it.

*When you think harmony, do not think numbers or letters or Do-Re-Mi symbols. Think sounds. It is a good rule of music not to try to grasp more than you can hear, mentally or physically. Therefore, if some of this now seems over your head, come back to it later, when your ear has improved, and see how simple it really is.

Curiously enough, each individual family of this tribe is made up in the same way, so that the groups of relatives are duplicated all over the country in every detail.

They all take their pattern from the famous C family, the natural aristocracy of Scale society. The C's trace their pedigree right back to Guido of Arezzo himself, and point with pride to old Sir John Do as a most popular ancestor.

THE C family, which is a model of its kind, starts naturally with Father Tonic, who is the key-note to all their success. He is of the strong, confident type, absolutely in unison with himself, level-headed, and of unshaken purpose. He gets at the root of things, and keeps all about him in harmony.

Father Tonic's greatest weakness is for his son, little Octave, whom people call his "living image," and whom he is inclined to spoil with excessive affection. He is never so happy as in a congenial family group, with little Octave, Mother Dominant, and Uncle Mediant, all sitting on the steps together.

MOTHER DOMINANT is also a strong personality, inclined to lord it over her unmarried sister, Aunt Subdominant. But she is a wonderful housekeeper, up at five every day of her life, and always ready with the keys to her well-stocked larder.

Father Tonic considers both Dominant and

Subdominant absolutely perfect, and is quite ready to sing with either one of them at any time. (There have been intervals, to be sure, when this perfection was diminished, but someone was always sure to augment it in turn, and so the results just about balanced.)

AUNT SUBDOMINANT got her name from a joking remark that she was exactly as far below Father Tonic in the social scale as Mother Dominant was above him, which made her almost as important in the family, but nobody takes this very seriously. She belongs to the Fourth Estate, and is practically self-supporting.

As for Uncle Mediant, he is not actually a relative at all, but he has always been so kind and helpful that he is considered an indispensable member of the family. He utterly disproves the theory that "Three's a Crowd." Lots of people affectionately call him "Mi" for short, and he has become famous to the public as "Happy Mediant." He has straightened out many a difficulty and brought harmony out of threatening discord, and he makes a wonderful go-between when little Octave and his mother want to get Father Tonic's attention, but don't like to disturb him.

(Uncle Mediant has occasionally been reduced to minor circumstances, but in military circles, where the bugle is his pet instrument, he has the permanent rank of Major.)

THE C family has a cousin, Relative Minor, who suffers from an inferiority complex, even though his initial is A. This is characteristic of all the Minors in the Scale tribe. They are the poor relations of the major portion of the population, always subdued in spirit, sometimes almost melancholy.

There are other Scales who are really quite outside the family circle of Tonic, Dominant, Subdominant and Relative Minor. Perhaps it is their own fault, although it is whispered that they all suffer at intervals from a chromatic affliction.

RAY SECOND has caused innumerable discords in his time, especially when he got mixed up with some of the less scrupulous of the Minor fraternity. (Of course, the up-to-date free-thinkers claim that they are all musical beings anyway, and a little discord never did hurt anybody.)

The gossips also throw up their hands with a meaning "La!" over the escapades of Old Man Sixth, who has often been kept sternly out in the cold. Aunt Subdominant, however, occasionally lets him in by the back door, and it is whispered that there is an old romance between them, which might have come to something if he had only developed his major virtues.

SI SEVENTH, uncouth but good-hearted, is recognized in many circles as a Leading Tone, and his bad manners are excused on the plea that he is a self-made man. He has a habit of keeping just half a step away from little Octave, and for this Mother Dominant once farmed him out to the Minors, and he came back sadly diminished. It is now generally agreed that he will come to no good end.

The C family are very proud. They claim that they need no Tonic outside of their own, and while everything is all right in modulation, some people had better not try to get in without a proper introduction. They admit the kinship of the G's and the F's, by way of Mother Dominant and Aunt Subdominant, and they are glad to do what they can for their poor but honest relatives, the A. Minors.

OF the rest of the Scales they are a little suspicious. There have been some rather questionable real estate operations, with an alarming increase in flats, and on the other side there are open accusations of sharp practice, involving some suspiciously complicated signatures. In fact, the C's have complained bitterly that when you get right down to it, there is no difference between a G Flat and an absolute F Sharp.

But somehow the Scales continue their curiously interlocked existence, and the general result has been harmony. Each family has its own Tonic, Dominant, Subdominant and Relative Minor. With the C's setting the standard by admitting the G's, the F's and the A Minors to their family circle, the rest proceed in exactly the same fashion, each welcoming the association with a simpler and more aristocratic Scale above, and making the best of the obvious relationship which can be claimed by those below.

THUS the G's "claim kin" with the C's, but admit it also with the D's and the E Minors. The D's in turn, point with pride to their G connection, and suffer the entanglement with the A's and the B Minors. The A's have to admit the E's and the F Sharp Minors to their little group, and from there on the whole genealogy becomes more and more filled with such apparently accidental relationships.

Yet if you make the entire round of the Scale tribe, and examine the signatures through every step of their correspondence, you finish inevitably where you began, on the firm level of the natural aristocracy of the C family, which remains the model and pattern for all the rest.*

THESE ARE ACTUAL FACTS

This Fable merely suggests what many a person with the Common Sense of Music, including perhaps yourself, may discover by instinct, following the guidance of an absolutely untrained ear; for that which sounds "right," even to the uninitiated, represents a mathematically correct system whose completeness is positively astonish-

*The Key to this Fable may be found in the chart of the Scales in Appendix A. Work it out on the piano.

ing. No problem of algebra, physics, chemistry or auction bridge contains anything more fascinating than the eternal cycle of the diatonic scales in music.

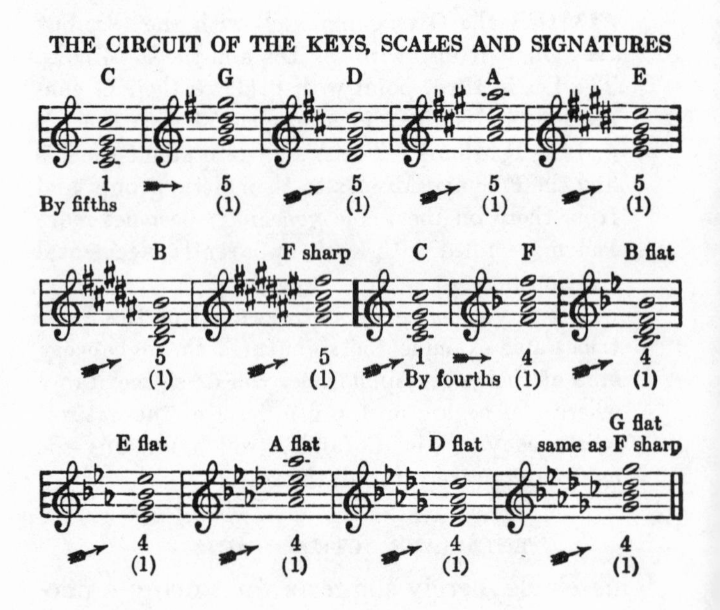

If you want to play the piano by ear, start with the simple keys, C, G, F and perhaps D and B flat. None of these will involve you in more than two sharps or flats at the outside, and while some people claim a fondness for the black keys, it is generally admitted that the smaller the signature and the fewer the "accidentals," the easier it is to play. The five keys suggested are more than enough to allow for the proper pitching of any tune for voices of various kinds, and that is usually the chief consideration in everyday piano-playing. There are lots of pianists of the "natural" type who can play in one key only, and their value for accompanying group-singing is necessarily limited.

Try to develop an equal facility in several keys, always hearing the constant relationships, and thinking in harmony rather than in terms of melody alone. Grow accustomed to the sound of closely related chords, no matter what the key in which you start.

You will find that you can get along with a few chords, a few keys, and a limited range of style. (Incidentally this also applies to playing the guitar.) If you can read notes, so much the better, but your ear will tell you in the long run what is good and what is bad in harmony, and your fingers will necessarily keep within the limits of their physical dexterity.

OUR NEW FREEDOM

The subject of harmony has been hedged about with restrictions in the past, but the modern point of view seems to be that anything will harmonize with anything in music. That is the gist of the theory of Schoenberg, whose scholarly dissonances have disturbed many an orthodox composer.

The trick of creating ultra-modern music is not such a difficult one, for it consists largely of writing deliberately in two or more keys at the same time, and particularly in making tones harmonize with the half-steps on either side of them. Reduced to terms of absurdity the principle works out in this fashion:

MISERERE FROM "IL TROVATORE"

Try this on your piano, or leave it to the nocturnal prowling of the cat. It is not an epoch-making discovery in any case:

MISERERE WITH MELODY HALF TONE HIGHER THAN KEY OF ACCOMPANIMENT

SAME WITH MELODY HALF TONE BELOW KEY

Unless you are a real modernist at heart, don't play too much with the fire of dissonance. But if you once acquire that independence of ear

which marks your budding futurist, may the gods of harmony have mercy on your soul and on your neighbors! It is an insidious germ, which the best of us may catch without warning, and perhaps a new health is to be discovered in the future, by way of apparent disease.

But do not worry if your taste remains stubbornly commonplace for a time. There is a beauty in simplicity as such, and Nature herself is full of platitudes.

Do not seek originality at all costs, therefore, but follow the normal dictates of your sense of hearing. Think in harmony, and your musical horizon will eventually broaden beyond every possible boundary.

CHAPTER IX

A MATTER OF FORM

BY THIS time you ought to have a very fair idea of some of the fundamentals of music: of rhythmic time, which is the physical stimulus, and brings the most primitive and obvious response; of melody, which defies analysis, yet seems to exert the surest and most consistent emotional appeal; and of harmony, which adds still further emotional qualities, but makes also certain demands on the intellect.

As the brain enters more and more into the appreciation of music, it inevitably develops an interest in the subtleties of form, system, organization, technique, or whatever you wish to call it.

Form in music is very much like form in athletics. It is simply the means of securing the greatest effect with a minimum waste of energy. It is the same as system and organization in business, and it has its parallels in architecture, in sculpture, in painting, dancing, writing, and driving an automobile.

ARE YOU IN GOOD FORM?

Your golfer or tennis-player builds up his form because he knows that it will help him to get the best results with the least effort. He may hit a ball with power and accuracy by sheer brute force, yet if he develops the technique of timing, of following through, foot-work, shifting weight, etc., he will become just that much more skillful at his game.

Your business man may have tremendous assets of personality, good-will, capital, imagination, and driving energy, but if he does not systematize his efforts, much of these natural advantages will go to waste.

A COMPOSER'S EQUIPMENT

With your composer of music, melodic invention is the raw material. It is what strength and energy are to the athlete, personal and financial assets to the business man, clay or marble to the sculptor, building materials to the architect, colors to the painter, and words and ideas to the writer or the orator.

Now if a composer wrote nothing but melody from start to finish, it would not only be a terrible waste of material, but his listeners would soon grow sick of this constant sameness, just as children do if they eat jam with a spoon. (See page 77.) The trick of writing interesting music is in creating enough variety and contrast to avoid monotony, yet reminding the hearer with sufficient frequency of the central melodic thought, so that the memory and the imagination will be constantly stimulated.

THEY ALL TRY FOR FORM

This is true even of the simplest popular music. We like tunes that have a faint reminiscence of something we have heard before, but put in a new way. We soon grow tired of the same thing over and over again, yet we do not want anything so completely original as to offer no familiar landmarks whatever.

Form in music concerns itself first of all with the basic truths of tonal relationship. It gives unity and design to even a primitive melody, and, in its higher development, it makes such melodic material flower and expand like the most wonderful works of Nature herself.

The creator of a good tune instinctively expresses his musical idea so as to throw the high light on its most significant portion. The skilled composer, with a complete mastery of formal technique, does the same thing with his original material, but on a more elaborate scale.

CONSERVATION OF ENERGY

As the strength of a composer lies in his melodies, he needs the conserving power of form just as much as the athlete, that his strength may not be wasted. Popular songs become wearisome because they endlessly repeat the same strain of melody. But the best of the popular music, as well as all good folk-music, has enough of form and design to keep it fresh and interesting to the average listener.

Take as an example once more the familiar tune of Old Folks at Home. Its main idea, musically, lies in the opening phrase, starting on the third step, working to the characteristic jump of the octave (which is the feature on which the memory lingers) and getting back again by the simplest of steps to the ground floor. The first time this snatch of melody appears, it is left incomplete, as though a question had been asked, but it immediately repeats itself, this time coming to a full close:

To make sure that the entire musical sentence has been grasped by the listener, Foster now repeats it with both endings, the question and the answer. Then comes his master-stroke of formal simplicity. He introduces a contrasting period which really changes both the key and the character of the melody, going first to the dominant, then back to the tonic, then to the subdominant, the nearest relatives of the key-note, and finally coming back to a closing reminder of the original strain, which is exactly what he wants to leave permanently in our memories:

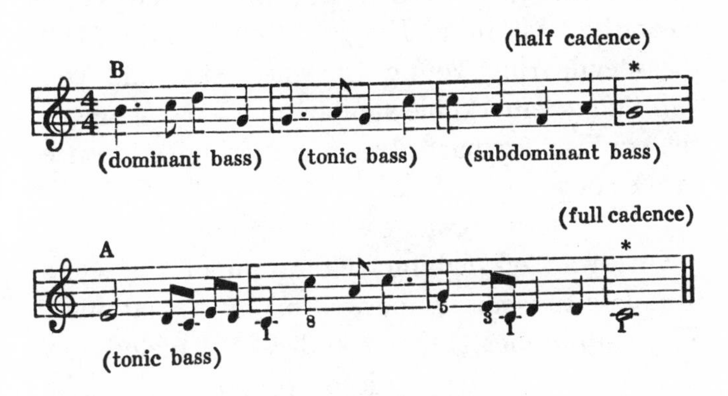

The form of My Old Kentucky Home is almost identical, with one central idea repeated five times, interrupted only by the contrasting period, "Weep no more, my Lady," etc. In fact, this arrangement of material is so common in the song literature of the world that it has been given the general title of "song form." Fundamentally it consists of two parts, the central or significant idea and its contrast, with the former stated at least twice, and probably more often, and the contrasting section interrupting once, where it will serve to draw the greatest attention to the final reminder of the chief melody.

If you call the main idea A, and the contrasting idea B, then your arrangement is essentially that of A-B-A. But it may also be A-A-B-A, or A-A-A-A-B-A. Listen to such tunes as "Carry me back to Old Virginny," "Drink to me only with thine Eyes," "Believe me, if all those endearing young Charms," etc., and you will find a remarkable similarity of arrangement, the contrasting part always occurring only once in the song.

THE MUSICAL SPICE OF LIFE

One way of making reiteration of the same tune less tiresome is the writing of "variations." This simply means that you dress the melody up in a variety of ways, decorating it with additional notes, in various figures, possibly changing the rhythm, or turning the tune from major to minor or vice-versa.

In the simplest variations, the tune remains

clear and prominent. But the form is so flexible that some composers have written variations whose original could scarcely be distinguished.

Take any simple tune, and see how many ways you can play it, by simply decorating it with consistent figures, and changing its rhythm and key. A good melody for variations is the little ABC or counting song that so many children sing. (Some day, incidentally, try and hear the elaborate and diabolically clever variations on this tune written by Dohnanyi for piano and orchestra.)

Here is the first part of the tune unadorned:

A B C TUNE

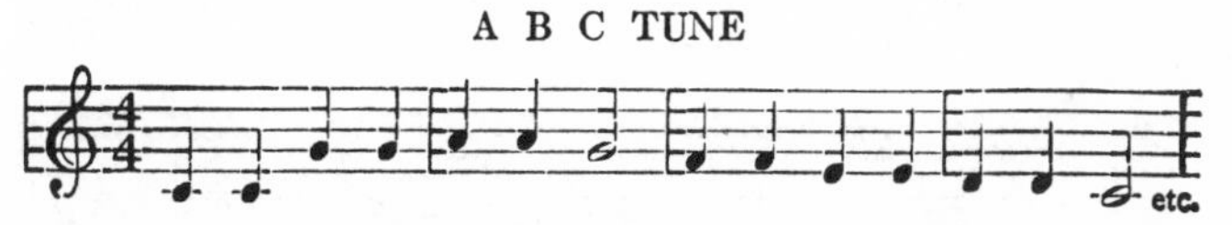

Here it is with an adornment of three extra notes to every note of the melody, which, however, keeps its original time exactly as before:

Here it is with five notes added to each tone by way of decoration, giving the effect of a six-note figure in place of each individual tone:

Such a process can be continued indefinitely by simply varying the number of notes added, and the details of arrangement. Now put the tune into waltz time:

This also can be varied by adding extra notes

to each note of the tune, without interfering with the rhythm:

Try it also in several other rhythmic arrangements:

Finally put the tune into the minor key, to which all the effects above can also be applied:

There is still the possibility of breaking the tune up into sections, playing it in other keys than the original or its minor, and entrusting it to different instruments or combinations of instruments, all of which may aid in the formal elaboration.

In this connection, look up the slow movement (second) of Beethoven's Fifth Symphony, which consists largely of variations on a tune first sung by 'cellos and violas:

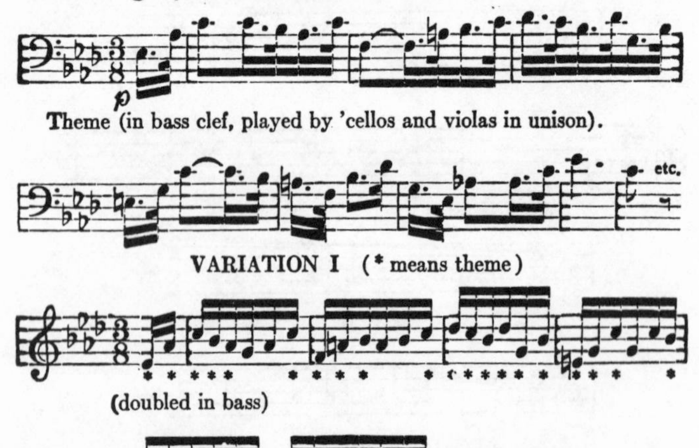

VARIATION II

(The same general figure in two other variations, given to different instruments, including the bass-viols.)

(Later also a touch of minor

and some counterpoint by full orchestra.)

Mozart wrote a beautiful set of variations on a pastoral air (Pastorale Variée) and Brahms, Reger and other modern composers have created some truly astonishing works in this form.

Liszt, in his paraphrases of the Rigoletto Quartet and other music, set a style which goes beyond the simple variation idea, and really makes a new tune out of an old one. The Schulz-Evler arrangement of the familiar Blue Danube Waltz is a brilliant example of such workmanship, and Godowsky has gone even further in his amazing transcriptions of other waltz-tunes.

WHEN TUNE MEETS TUNE

You can build up your musical form still further by making different tunes harmonize with each other, or the same tune with itself. For instance, try singing The Long, Long Trail while someone else sings "Keep the Home Fires Burning." You will find that the two may be combined quite easily, if you start them both on the same down-beat. (The Long, Long Trail begins on an up-beat, and has two tones before the first down-beat.)

You can do the same thing with Tipperary and "Pack up your Troubles."

The Civil War might have ended sooner if everybody had only realized that Dixie and Yankee Doodle could be sung simultaneously, in a very respectable harmony:

Perhaps you remember also that old song "Because You're You," in Victor Herbert's Red Mill, in which someone always took special pride in imitating the melody just one measure behind the leader:

Another favorite was the combination of The Spanish Cavalier and Solomon Levi (using the first half of the second tune):

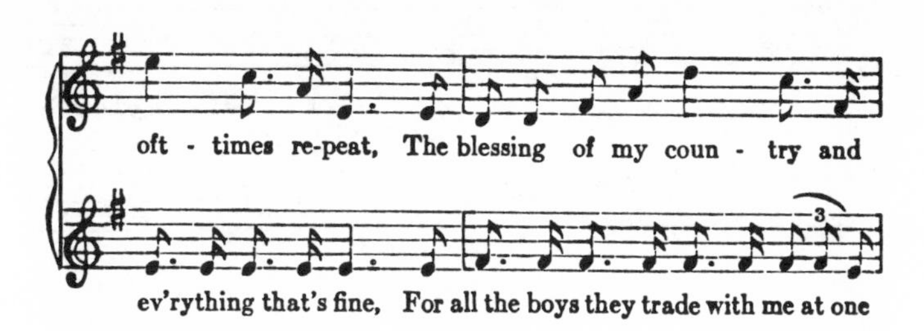

Perhaps the most interesting of the lot, musically, is the decoration of the first section of Old Folks at Home with the lilting strains of Dvorak's famous Humoresque, which gave a great motion-picture its title not so long ago:

OLD FOLKS AT HOME

(Such musical coincidences provide splendid material for song-contests, with half of a crowd singing against the other half.)

Musicians use the term "counterpoint" to describe this simple trick of making one melody harmonize with another. Harmony really began with the process of having several voices sing independent tunes, each one probably considering itself the most important, as is still the case in some quartets.

EVERYONE FOR HIMSELF

The music which existed before much distinction was made between melody and accompaniment was called "polyphonic" or "many-voiced," and many choruses and instrumental numbers are still written in that way.

When a tune is made to harmonize with itself (by starting it in a second voice after the first is well under way), it is called a "canon," which strictly means nothing more than "law" or "rule." (Remember, of course, that a tune is the same no matter what key it is played in, and this fact gives unlimited opportunities for self-developed harmony.)

Schubert has some beautiful examples of counterpoint in his Unfinished Symphony. Listen for a passage in the opening movement where the first violins are imitated by their seconds in The Song of Love melody, with a third part eventually joining in:

The opera Carmen also exhibits clear and charming counterpoint in its music between the acts, particularly one intermezzo, in which a flute part soars harmoniousy above the principal melody:

Bach wrote his Inventions for the piano in two and three parts, and some of these are in "canon," others merely contrapuntal. (Strictly speaking, the word "counterpoint" refers to the process of setting down music "point against point," or note against note. A contrapuntal melody is often called a counter-melody, and appears thus frequently in modern jazz.)

But the most astounding examples of counterpoint occur in the Wagnerian operas, in which several melodies are sometimes going on at the same time in the orchestra alone. Near the close of the Meistersinger Prelude, for instance, the violins are playing a part of the Prize Song, while the opening theme comes out strongly in the basses and the middle parts fill in with the pompous march-tune to which the musical tradesmen assemble:

In that elaborate and difficult type of composition known as a "fugue" (the caviar of musical culture), counterpoint, "imitation" and canon all play a part, and scraps of melody are made to prove relationships as insistently as heirs facing a family lawyer.

Literally a fugue is a flight, and it always follows the general plan of a pursuit, the Eliza of one theme keeping just ahead of the bloodhounds of another, and the actual tones and rhythms providing as much excitement for the composer (and in rare instances the listener) as though they were the living characters of a drama. (Fugues have been written chiefly for the organ, with Bach as their greatest master; but you will find fugal passages also in symphonies, choral works, and other music in the larger forms. Milton picturesquely described an organist whose "volant touch . . . fled and pursued transverse the resonant fugue.")*

When people sing a "round," they are singing an infinite canon, for the tune could go on forever harmonizing with itself, in several parts. This is a good way, incidentally, to grow accustomed to singing in harmony. First learn the tune. Then stick to it even when the parts become absolutely interlocked. You will find it more and more easy to learn parts that do not seem to have any definite relation with the tune itself.

Appendix B contains several rounds, which anyone can sing. Divide a crowd into evenly balanced groups, and teach them these rounds, and you can make them sound like a regular chorus.

This principle of self-relationship in tunes is applied also to the building up of melodies them-

*See the discussion of this and other poetic passages in the author's doctoral dissertation, "Milton's Knowledge of Music," published by G. Schirmer, New York.

selves. You can lengthen out a melodic snatch by simply repeating it in another key, or you can imitate it without absolutely copying it, or you can "invert" it by making the tones move upward where originally they moved downward, and vice-versa. You can even play it backwards, or you can "augment" it by lengthening each tone and thus slowing up the time.

Various popular composers have made use of such common features of musical form. You will find, for instance, a clear and clever structure in Irving Berlin's Alexander's Rag-time Band. Disregarding the verse, which in itself follows a definite form, the chorus first shows a little chromatic motive on only two tones, repeated three times and then working to the logical key-note:

After that, the composer simply takes the same combination and puts it up four steps, repeating it in the key of the subdominant (or fourth interval) with a slight difference in the finish:

Next he introduces a contrasting musical idea in imitation of a bugle-call, followed by an actual bugle-combination on the key-note:

Then he prepares for a general repetition by modulating first to the dominant and then back to the original key:

Now comes the restatement of the first phrase and its imitation, and Mr. Berlin is ready for a quite individual finish. His text leads him to suggest the melody of Old Folks at Home, which he actually quotes just before and on the words "Swanee River," and a final reminder of the "Ta-ra-ta-ra" effect brings the chorus to a close:

Lou Hirsch achieved something similar in his chorus of The Love Nest, one of the most popular tunes of recent years. The actual material of this chorus consists of two short phrases, both reminiscent, but both justified by the skill with which they are used.

He starts naturally with his first phrase, but immediately repeats it in the key of the subdominant (four steps higher) as Mr. Berlin did in his Alexander song:

(Incidentally, the use of the triplet against two eighth-note beats gives the phrase quite an original and attractive character.)

Now comes the second phrase (lifted bodily but perhaps unintentionally from a song by Oscar Straus), and this also imitates itself immediately in another key:

The incompleted cadence leads logically to a repetition of the first part, including both phrases, but omitting the second imitation, after which Mr. Hirsch has merely to end his chorus, which he does by once more imitating his first phrase, with just a suggestion of minor key:

Even though Mr. Berlin and Mr. Hirsch may have been quite unconscious technicians in building up these fairly obvious choruses, the formal structure is nevertheless entirely clear. In fact, it has been characteristic of the history of music that at all times there were natural musicians working out by instinct the same principles that the scholars of the day, or perhaps another day, evolved laboriously in the seclusion of their studies.

NATURAL AND CONSCIOUS MUSIC

While the monks of an earlier time created painstakingly some rules of music which are still looked upon with veneration, Nature's own singers were melodizing and harmonizing without the help of a book or a written note, and it is this folk-music which has proved permanently most significant.

In every period there has been such a parallel productiveness of the trained and the natural musician. People have sung or played "by ear," and invented melodies "without knowing one note from another," and because they were unconsciously following universal laws, their work often took its place with the conscious art of their time, or a later time. In many instances these naïvely honest folk-tunes provided the real inspiration for symphonies and other masterpieces of music.*

MORE ELABORATE WORKMANSHIP

The elements of form which are found even in simple folk-tunes and popular music are merely broadened along logical lines in the greater classic compositions. The principle is always the same. Essentially it has to do with unity through contrast. That is to say, a piece of music, like a story, or a play, or a picture, or a piece of sculpture or architecture, generally presents materials of a conflicting nature, and succeeds eventually in creating a unity through the very conflict which is so necessary for the sustaining of interest.

STRENGTH IN UNITY

We do not care about a book or a play in which we know at every moment exactly what

*While rag-time is unquestionably the folk-music of modern America, and the only American music which has been recognized in other lands as characteristically national and individual, it is by no means necessary to think of it as the final word or the only medium of our musical self-expression. It has scarcely begun to reach beyond the stage of the obvious, and is at present little more than an unmistakable expression of restless energy and occasionally of a downright animal vulgarity which no honest and normally healthy human being need deny as a natural part of his make-up.

If there is ever to be a typically American music that will command universal respect and sincere liking, it must be built largely upon elements which are prevalent today in a cheap and commonplace form, but which may well produce in time something equally sincere and natural, but possessed of a true dignity and a permanent beauty.

is going to happen next. We want to be excited and stimulated by an actual battle of minds or personalities or world forces. Yet we want to be assured in the end that all is as it should be, a happy ending if possible, but a logical ending above all else. We want the problem solved, the conflict decided in no uncertain terms.

We do not like an incoherent picture, which is one reason why we do not like futuristic painting. We welcome contrast, but we demand unity nevertheless. We abhor a shapeless building or statue, yet we would never be satisfied with a mere evenness of architecture or sculpture. Unconsciously we admire the structure whose artist has made use of varied materials, whether in colors, tones, words and thoughts, or clay, wood and stone, and succeeded in bringing these contrasting materials to a final and inevitable unity.

Object and design, system and organization, these are the fundamentals of form, in art, business or athletics. The ancient Greeks themselves used the word "harmony" to indicate "system," and the original idea of "symphony" is nothing more than a "sounding together." Just as form in athletics is organized effort, so form in music is organized material, and the material has always been and will always be the same: tones and time, with their possible elaborations.

DON'T LET THIS FRIGHTEN YOU

It is the underlying principle of unity through contrast that has developed the so-called "sonata form," a system found in all the masterpieces of absolute music. Every great composer has written sonatas of some kind, even though he may not have used that title for them. A sonata is simply a "sound piece," consisting of several "movements," or divisions, broadly related, but quite capable of independent performance.

In every sonata at least one movement, and generally the first movement, is in "sonata form." This means that it has two basic melodies, known as the first and second themes, in different keys, and otherwise offering a certain amount of contrast. There may be other melodic material, as well as connecting links, and each theme or subject may be developed in a variety of ways for itself alone. But the sonata structure as a whole must present on a larger scale the same kind of conflict that is represented by the contrasting themes themselves.

INTRODUCING THE CHARACTERS

The composer's object is first to gain the attention and interest of his hearers for the melodies as such, just as the novelist starts out by creating a certain sympathy for his chief characters. He presents each subject in turn, with sufficient musical background to throw the melodies into strong relief, and this section of his sonata-movement is called the "exposition." (Exactly the same term is used in play-writing, of the opening portion, which presents the general situation and the principal characters, and it is also common in oratory, debating and journalism.)

After the exposition, which in the older form is repeated entirely, so that the hearer may be thoroughly familiar with the subject matter, there follows a section of "development," in which the two themes are turned loose to fight it out for themselves. This part of a sonata-movement is sometimes called the "free fantasia," and in it the composer has every opportunity to use his imagination, to play with his contrasting tunes as he would play with toy soldiers, to break them up into pieces if he wishes, and then put them together again, to lead them far from their home keys, only to bring them back again in safety. The development in sonata-form is the same as the action in a play, or the plot in a story. It provides the excitement and it tests the character of the subjects themselves to the utmost.

INVENTION VS. SCHOLARSHIP

While the creation of significant melodies, like the creation of significant materials in fiction, requires inspiration and a true inventive power, the development is largely a matter of workmanship, of deliberately reasoning out the variety of things that might happen under given conditions. To an inexperienced listener, the development section of a sonata-movement often sounds utterly meaningless, for he does not realize what the composer is doing, and his ear is not sufficiently trained to keep track of all the ramifications of the musical plot.

But before the movement ends, he is likely to have the satisfaction of a familiar experience once more, for in the "recapitulation" he will hear again the original subject matter, in the primary key, now happily freed from conflict and joined in a greater unity than would ever have seemed possible. It is the solution of the problem, the ending of the play, the final effect of the picture, or statue, or building, after the observer has secured the right perspective and accustomed his eyes to the necessary relationships of color and outline.

THUS ALL ENDS HAPPILY

By way of a final flourish, such a sonata-movement generally ends in a "coda," or tail, representing a perhaps unnecessary reminder that everything is really over. It is the Amen to the benediction, the spire to the church steeple, the epilogue to the play. With this definite finish, the sonata-form is complete.

Sonata-form is the structure to which every great piece of absolute music adheres, at least in part. Sonatas have been written for the piano, the violin, the 'cello and other instruments. A symphony is merely a sonata written for orchestra. Generally it has four movements instead of the three with which most of the regular sonatas are content. A concerto is similarly a sonata for a solo instrument with orchestral accompaniment, and a string quartet, quintet or trio follows the same form, with four, five or three instruments to tell the story.

UNITY AND CONTRAST

If all this seems a difficult and complicated matter, keep in mind the fact that sonata-form, like all other musical form, is nothing more than the organization of material in such a way as to bring out the double significance of unity and contrast. It is much the same as the simple song-form on a larger scale.

You have a pair of tunes, to start with. You

have an independent development of these tunes, parallel to the contrasting parts of a song-melody; and you have finally a restatement of the tunes themselves in a newly discovered unity, very much like the final reminder of the opening section of the song itself. (See page 221.)

The underlying purpose of the composer is always to make his melodic material as interesting as possible to the hearer. The mere repetition of his tunes would only create boredom, but by constantly using the trick of contrast, by introducing even a few of the numerous devices known to musical elaboration, he can create a diversion which will then emphasize all the more the beauty of the melodies themselves, when they are heard again, in part or as a whole.

SOMETHING MORE THAN MELODY

It is by their themes that we remember symphonies and sonatas, but in actual performance this memory may be enhanced by the ever fresh delight in pure craftsmanship, which reveals new devices and new beauties with each hearing. It is thus that the intellect enters into the appreciation of music, for after we have responded physically and emotionally to the rhythmic and melodic inspirations of a great composer, we still have left the limitless field of pure reason, which tells us not only "This is beautiful," but also "This is admirably clever."

The symphony is the Gothic cathedral of music, the ultimate flower of all the seeds sown experimentally by the natural and the cultivated musicians of the world. Just as the Greek columns and the Roman arches had to precede the Gothic structure, with its wealth of decoration, and its inevitable logic of line, so the song-form and the simple devices of contrast and elaboration have to lead up to the symphony.

TAKE IT SLOWLY

Don't worry if you can't appreciate a symphony at a first hearing. Listen first for the tunes, and try to get them permanently into your memory. And if you are not quite ready for anything so involved and elaborate as symphonic development, there is plenty of other music to satisfy your instinct for beauty, and to build up gradually your intelligent appreciation of unity and contrast in form.

The basic principle extends beyond the movement or movements that may be in strict sonata-form. Often this structure is found only in the first movement of a symphony, although Mozart displays it in all four parts of his melodious work in G minor. The second movement of a symphony is usually the slow part, again contrasting with the opening movement, which, as a whole, generally has a marked life and swing to it. Often a composer writes his slow symphonic movement as a theme with variations, which is practically what Beethoven did in his Fifth Symphony. (See above, page 226-7.)

THE REST OF THE SYMPHONY

The third movement of a symphony is likely to be the liveliest of all, often called "Scherzo," which connotes a cheerful mood.

The Finale should have power and dignity, but also plenty of life, and it is often, like the first movement, in strict sonata-form. Tschaikowsky created a famous exception in his Pathetic Symphony, when he gave his Finale the atmosphere of absolute despair, after writing a third movement that overflowed with exultation, in march time.

A form often found in a symphonic movement, as well as independently, is the Rondo, which is similar in structure to the Rondeau form in verse. It has one central theme, which it repeats again and again, alternating it each time with one or more contrasting themes.

COLORING STILL POSSIBLE

After using all the devices of form in music, from the simplest treatment of tones and time to the most elaborate decorations and complexities of symphonic architecture, a composer still has at his disposal the resources of instrumental and vocal color, or "timbre."

The term "color" has been very loosely applied to music, just as people also speak loosely of "tones" in pictures. But there are actual effects of sound that clearly suggest a variety of color, and this obvious relationship has led many a philosophic investigator to work out possible systems of absolute parallels.

PHILOSOPHY ONCE MORE

There was a medieval theory that all sounds in the universe were part of one great harmony, and that the elements in Nature, the laws of astronomy and the colors of the spectrum fitted into this system in mathematical fashion.

A man named Robert Flud (who Latinized his name for purposes of scholarship into De Fluctibus) drew up a table of all the factors in the universe having a possible musical value and he made the seven colors of the spectrum balance the seven tones of the diatonic scale exactly.

There have been plenty of other experiments

with the so-called "universal harmony," and color has always entered into them. The church fathers evidently believed in such a system, including the "Music of the Spheres," which Milton immortalized in his poems. More recently we have had the "color symphony" of Scriabine, in which an organ was used to throw colors on a screen, supposedly harmonizing with the music, another by Arthur Bliss, and finally the "clavilux" of Thomas Wilfred, for which symphonies and other musical forms can be composed in colors alone!

HOW COLORFUL IS MUSIC?

Much of the association between color and music must be considered a matter of habit and tradition. Certain sights bring to mind certain sounds, and we readily credit the sounds with the color which originally went with them.

But it is quite possible that a pronounced quality of tone may consistently suggest a definite color. When we hear of the "scarlet" tones of a trumpet we are inclined to agree, and similarly it is not difficult to think of a flute as playing light blue tones in its lower register, with perhaps a suggestion of silver above. The viola has been accused of a dark brown color, but this, as well as the silver of the flute, may be merely the result of the actual color of the instrument.

COMBINING MANY QUALITIES

When musicians speak of "tone-color" they really mean individuality of timbre or quality. Obviously, therefore, an orchestra has wonderful opportunities for a variety of tone-color.

Even among the stringed instruments, the violins are quite different from the violas, 'cellos and bass-viols, in the individual quality of their tones.

An oboe sounds absolutely different from a clarinet (although many people can't tell them apart, by sight or by ear), and a French horn has an individuality of tone that easily distinguishes it from other brass instruments. With such distinctive tone-quality as we find in the harp, the drums, triangle, etc., added to all the other factors in an orchestra, it is not difficult to imagine the variety of color that may be heard in actual performance.

Even in dance-orchestras you hear quite individual effects, in the almost human voice of a saxophone, or the insistent strumming of a banjo-mandolin; and the difference between a muted trombone and the same instrument "played straight" is unmistakable.

COLOR ADDED TO FORM

A great composer, therefore, takes into account the possible variety of tone-color at his command, and makes this a definite feature of his formal development. In a symphony orchestra, for instance, he can present his melody in a new light by simply giving it to a new instrument or combination of instruments to play, and even in a string quartet he has at his command a variety of color as well as of pitch.

A singer colors his voice, either by instinct or by practice, and he has a greater range of quality at his disposal than any artificial instrument. We recognize even a speaking voice by its individual quality, and the four different types of voices, soprano, alto, tenor and bass, are quite easily distinguished even by unmusical listeners. This matter of vocal coloring is of the greatest importance when it comes to interpretation.

PITY THE POOR PIANIST

The violinist or 'cellist commands a range of individual tone-color similar to that of the singer, but the pianist has a hard time because his tones are all ready-made, and he can color them only as he builds up combinations. There is a certain variety of color in the mere difference of volume which he draws from the instrument by the varying force of his finger-blows, but if he wants a real individuality of quality, he can secure it only through his personal mastery of tone-blending, with the help of the pedals and the pianistic methods of the composer he is interpreting.

WHERE COLOR REALLY HELPS

Color as a factor in form may well be limited to such combinations of instruments as find their climax in the full orchestra, and every great writer of symphonies is necessarily a master of instrumentation.

When the imaginary colors of the orchestra are supplemented by the actual colors of opera, ballet or pantomime, or by such effects as are growing more common and more artistic every day in the motion-picture theaters, then indeed the musical imagination requires very little help for the assurance of complete understanding and enjoyment.

THE LANGUAGE OF MUSIC

In its last analysis, music is a language, and it grows to the fullness of form, color and content very much as do the materials of language itself. It would be absurd to teach children to speak by starting them on the alphabet, yet that is what too many people still try to do with the language of music. We let children gain their first vocabulary and considerable fluency of speech entirely by imitation, and in exactly the same way we should let them, and adults as well, pick up the essentials of musical language "by ear."

BUILDING A VOCABULARY

After they have become accustomed to the sounds of music, and can perhaps utter them with some confidence, there is time enough to begin the study of musical spelling, grammar and rhetoric. They will find the notes of music literally corresponding to the letters of the alphabet, and chord-combinations corresponding to words of varying simplicity or elaborateness. They will find that these letters and words can be built up into phrases, clauses and whole sentences, that sentences grow naturally into paragraphs and paragraphs into chapters.

Gradually the meaning of unity and contrast in expression will grow upon them.

They will find that a musician has a way of creating dramatic or lyric or descriptive effects, just as a poet or a playwright or a novelist does.

They will discover the value of a proper introduction to a work of considerable scope; they will follow with complete sympathy the exposition of musical material, whether it be purely melodic or of a definitely dramatic character.

They will even learn to appreciate the complexities of development, and look forward with expectant enthusiasm to the climax of recapitulation, when the essential unity of the whole conception becomes manifest at last.

They will maintain their interest through a solid peroration, if necessary, and share with the composer, at the finish, the consciousness of a logical and satisfying close.

READERS, ATTENTION!

That is the ideal of the appreciation of the musical form divine, and it is by no means an impossible one. If we can progress from the "Da-da" of the cradle to an intelligent reading of Shakespeare, why can we not with equal ease advance through the logical steps of rhythm, melody, harmony, form and color to Bach, Beethoven and Brahms?

The language of music is universal, for it is delivered through tones that everyone can hear, and in symbols that anyone can understand. And it has the vast advantage over any and every spoken language that even when it is imperfectly comprehended, it rewards the listener with a direct thrill of pleasure that no one can take away from him, and for which there is no substitute.

CHAPTER X

AS COMMONLY INTERPRETED

WHICH is more important, the telegraph-boy or the message he delivers? How significant in such a situation is the man who sent the message and the man who receives it?

The probable answer is that the boy is the least significant of the lot. The message itself is certainly the most important, and after that comes the sender, and perhaps the receiver.

Of course if a messenger is absolutely necessary he becomes relatively important, and if he has a chance to forget or distort or completely bungle the message, his final significance is almost immeasurable. But this emphasizes all the more the vital importance of the message itself.

HOW DO YOU GET IT?

Just as any message requires the co-operation of the sender, the bearer and the receiver, so every musical performance has as its necessary factors the music itself, the composer, the interpreter, and the listener.

The modern tendency is to glorify the interpreter at the expense of the composer and of the music itself. This is only partly the fault of the interpreters themselves. Chiefly it is the result of a non-receptive attitude on the part of the listener.

ATTRACTIVE LITTLE FELLOW!

We grow so interested in the messenger-boy, the cut of his uniform, the appeal of his personality, the exciting story of his adventures on the way, that we often forget completely just what message he has to deliver.

We overlook the fact that someone gave him the message in a very definite form, and we accept a garbled version, sometimes even a self-contradictory one, without stopping to inquire carefully what the composer may have meant.

There is all the less excuse for this because in so many cases it would be a comparatively simple matter to find out in advance what the composer's intentions were, and to refuse to tip the boy when he obviously fell down on the fundamentals of his errand.

STIMULATING MATERIAL

Many people who think they are listening to music are really not listening at all. They allow themselves to be pleasantly stimulated by musical sounds, but they would receive a similar and perhaps equally significant stimulus from an electric fan, or a cup of coffee, or a brisk rub-down.

The big successes of the concert-stage to-day are made through a combination of factors only partly musical. The great artists are essentially great personalities, with a box-office value that depends on many things outside of their musical ability. People who go to concerts only when the well-advertised and highly press-agented sensation comes to town go purely and simply for a new form of excitement, and the psychology of such concert-going is exactly the same as the psychology of World Series baseball. Only, your real baseball fan will stop and watch a game of "movin's-up" on a back lot instead of waiting for Babe Ruth to do his home-run act.

THE CRAZE FOR SUPERLATIVES

Out of the "nothing but the best" attitude toward music, which has been deliberately or unconsciously fostered by the scholars and critics of music, there has grown an automatic monopoly of the concert-field by a few artists known as "sure-fire" box-office attractions. Fortunately, they are in general worthy performers, with a true regard for the ideals of their art.

But the world, and particularly America, is full of other worthy performers, equally aglow with the sacred duty of interpreting the universal message of music, and because they have not yet established a "name value" they find it difficult, if not impossible, to get a hearing. Until we stop eternally asking who is singing or playing, and begin to take an interest in what is to be sung or played, we cannot honestly consider ourselves a nation of music-lovers.

There must be standards of performance, of course, and it is unwise for a talented amateur to rush into a professional career without sufficient preparation. But in the home, where professional standards do not hold, almost any kind of performance has its significance, if only for the performers themselves. It has been said that chamber-music, such as string quartets, trios, etc., is written for the fun of the players rather than the listeners, and there may be something in that point of view. Certainly it is the type of music which gains public appreciation with the greatest difficulty.

But music is in a sense a religion, and if, in comparative privacy, a halting and unskilled performance is heard, may it not be regarded in the same light as the naïvely incoherent prayer of a child? Religious devotion is possible without the practiced art of ministerial guidance, and with music also the sincerity of the spirit may be more significant than the effect of the performance.

The true music-lover needs but little stimulus to his imagination for calling up spiritual realities which his soul has already made its own. A few notes at the piano may create for him the memory of a symphony orchestra, and the humming or whistling of a tune may be enough to suggest the voice of the greatest singer.

STANDARDS FOR LISTENERS

But since the public performance of music is now so common, it is well for the average listener to develop certain standards of interpretation as well as composition, so that he may really judge the musical value of what he hears, quite aside from personal and other considerations. Let him concentrate on the symphony rather than the conductor, on the song rather than the singer, on the opera rather than the artists.

The interpreter is after all only the messenger, and if we exaggerate his importance, we may overlook all too easily the significance of the message itself.

THE AVERAGE APPEAL

In general, as has already been pointed out, the concert-going public listens for only two things, tonal beauty and technical skill. If a singer can utter pleasing words in appealing tones, and perhaps introduce an occasional top-note or a startling bit of vocal gymnastics, popular success may be considered certain.

A violinist, similarly, is asked to stimulate the emotions with sensuously beautiful sounds, and even more frequently to stir up excitement by astonishing feats of physical dexterity.

The pianist in particular is expected to perform miracles with his well-trained fingers, and a perfect technique is now taken almost for granted among the real top-notchers. But he must be more than a prodigious automaton of mechanical skill if he wishes to win lasting fame. In his case also the tonal beauty of the performance is most important to his audience, and in this respect his task is a difficult one, for the piano does not permit such obvious individuality of tone as the singer or the violinist may produce.

In every case, however, tone and technique are demanded by the worshipers at music's shrine, and this habit extends even to the appraisal of orchestral performances, chamber-music, opera and oratorio.

WHAT OF THE COMPOSER?

But this is only the beginning of music-appreciation. Every composer had his own definite ideas and intentions, and he probably took it for granted that the mechanical difficulties of his work would be adequately overcome, and that his tonal conceptions would receive their just due from the interpreting instruments or voices.

But beyond this he must have hoped for an intimate understanding and an inevitable revelation on the part of his interpreters. He must have dreamed of the perfect performance which would transfer directly to the listener the inner meaning of his entire composition, and in most cases he probably never heard such a performance actually given.

ANYONE CAN DO THIS

There are some matters of misinterpretation so obvious that even the inexperienced hearer will immediately detect them, just as he will also detect, as a rule, such manifest faults as playing or singing out of tune, creating raucous, strident or otherwise unmusical tones, scratching or whistling on a violin or 'cello, and "breaking" or getting out of breath in singing.

Often, however, there are crimes in interpretation more flagrant than any of these physical imperfections, yet they are allowed to pass unnoticed even by supposedly critical ears. If the listener acquires the habit of analyzing interpretation, instead of merely exposing himself to sensuous effects, he will find that music possesses a limitless fascination, which will add a vital interest to every performance, from the amateur's stumbling attempts to the ultra-brilliant mastery of the virtuoso or the prima donna.

A SINGER'S METHOD

Consider first the field of song, which offers the greatest opportunities for "faking," through personal appeal and the character of the material presented, and at the same time offers perhaps the widest range of potential finesse and subtlety of interpretation. Every singer knows that the words and music of a song may do practically all the work, given a fairly pleasing voice, an attractive presence, and the ability to make the text understood. Too many songs, in fact, rely almost entirely on the appeal of their words, and the mere power of association may thus create a most impressive effect. (See the discussion of "heart-music" on page 56.)

It is actually a difficult matter to analyze vocal music, because of the big part played by the text, the facial expression of the singer, and the downright acting that even the concert-stage permits.

The ideal of a great song-writer is unquestionably to express most musically and most fittingly the mood and details of an inherently beautiful poem. This means that he must follow the meaning and accent of the words as closely as possible, yet at the same time create a purely musical composition which is in itself worth while. The greatest songs are those which achieve the most accurate interpretation of their text, with the least sacrifice of musical beauty as such.

THERE IS A DISTINCTION

Song-writing of an obvious character is an easy matter, and it has its parallel in song-interpretation of the same sort. But song-writing of the highest type is a rare and difficult art, requiring actual genius for its complete realization, and again there is a parallel in the field of interpretation.

In judging a concert-singer, it is quite natural

to look first for a voice of unusual quality, and perhaps range and volume as well. The "voiceless interpreter" has occasionally won success, particularly with over-precious listeners, but for a real career a beautiful voice is essential. (Rossini said that the three necessities of singers were Voice, Voice and Voice.)

PLANTING THE WORDS

Assuming the possession of at least a satisfying vocal ability (the kind that puts a hearer at his ease, instead of making him worry every moment over possible disaster), the next requirement for good singing would seem to be a clear enunciation of the text. In this the singers of vaudeville, cabarets and musical comedy are far in advance of those in concert and "grand" opera. Popular entertainers are forced "to get their words over," for to their audiences the text is often far more important than the music. (They have also as a rule the advantage of light accompaniments and a fairly obvious line of thought to express.)

Concert-singers, and particularly grand opera stars, are too much inclined to sacrifice clear enunciation for tonal beauty, and this is encouraged by the common practice of singing in foreign languages, which few of their hearers understand in any case. On the other hand you will often find that American singers actually pronounce and enunciate their own language in more slovenly fashion than a foreign tongue, simply because they take it for granted instead of giving it special and painstaking study.

SCIENTIFIC BREATHING

A singer is expected to breathe without undue exertion, avoiding the interruption of a natural phrase or clause of the text and, of course, never breathing in the middle of a word. The tones should come out evenly and smoothly, without a "wobble" or other evidence of nervousness and spreading breath.

The technique of singing makes it possible to control the breath from the diaphragm, instead of depending on the muscular activity of the upper chest. The tones may be definitely focused or "pointed" in a forward and upward direction, bringing into play the cavities in the head which contribute resonance and individual quality, and the final touch comes from the formation of the lips, which, you may notice, generally suggest a "fish-mouth," or the blowing of smoke-rings.

WHICH TYPE ARE YOU?

Some people have a natural "placement" of their voices, but in most cases they both sing and talk "right on the vocal chords," which means not only a lack of volume and quality, but a speedy fatigue, expressed by hoarseness and the gradual descent to a mere whisper. Singing through the nose is an excellent way of acquiring endurance, and you will hear much of it in those resorts which make constant physical demands upon their entertainers. But it is hardly conducive to beauty of tone, which, in the long run, is more important than either strength or endurance.

Listen to public speakers and decide for yourself whether they are using their voices to the best advantage. Then watch a great operatic or concert-singer and see how he or she makes every tone carry, from the softest whisper to an absolute shout, always with an individual quality, and never seeming to tire. The whole body enters into such singing, and the mind and soul as well.

TECHNIQUE MUST BE HABITUAL

Great singing is impossible until all technical details have become a matter of habit and the entire mechanism is at the command of the singer's will. "The greatest art is that which conceals art," and we resent the type of performance which perpetually reminds us that the wheels are going 'round.

It might almost be said that there are only two kinds of singers, those who make it seem hard, and those who make it seem easy. We like to listen to the latter, but with the laborious technicians we feel that we are doing similar hard work, and instead of relaxing and enjoying ourselves, we become as nervously weary as though from the strain of actual effort.

NO CONSCIOUS TECHNIQUE

When a singer is not forced to think at every moment of mechanical details, it becomes possible to concentrate on the subtleties of interpretation, and it is then that merely pleasing sounds become translated into significant art. If a soft tone is to be sustained, creating an atmosphere of complete calm, of ethereal serenity, the effect is ruined the moment a listener joins the singer in such thoughts as "Will the breath hold out? Can the tone be kept from wobbling?"

If a climax comes on a high note, the hearer, as well as the singer, should feel "It could have been several tones higher without causing any worry," instead of "This is positively the limit, and the strain may prove too great."

A well-trained singer practices the physical details of the art until there is no uncertainty as to the ability to reach a certain note, or to stay on the pitch, to perform rapid passages with sufficient flexibility and to emit pure tones without any rasping interference.

KEEPING IN TUNE

Singing off pitch is far more common than is generally realized, and while the usual tendency is to "flat" there are plenty of cases of persistent "sharping." The conductor is often quoted who stopped in the midst of a rehearsal and asked the prima donna to "sound her A" for the orchestra, and he has good company in the irascible singing-teacher who burst out "I play for you the white keys and I play for you the black keys, but always you sing in the cracks."

While there are certain traditions of style in the interpretation of vocal music, including the purity of the "bel canto" school (which treats the voice absolutely as a musical instrument), the rather exaggerated mannerisms of opera, the repose of oratorio, and the sentimental realism of German Lieder-singing, a well-equipped vocalist enjoys considerable freedom in the presentation of his material. His chief concern is to express clearly and beautifully the thoughts of the composer and the writer of the words.

THIS COULD NOT BE OVERLOOKED

Obviously it would be absurd to shout a lullaby at the top of your voice, but singers are daily guilty of equal inconsistencies. You will hear hunting-songs and patriotic sentiments uttered in a weakly deprecatory style, and flaming passion presented with the coldness of chiselled marble. You will find a curious readiness to alter the clearly marked intentions of a composer for the sake of an astonishing effect, as witness the common practice of ending a song on a high note, even when it is absolutely out of place. (Caruso himself used to finish his "Celeste Aida" with a stentorian B-flat as a sop to the gallery, although the score calls for a soft, spiritual effect.)

The careful interpreter must watch his pronunciation as well as his enunciation, particularly if he is singing in a foreign language. A singer once made the father in the "Erlking" hold in his arms his "eighteenth child" by overlooking the two little dots which turn the "ah" of "achtzehnte" into the "ae" of "ächzende" ("groaning").

The art of acting makes operatic interpretation a fairly intelligible matter. But on the concert-stage there is a definite limit to the dramatic support which can legitimately be given to the voice. Strictly speaking, the voice should do it all, by its coloring of tones and enunciation of syllables, with perhaps a little help from the facial expression and the carriage of the body.

But some singers do not hesitate to use actual gestures in concert-singing, and similarly there are operatic artists who will cheerfully spoil an illusion by taking a bow, or even repeating part or all of an aria. (For this also the public is chiefly to be blamed, for we break into an artistic continuity with our insistent applause, and encourage a disregard of form by our continual worship of personality.)

THE MELTING-POT OF ART

Opera has so many elements outside of the music itself, that its interpretation actually has little to do with purely musical standards. In general the sustaining of an illusion must be considered of primary importance, but the older. frankly artificial operas invariably sacrifice realism for musical effect, largely of a technical character.

Traditions are so closely followed in opera that a novice must learn the rôles with the assistance of experienced teachers, who know exactly what gestures and stage manœuvers are necessary at every point. The lack of local opera companies, such as are common (and generally terrible) in Europe, makes this kind of training difficult to secure in America, for experience alone can perfect all the details of such a complicated technique.

ACHIEVING THE BALANCE

The more modern composers of opera have tried for a balance between realism and musical beauty, and in this Verdi, Puccini, Mascagni, Leoncavallo, Bizet, Gounod and Massenet have been particularly successful. Mozart, Gluck and Weber thought more of their music than of their stage illusion, and this tendency was shared by Rossini and Donizetti, although both Mozart and Rossini were masters of a completely convincing type of musical comedy.

Wagner generally renounced realism altogether, and created heroic effects in a mystic sphere which resulted in music of "absolute" significance. (See page 86.)

(One of the chief requirements of opera nowdays seems to be that the singer shall be heard above the noise of the orchestra, and this necessarily interferes with any consistent subtlety of interpretation, vocally or dramatically.)

THE CONTRAST OF ORATORIO

As compared with opera, oratorio is a very quiet and self-contained proceeding. It requires a highly developed vocalism on the part of the soloists, but the dramatic opportunities are comparatively few, and the sacred nature of the subject matter demands a consistent dignity, even a sublimity of mood.

Handel's Messiah and Mendelssohn's Elijah are the two best-known oratorios, but there are many minor works well worth hearing, including cantatas, requiems, masses, anthems and single choruses of a sacred or secular character. Bach and Beethoven both wrote huge masterpieces of sacred music, and Haydn, Mozart, Rossini, Berlioz, Verdi, Brahms, Sullivan and Dvorak all had success with the same type of composition, with Elgar perhaps the best of its modern exponents.

APPRAISING A CHORUS

Choral singing must be judged first on the basis of general vocal quality, correct intonation (or singing in tune), precision of attack and release (that is, all the singers starting and stopping exactly together), and the ability to create effects of contrast and "shading." Details of interpretation are the responsibility of the conductor, and the credit for technical smoothness of performance also belongs chiefly to him (or to his hard-working assistant).

Choral singing can be carried on by amateurs to a high degree of excellence, and even untrained singers may enjoy themselves and create real pleasure for their neighbors in a "community chorus" which sticks to the easier and more popular pieces. There is no finer effect in music than that of a big mixed chorus, accompanied by a full orchestra, and this is also an important factor in most successful operas.

"WHERE MEN ARE MEN"

A male chorus or quartet has an absolutely individual quality of tone, often more attractive than the color of mixed voices (soprano, alto, tenor and bass), and fortunately there is plenty of good music for both combinations. Women's choruses have not proved so successful, partly because so little good music has been written for them, but partly also because they lack the balance of harmony provided by a real bass part.

People in general are not sufficiently aware of

the fun of singing in harmony. Men who have sung in college glee clubs never forget the experience, and in some cases they are able to keep it up after graduation, as in the University Glee Club of New York.

But the Anglo-Saxon self-consciousness seems to interfere with an unrestrained vocal enthusiasm, in school, in church, and in general community gatherings. In the old days men sang lustily enough when their inhibitions had been artificially removed, and they still do so on occasion, proving that it is a normal procedure for man to express himself in song, if he can only stop being self-conscious about it.

STRINGED INSTRUMENTS

Violinists and 'cellists have much the same problems in delivering their art to a critical public. People claim to love the 'cello, "its voice is so human," but how many of them ever pay good money to go to a 'cello recital?

While the 'cello is a splendid solo instrument, it requires a Casals to make it interesting for an entire evening. Its normal tones are of a deep and thrilling beauty, but it is too clumsy to achieve the delicate flexibility characteristic of the violin.

A 'cellist naturally hesitates to fill a whole program with broadly lyric pieces, and when he introduces some technical excitement, the effect is too often painful. A truly great 'cellist never suggests the homely analogy of "sawing wood," but makes the difficult passages sound just as musical as the singing tones.

Except in rare instances, however, the violoncello (which is its full name) appears to best advantage in an orchestra or string quartet.

"FIDDLERS' LUCK"

The violin, on the other hand, is a versatile instrument, and one of the most popular of soloists. With its four strings sounding the treble E, A, D and G, it can sing far above the human voice, and at the same time suggest a fairly respectable bass.

It can harmonize its own melodies, playing two tones simultaneously, and adding a third or even a fourth if necessary. It can execute rapid passages without scratching or whistling or losing the pitch, and it can sustain melodies with both sweetness and power.

Finally it has at its disposal a variety of trick effects, such as plucking the strings (pizzicato) in the manner of a banjo-player, beating them with the stick of the bow instead of drawing out the tone by the hair, clamping a "mute" (sor-

dino) on the bridge so as to stop its vibrations and produce a soft, reedy sound, and creating "harmonics" or "flageolet" tones which have the crystalline quality of the flute itself.

THIS INSTRUMENT NEEDS SKILL

A violinist, like a singer, makes his impression chiefly by the beauty of his tones and the dexterity of his technique, but few of us realize the infinite details involved in such skill, and we are still less concerned with the traditions or individualities of interpretation.

It is sometimes said that anyone can learn to do the astonishing feats of fingering demanded of a violinist's left hand, but that it takes genius to work out the full possibilities of the right or bowing hand. The fingers of the left hand actually make the tones by stopping the strings at certain intervals, and, as everyone knows, it is the easiest thing in the world for a fiddler to play out of tune.

He can give the tone also a human quality by a slight quiver of the left hand, which produces a vibrating ("vibrato") effect, and a sentimentally-inclined violinist, like a singer, is more than likely to overdo this. A pure, non-tremulous tone is always harder to produce than one of mixed quality.

THE IMPORTANCE OF BOWING

But after the fingers of the left hand have done the work of correctly stopping the strings (and this must become absolutely habitual before a violinist can play successfully in public), the big part of the job still remains to be done by the bowing hand and arm. It is the bow that really fixes the quality and volume of the tone, varying from a strong, solid pressure to the lightest of whispering touches, producing passionately emotional sounds by a savage attack or a gradual enticement, using its full length for a broad, singing melody, or throwing out crisp sparks in flashing designs from either tip.

The wrist of the violinist is the controlling factor in all these accomplishments, with some aid from the fingers and the fore-arm. A good violinist does his bowing practically from the elbow, otherwise his bow would not travel in a straight line across the strings, and shrieks of protest would result.

MODELS NOW ON EXHIBITION

Watch a real master of the violin in action and see how high he holds the instrument, how freely he bows, and how easily and accurately he runs the mechanism of his left hand, which must also be in free motion, not clutching the neck of the violin as though to strangle the fingerboard. If a violinist once begins to think consciously where he is placing his fingers, he is lost, for, as with a singer, all this technique must become automatic, a habitual response to the sense of touch and feeling.

After you have acquired some appreciation of the skill which lies behind the physical beauty of a violinist's performance, you are ready to analyze his interpretations from the purely musical standpoint. You will naturally object to an oversentimental style in strictly formal classics, and you will be equally disappointed in the coldly mechanical exposition of music that is aglow with emotional fire.

Violin music rarely indicates a definite program, even by title, being mostly of the "absolute" sort, yet the intentions of its composers are by no means enigmatic, and can often be gathered at a first hearing. There is just as little sense in playing Dvorak's Humoresque portentously as in making a jazz tune of Beethoven's Finale to the Kreutzer Sonata.

INTRODUCING THE ORCHESTRA

In the orchestra the violin is the most important instrument, and a good body of string players is absolutely essential to any adequate performance. Just as a string quartet, composed of two violins, viola and 'cello, can make beautiful music, in complete harmony, so also these same instruments, in larger numbers, and with the addition of double-basses (or bass-viols) form the foundation of the full symphony orchestra.

Many of the older orchestral works are played chiefly by this quartet or quintet of strings, but as music advanced, it was found possible to utilize more and more the wind-instruments (flute, oboe, clarinet, bassoon, horn, trumpet, trombone, tuba, etc.) and those of percussion (drums, cymbals, chimes, triangle, etc.), with which modern compositions secure their most colorful effects.

THESE FIGURES ARE MODEST

A regular, up-to-date symphony orchestra may include from eighty to one hundred performers, of whom more than half are playing stringed instruments. Twelve or fourteen first violins at the very least are necessary to secure the proper balance of tone, and there should be almost as many second fiddles. Eight or ten violas are needed for the tenor part of the orchestral string quartet, and there should be an equal number of 'cellos, with eight double basses for the foundation.*

Nearest to the strings in quality and actual position are the "wood-wind," whose full choir includes two or three flutes, with perhaps a piccolo besides (similar to the military fife in sound and appearance), two oboes, two clarinets, an English horn (cor anglais), two bassoons, and perhaps a contra-bassoon and bass-clarinet.

*For the drawings of the orchestral instruments, as well as the seating plan of the orchestra, the author is indebted to the Symphony Society of Portland, Oregon.

LOOK THEM OVER

In time you will be able to distinguish these instruments by sight as well as sound. The flute and piccolo are easy, because of their cross-position at the mouth, like that of a harmonica, and the unmistakable purity of their tones. The lower register of a flute sounds quite different from its upper tones, and the piccolo (or "little flute") reaches the highest notes with piercing shrillness.

The oboe (or hautboy), formerly the leading instrument in the orchestra, and still the source of pitch for all the other instruments, which have to tune to its A, has a nasal quality of tone, something like that of a bag-pipe, and its sound is not always pleasing to the ear. It looks very much like a clarinet (whose tones are more liquid and flexible) but there is a decided difference in the method of blowing, for the clarinet has a chisel-shaped mouth-piece, containing a single reed, while the oboe has two open reeds, which are held by the lips of the player.

WHEN IS A HORN NOT A HORN?

The English horn is really an alto oboe, with a richer and more melancholy timbre, and it differs from the regular oboe in being cup-shaped instead of bell-shaped at the lower end, while its reeds project in a curve. Listen to it some time in the Largo of Dvorak's New World Symphony.

The bassoon makes a noise something like the croaking of a frog, and has often appealed to a composer's sense of comedy, as in Wagner's Meistersinger Overture. It is much longer than

the other wood-wind instruments and looks like a good, solid piece of sapling, with a curved mouthpiece protruding from the middle, like a budding twig.

All of these instruments are exceedingly difficult to play well, but in school orchestras and for dance music the simpler saxophone (which is really a clarinet disguised in brass) may be substituted with good effect in several different parts.

STRIKE UP THE BAND!

In the brass choir, which always sits far back in the orchestra, because of its overwhelming power, the four French horns are most easily distinguished, with their big, bell-shaped ends, into which the players often poke their fists, and the snail-shell curlicue of their brazen bodies, suggesting the old-fashioned hunting-horn (called by the Germans Waldhorn, or "forest-horn"). Their tone is mellower than that of the commoner members of the brass band, and they are capable of beautiful "muted" effects, as well as rasping sounds.

A horn-player is facing a difficult proposition at all times, and his most golden tones may unexpectedly "break" if his lip and wind are not in the best of condition.

The trumpets in an orchestra look and sound much the same as the familiar cornet, the latter being easier to play because of the "pistons," which help the performer in changing from one key or interval to another. Cornets are often used in place of real trumpets, and they are es-

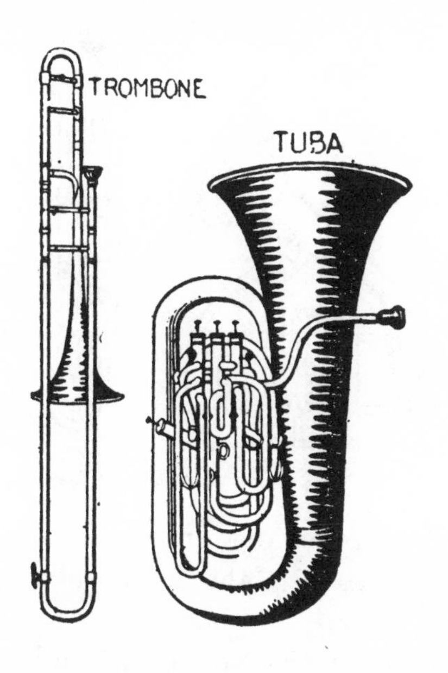

sential to a military brass band, in which clarinets, oboes, saxophones and alto-horns take the place of stringed instruments. (A good brass band can interpret much of the music originally written for orchestra, and is by no means to be despised, particularly as a purveyor of soul-stirring marches.)

The slide-trombone has become the laughing hyena of modern jazz, and its active participation in the orchestral effects of the concert-hall may be recognized without special guidance.

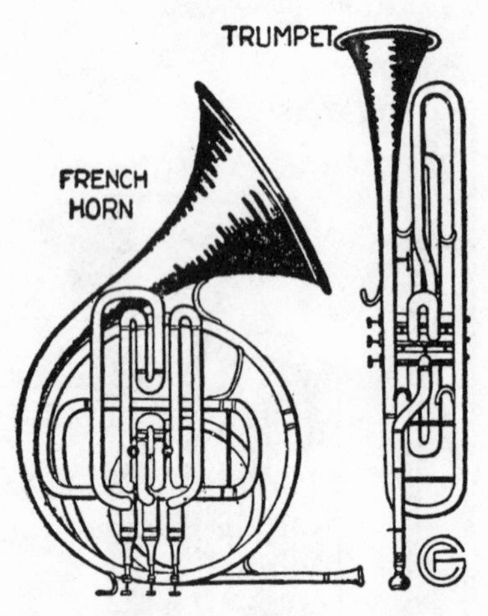

The trombone plays the tenor parts in a quartet of which the bass is the huge tuba, wrapped python-like about the body of its master, or eclipsing him with its fat and gleaming horn, a paradise for imaginative soap-bubble blowers.

(The wind instruments of an orchestra are all really soloists, and sometimes they are heard individually or in more intimate combinations on the concert-stage.)

THE LORD OF PERCUSSION

In the very last row of the orchestra stands the drummer, often with several assistants. The master of the "traps" in a dance-orchestra can handle all his effects by a species of hand and foot-jugglery, but the head of the percussion department in a symphonic college approaches his task with more dignity.

His real skill is shown in the command of the kettle-drums, or "timpani," which are literally copper kettles, covered with drum-heads which can be tuned to different pitches. Usually there are three of these drums, sounding the bass notes most likely to occur in a composition, but often the drummer has to change their pitch in the course of a performance, which he does by a frantic twisting of the screws around the edges. He plays with two sticks with felt-covered heads, and can produce a great variety of effects, from a lusty thumping to the softest "tremolo" or "long roll."

(The xylophone, cymbalom and similar instruments carry the principle of kettle-drumming right through the musical scale and are valuable aids to small orchestras and dance-music, as well as interesting soloists.)

When the orchestral drummer is not busy at the copper kettles, he may tap out bell-like tones from a triangle or use a hammer on a set of chimes, suspended on a frame. If a bass-drum, snare-drum and cymbals are needed, with perhaps a tambourine or castanets for Spanish effects, he sends a hurry call for help. (The biography has not yet been written of the man whose job it is to bang the cymbals together just once in an entire composition, after which he has "nothing to do till to-morrow.")

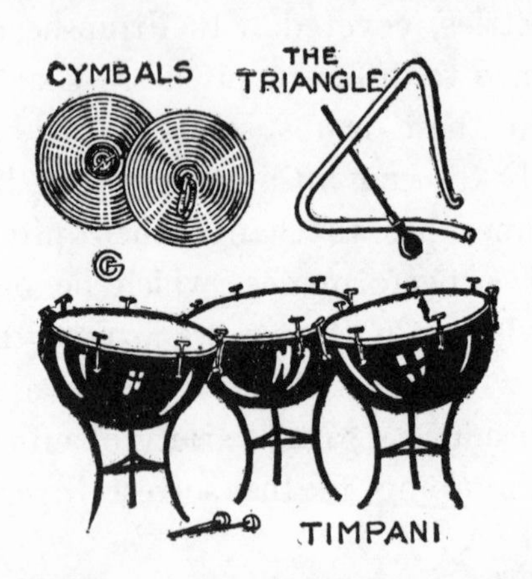

Some modern orchestral music calls for a celesta, which is like a little tinkling piano, producing ethereal effects, and occasionally a regular piano fills in as part of an orchestra. Finally there is the harp, related to both the percussion and the string choirs, but usually quite independent in its parts. It sometimes appears in pairs, and it has won considerable popularity as a soloist and as an accompanist to the human voice. (The side-walk harp, also known as the ferry-boat harp, aided and abetted by a fiddle in scraping up pennies, has an archeological rather than a musical significance.)

THE SEATING PLAN

A symphony orchestra is commonly arranged on the stage as follows (with the strings on a small scale):

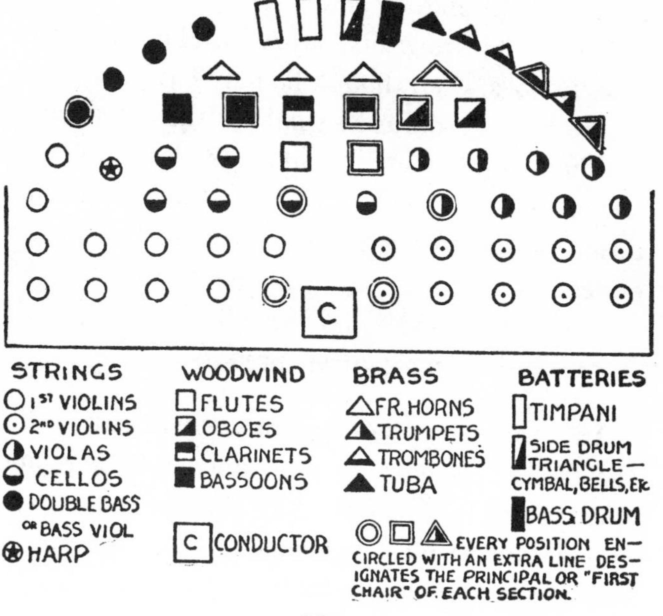

This is partly for the balance of tone, and partly that all the players may clearly see the leader. As with a chorus, it is the conductor's place to train his men in precision of attack, beauty of tonal quality, and accuracy of technique and interpretation.

He does far more than beat time during a performance, for he must work out every detail of musicianship and remind each individual at the proper time with an economy of gesture or personal distraction (a rule which "prima donna conductors" often reverse, for the sake of holding the attention of their audiences).

He should know his "score" by heart, and he usually does, even though he may have the music before him. He must signal for the entrance of any important part, and indicate clearly, by the larger or smaller sweep of his baton, the infinite gradations between the loudest and the softest effects.

TECHNICAL DETAILS

In a well-trained orchestra you will notice that the violins all bow up and down together, and this system is worked out to the best advantage by the concert-master, who sits in the chair nearest the conductor's stand and acts as a first lieutenant, besides taking such solo violin parts as may occur in the course of a piece.

Symphonic interpretation is a most complicated matter, but a good conductor will let his audience hear every detail of musical development, as well as the significant bits of orchestration, and not depend merely on the beauty of the melodic material and the overwhelming impressiveness of the masses of sound his men can produce.

THE HARDEST SOUNDS EASIEST

It is sometimes more difficult to give an interesting performance of a fairly simple classic than to excite an audience with the sensational climaxes of a "self-playing" modern work. A good conductor, with a thoroughly prepared orchestra, may lay down his baton through long stretches of Tschaikowsky, but he must be on the job every minute during a symphony by Haydn, Mozart, Schubert or Beethoven.

If a symphonic classic sounds dull to you, don't blame it entirely on the composer. Perhaps he wasn't given a fair chance by his interpreters.

Orchestral conducting enters also into opera and the great choral works, where one man is responsible for the performance of singers and players alike. (But in opera he at least has the assistance of a prompter, who sits under the mushroom at the front of the stage, and utters, often too audibly, the opening syllables of every phrase.)

THE KEYBOARD INSTRUMENTS

There still remains the piano, with its wind-blown relative, the organ. It is doubtful whether organ music will ever become truly popular, for its long-standing association with the church has put it permanently in the class of "free entertainment." But there is all the difference in the world between the little reed-organ or harmonium of a country home or church, and the pipe organ which now figures in so many public auditoriums, not to speak of the more elaborate private dwellings.

If you watch an organist at work, you may think he is playing dominoes, or running a switchboard, for he is constantly pulling or turning over certain "stops" and oblongs, inscribed like a Mah Jongg set, and the result is a constant variety of tone-color.

His fingers move over three or four keyboards, called "manuals," and his feet go searching among a full set of wooden pedals that provide him with another deep-toned scale, with which he occasionally makes a stained-glass window rattle in sympathy.

"IMITATION'S ARTFUL AID"

The organist has at his command not only the natural organ-tone, produced by the pipes called "diapasons," but he can imitate practically any other instrument, including all the wood-wind and brasses of the orchestra. He even has a "vox humana" stop, which supposedly reincarnates the human voice, and the insult is not absolutely flagrant.

The modern trick-organs contain chimes, animal imitations, and sometimes piano attachments, in addition to the reeds and "string tone" of the conventional instruments, and there is always a "tremolo" stop, which can be worked to the heart's content of the sentimentalist.

TWO-HANDED PERFORMERS

Good organ-playing demands a complete independence of the hands. The right may know what the left is doing, but each must go its own way, for the variety of effects on the different keyboards makes possible the most elaborately "polyphonic" style.

That is why Bach wrote his fugues for the organ, and why so much of its music smacks a little of mathematical experiments. An organ recital is stimulating if the performer has a command of both the classic and the modern music, but in general people are most interested in the trick effects.

With the development of the motion-picture industry in America, a school of impressionistic and realistic organ-playing has arisen which keeps many a first-class musician busy, and at the same time does its share of pioneer work toward the general appreciation of the art.

GETTING NEARER HOME

The piano (a convenient shortening of "pianoforte," which strictly means "soft and loud") is the most practical of all musical instruments, particularly for use in the home. But its full possibilities are only slightly appreciated as yet, and its players have perhaps the hardest task of all in securing an intelligent hearing.

A pianist is handicapped at the outset by the fact that every tone begins to die away as soon as it is struck. He cannot swell on a single note, as can the organist, the singer and the violinist. He cannot vary the color of his tones by personal control, for they are created for him by the mechanical action of a hammer striking a set of strings, as a result of his own blow upon a key, or lever.

To be sure, he cannot play out of tune, but his technical command of the keyboard must be none the less certain, for the striking of a wrong note, or that overlapping to an extra key which produces "blue" tones, will inevitably be noted by all his listeners.

Insufficient technical equipment comes out more quickly in a piano recital than anywhere else in the concert world, and this alone is the cause of most criticism. But even assuming a perfect command of all technical effects, a pianist must do something more to interest an audience.

He must in some way give his playing individuality, and too often he is content to do this through meretricious externals, such as the tossing of the head, the exaggerated motions of the hands, artificial grimaces and bodily contortions.

HOW MUCH DOES HE KNOW?

A pianist is sometimes hardly conscious of just how he achieves his effects. His technique, as with the singer and the violinist, becomes automatic, and he produces tone-combinations as the direct result of thought and will-power.

In so far as individuality is possible (and this depends somewhat also on the particular instrument that is used) it arises from the almost subconscious blending of tones and overtones, for which the composer himself may have provided only the initial suggestion.

COLOR ON CANVAS AND KEYS

The modern painter does not work simply with the primary colors. He blends all possible shades, on his palette and on his canvas, and no one can tell where one begins and another leaves off.

So also the modern pianist goes beyond the primary colors of actual tones and limited degrees of volume, and blends all his resources of touch and pedaling into a complete tone-picture of which the notes themselves are no more than a skeleton.

Clean, correct piano-playing should be interesting if only because of the wealth of musical material that it brings to the attention of the listener, but the concert field is overcrowded to-day with talents far beyond such adequate performance, musicians who have the intangible gift of directly thrilling an audience, if only one can be gathered for their support.

It has been said that there is too much good piano-playing nowadays, but that is as absurd as to say that there is too much good food. The demand is simply not equal to the supply as yet, and as soon as enough people work out their potential enthusiasm for piano-music as such, the laws of economics will assert themselves with the same old dependability.

CREATORS LEAVE THEIR MARK

No matter what kind of music you are hearing, remember always that the composer's message is of primary importance. You will find after a time that it is not difficult to distinguish the styles of composition which mark different periods of history, different countries and even different individuals.

However unskilled or independent the interpreter may be, he cannot completely obliterate those characteristic marks of nationality, of form and style, of historic background and of individual genius which are found in most great music.

DEVELOPING MUSICAL SENSE

The "music memory contests" in our schools are admirable for encouraging the hearing and retention of a lot of compositions. But they fail in their purpose if the winners are not able to add to their parrot-like repetition of names, keys and numbers some direct recognition of tendencies, forms and individual styles.

After learning to recognize one Nocturne of Chopin, they ought to be able at least to guess at other pieces of the same type. They should have no great difficulty in distinguishing compositions of the classic school from the markedly romantic or modern. Beethoven and Debussy should produce decidedly different reactions, and a sonata-movement should not easily be confused with a Sousa march.

(If such a logical development of musical sense were taken into consideration, there might not be so many tie scores in these memory contests.)

AN AID TO RECOGNITION

The distinction between periods, composers, styles and forms may be stimulated by the harmless methods of parody, for we often remember best the things at which we have laughed. For instance, it is not difficult to suggest the ways in which various composers might have made use of so familiar a tune as our own Yankee Doodle.

It would certainly have been done in the grandiose manner of an old-fashioned chorale, with the melody slowed up over heavy chords. The infant Bach would probably have made of it at least a little two-part invention, with the second half of the tune harmonizing in counterpoint with the first half.

Beethoven could have turned Yankee Doodle into a really beautiful slow theme by changing the rhythm into triple time, and Chopin would have decorated the tune in charming fashion, at the same time putting it into a minor key, with the suggestion of a Nocturne.

America's MacDowell might have made of it a salon piece, "To a Yankee Doodle," short and sweet, with rather exotic harmonies, and Tschaikowsky would hardly have resisted the temptation of a five-beat rhythm, and a pathetic melancholy of mood.

On the operatic side, Puccini's individual tricks of harmony would create without difficulty the leading motifs of a "Madama Yanki-Doo," and for the modern school Debussy should contribute a Yankee Doodle Arabesque, built on the whole-tone scale.*

THIS CAN BE SUNG ALSO

Transferring the parody to vocal music, one could take such a verse as "Jack and Jill," and imagine without much effort its treatment in various styles. Oratorio would make of it a recita-

*Such a series has actually been evolved by the author, and may shortly be had in published and recorded form.

tive and aria, preluding the actual lines with a portentous announcement of the impending tragedy, and then telling the story in a series of long-drawn phrases, in which one syllable carries on for more than a dozen notes.

Such a song-writer as Franz Schubert would set the verse in a naively sentimental fashion, perhaps using a constant figure in the accompaniment, and keeping it going long after the song was really over.

The old Italian opera might require at least a sextet to do justice to "Jack and Jill," with a "cadenza" (or "stunt passage") by the coloratura soprano, accompanied by a flute. Wagner, on the other hand, would give each character a "Leitmotif," or musical tag, of sturdy masculine type for Jack, and gently feminine for Jill, with the text put into a violently alliterative German.

Incoherent harmonies and a vague melodic line would characterize the modern French version, and finally American jazz would seize upon it and deliver it to the mercies of a vaudeville team, with the chorus interrupted by maudlin "blues."*

But enough of parody and instruction! Give the composer himself a chance!

*This fancy has also been carried out in some detail by the author, and will be similarly available.

AS COMMONLY INTERPRETED

The Composer to His Interpreter

An Open Letter

Sir or Madame, whoever you may be:

To you I have entrusted my work for public performance. My reputation, such as it is, rests entirely in your hands.

I gladly resign to you the difficult task of presenting my musical thoughts to a listener's understanding. Without you I am nothing; and without a listener's appreciation we are both as nothing.

You have, I trust, conscientiously studied my intentions, in so far as I have been able to transfer them to paper. You have noted such directions as are unmistakable, and you have been guided by them in other details that must be left to your imagination. You are, I am sure, equipped with a physical and spiritual mastery of your art, and sincerely desirous of glorifying its materials, if they have proved worthy of your intelligent interest.

I have no wish to intrude matters of purely personal significance, yet my own life has entered into this work in most intimate fashion. I have starved at times, in order that it might be completed; and I have accepted patronage which was worse than starvation.

I have passed by the common pleasures of mankind, to devote myself more completely to my task, and I have shunned the easier ways of turning my talents to profit. I have risen in the night-time to preserve the thoughts that possessed me, and I have walked in the fields and forests by day, that inspiration might come from things greater than myself.

You also have made sacrifices, and learned to revere a gift which is your sacred trust. If you have suffered, let your sufferings reflect my own; and if you have found joy, let it illumine that joy which comes through creative achievement.

Do not, I pray you, distort or pervert that which I have committed to permanent form. If your skill should fail you, preserve at least the spirit of my work, and if your own æsthetic conscience be satisfied, I ask no further approval.

Accept the rewards that your accomplishment may bring you, but forget not the humility with which interpreter and creator alike must stand before the divinity of Music itself.

We are but tools for the fashioning of a mystic purpose, and we know not whence the spark has come, nor whither it may guide us.

To you I entrust all that is my final and universal self, and I gladly share with you my bondage in the joyful service of Beauty.

CHAPTER XI

NOW PLAY SOMETHING

MERELY reading this book is not going to turn you into a musical performer, nor even an intelligent listener. You will have to hear a lot of music before you can begin to realize the possibilities of its enjoyment.

But it is not necessary to play or sing, in order to have music of the best type in your home, nor do you have to depend constantly on your talented friends. Modern science offers you a ready-made performance of truly artistic merit through the records of the phonograph or talking-machine, and the wonderful re-enactment of human touch through the piano itself, when electrically controlled, or even pumped by the feet.

JUST GET THE HABIT

Musical self-education is a simple matter, and one which carries with it a constant entertainment. All you have to do is to listen to plenty of music, and then watch your taste and appreciation develop.

If you have access to concerts and good amateur performances, so much the better. But waiting for such occasions is like waiting for a banquet and starving in between times. We must eat to live, and we must hear music constantly if we are to keep alive a sense of beauty and harmony.

A new type of music-lover is possible to-day, created by the regular association with artistic performance, heard through the mechanical instruments of the home. The term "canned music" is no longer one of opprobrium. Paraphrasing an old pun, "We hear what we can in concerts, and what we can't we can." Or, as the Englishman put it, "What we can't, we tin."

ONE STEP AT A TIME

The progress of those who expose themselves consistently to music is often amazing. They follow the line of least resistance at first, listening only to the more obvious tunes and rhythms. But gradually they discover for themselves more and more of the music that has a lasting value, and as they return to it again and again, they continue to add the subtler and more complex works to their repertoire of appreciation.

Eventually they have not only built up a treasure-house of direct and inevitable enjoyment, of which no one can deprive them, but they have also increased their social significance by becoming live, responsive enthusiasts, instead of dull plodders along the routine paths of mere existence.

The statements that have been made in this book are not just theories. They are facts, proved again and again by actual experience. In this final chapter you may pick up a few hints toward making easy the practical approach to good music.

AN ORGANIZED ATTACK

Many compositions have already been mentioned by name, and if you played or listened to these as you went along, your taste may be well on the way to its goal. But in any case, it is possible to draw up a definite plan of attack which will carry you almost unconsciously over the top, to a command of the most impregnable strongholds of classic composition.

Don't try to do it all at once, and above all be honest with yourself. If you don't care for a piece at the first hearing, let it go for a while, and then come back to it later.

If you become tired of a piece, drop it absolutely, and don't listen to it again until you feel an insatiable desire for it. The chances are that your judgment was correct, and that you have passed by one of the obvious landmarks of musical progress.

YOU CAN BE GREEDY

But even after you have clearly reached the heights, and receive immediate and unmistakable thrills from the supreme beauties of music (and this is an experience not easily forgotten, nor carelessly to be omitted from a human lifetime), it is still quite possible to retain earlier and more obvious impressions, without discarding any of the material that once stirred your enthusiasm.

Our moods vary, and we may at one time demand a blatantly sensational excitement, while an hour later the most ethereal spirituality alone will satisfy us. The whole body of music can always be at our disposal, and we are entirely justified in following even the whims and caprices of a moment.

Remember that no taste is hopelessly bad, and that no music is without some redeeming quality that may lead the listener on to better things.

Your one and only need is to listen, always, sincerely, enthusiastically, intelligently if possible, but with a personal integrity that makes your reaction an individual matter, not simply the reflection of another's taste or judgment.

Since rhythm and melody are the primitive and physically appealing factors in music, it is easiest to gain a first interest through pieces that are markedly rhythmic or melodic or both. The popular music follows this rule in obviously simple fashion, and few people require much urging to give such pieces at least one hearing. (Often too it has a practical utility for stimulating exercise and eliminating social silences, which must not be confused with permanent musical value.)

A FEAST OF WALTZES

But if you like rhythm and melody, you can find it in thousands of pieces that rise well above the level of the commonplace. Does waltz-time captivate your fancy? There are waltzes in profusion, from the Schubertian Song of Love up to the solid achievements of Brahms himself.

Victor Herbert has written excellent waltzes, including Kiss Me Again and the recent Kiss in the Dark. Drigo's Valse Bluette is a good melody, and we have the similar Valse Bleu,

Amoureuse and "A la bien Aimée" of an older day.

Johann Strauss is remembered for his irresistible waltz rhythms alone, and he offers far more than just the Blue Danube. Light opera has contributed many other good waltzes, notably in Sari, The Pink Lady and The Merry Widow, not to speak of My Hero, in the Chocolate Soldier.

MORE ELABORATE STYLES

You will find the Delibes ballet-waltzes very easy listening, and they will lead you inevitably to the more elaborate caprices of Godard, Moszkowski and Rubinstein, and perhaps to the melancholy Valse Triste of Sibelius.

Tschaikowsky has his Flower Waltz, and the spectacular dance music in Eugen Onegin, and after that you are just about ready for the unique inspirations of Chopin himself. The Minute Waltz, with its reminder of the little dog chasing his tail, is an easy self-starter, and its logical followers are the one in E flat, op. 18, the famous C sharp minor, op. 64, no. 2, and the three in op. 70. There are many others from Chopin's genial pen, not intended for dancing, but for the pure delight of the hearer. Don't let the arithmetical titles scare you away from them.

GREAT MASTERS OF TRIPLE TIME

Schubert wrote lovely waltzes, some of which Liszt has embodied in his "Soirées de Vienne," and Beethoven did not scorn such modest compositions. Weber's Invitation to the Dance contains a whole string of them. If you discover the Brahms waltz in A flat, you will want to hear more, and he has some beauties in his collection.

There are Spanish waltzes that have a fiery swing all their own, and the Polish Mazurkas, also immortalized by Chopin, differ from the triple waltz-time only in the slight accent on the third beat. (The Viennese habit is to stress the second beat in similar fashion, although all triple time necessarily has its main accent on the first beat.)

GRANDMOTHER MINUET

A slower and more stately triple rhythm is that of the old-fashioned Minuet, best known by Paderewski's popular piece of that title. Beethoven wrote several charming Minuets, of which the most familiar is the one in G, effective on the piano or the violin; and Haydn, Mozart, Boccherini and other old-timers did their share in establishing the popularity of this dance-form. A good modern example is Bizet's Minuet from his incidental music to L'Arlesienne.

Perhaps you like livelier dance-rhythms than those in triple time (in which, incidentally, the Polonaises of Chopin should be included). What's the matter with Turkey in the Straw or Dett's Juba Dance or some of the Irish jigs and reels? The influence of the negro on dance-music may be felt in John Powell's Banjo-Picker and Eastwood Lane's Crap-Shooters, and we have an echo of the old English Morris Dances in Percy Grainger's Country Gardens and Edward German's Henry VIII.

THE PACE QUICKENS

Beethoven wrote some lively Country Dances, and there are fascinating Spanish dances in various rhythms by Albeniz, Granados, Chabrier and other composers. Characteristic and eccentric effects are found in Grieg's March of the Dwarfs, Liszt's Dance of the Gnomes and Cyril Scott's ultra-modern Danse Negre.

Marches of all kinds are of course plentiful, with Sousa still holding his throne. The French Marche Lorraine and Sambre et Meuse became deservedly popular during the war, and for an older Military March you can hardly improve on Schubert's. Elgar's Pomp and Circumstance lives up to its name; Tschaikowsky's Marche Slav is a tremendously dramatic piece, and the Knights of the Holy Grail, in Wagner's Parsifal, march to bell-tones of impressive solemnity.

MARCHING THROUGH OPERA

More obvious operatic marches are found in Tannhäuser, Aïda, Meyerbeer's Prophet and the Soldier's Chorus from Faust, with Mendelssohn's Athalia contributing a fairly familiar Priests' March. The same composer's Wedding March, with its companion from Wagner's Lohengrin, can scarcely require publicity, but people who know Chopin's Funeral March (which is part of a sonata) should look up also the even finer inspirations of Beethoven and Wagner along the same line.

Dance-forms are so common in music that every great composer has necessarily made use of them. You will find Gavottes all the way from Bach and Gluck to Czibulka and Glazounoff. The Polka has appealed to many a serious writer, including the austere Rachmaninoff.

Ballet-music as such has brought delightful whims from the invention of a Chaminade, a Delibes, a Bohm, or a Herbert, with the operatic writers keeping up their end, and a real climax appearing in the colorful pantomimes of the modern Russian school.

WORDS ALWAYS HELP

If your imagination demands that music should have a definite "program," you will find it most easily, of course, in the songs of the world. Starting with the simpler ballads and folk-music, including Stephen Foster's immortal melodies, you will soon advance to the works of Schubert, Schumann, Mendelssohn and Robert Franz, taking first the obviously melodious things (Serenade, "Who is Sylvia?" Hark, Hark, the Lark, "Du bist wie eine Blume," On Wings of Song, Widmung) and later reaching the deeper and more dramatic inspirations (Erlking, Two Grenadiers, etc.).

You will discover some wonderful songs among the works of Grieg (Ein Schwan, Ich liebe Dich, Im Kahne) and our own MacDowell (The Sea, Thy Beaming Eyes). Rubinstein, Liszt and others had their moments of lyric greatness, and eventually the path leads to Hugo Wolf, Richard Strauss and Brahms, the greatest of them all.

FRENCH AND AMERICAN SONGS

For a realistic fidelity to text, the modern French style of Debussy, Chausson and Fourdrain is supreme, and Reynaldo Hahn, Fauré and Paladilhe provide a pleasant introduction to this advanced school. (See particularly L'Heure Exquise, Après un Rêve and Psyché.)

Modern American song-writers have often imitated the French and German styles, but there are plenty of good, straightforward settings of English words, by Chadwick, Parker, Cadman, Rogers, Speaks, Homer, Huhn and others, which demand no preciousness of taste for their complete enjoyment. We have also the beautiful negro spirituals, as arranged by Burleigh, Coleridge-Taylor, Guion and Reddick, notably Deep River, "Swing low, sweet Chariot" and "Nobody knows de Trouble I've seen."

The great songs of the world have generally been transcribed for piano, and they are worth hearing in this form, quite apart from the words.

OPERATIC DEVELOPMENT

If opera has a real musical interest for you (and this is possible even without the trappings of its stage-craft), get your first impressions from such melodious yet convincing works as Carmen, Aïda and Faust. The "heavenly twins" of Pagliacci and Cavalleria Rusticana will bring you normally to Puccini, and his Bohême, Butterfly and Tosca music may give you permanent satisfaction.

The earlier Verdi need not detain you long, although you will find bits of Trovatore, Traviata and Rigoletto necessary to carry you past Rossini, Donizetti and Meyerbeer. But if you once reach Verdi's Otello and Falstaff, you are close to Wagnerian standards.

Mozart's lovely melodies ("Voi che sapete," "La ci darem," etc.) with a little of Gluck and Weber (at least the overtures to Oberon and Freischütz) may make the approach to Wagner easier, but there are individual numbers in The Flying Dutchman, Lohengrin and Tannhäuser (such as the famous Song to the Evening Star) which will eventually make you feel at home with those operas.

VERDI TO WAGNER TO STRAUSS

The greater Wagner is first discovered in his descriptively exciting pieces, such as the Fire-music and Ride of the Valkyries, while a few hearings of the Prelude and Love Death from Tristan and Isolde will make you want to hear the whole work. After that, the elaborate comedy of Die Meistersinger and the still more elaborate mysticism of Parsifal need not be considered out of reach.

Beyond Wagner there is still Richard Strauss

(whose Rosenkavalier contains fascinating waltzes and some almost Mozartian melody), Debussy's experimental Pelleas and Mélisande, Charpentier's Louise, and Montemezzi's "L'Amore dei tre Re" (Love of Three Kings), all masterpieces of their kind. And, if any intervals remain to be filled, we can call upon Massenet (Manon and The Juggler of Notre Dâme, rather than Thaïs), Saint-Saëns (whose Samson and Delilah is practically an oratorio in costume), and the Russians, headed by Moussorgsky (Boris Godounoff) and Rimsky-Korsakoff (Le Coq d'Or, etc.).

THE MUSIC OF DAILY LIFE

But even when words and plots are lacking, music may be distinctly descriptive or narrative in its character. The episodes of daily life are suggested in the world's lullabies (see especially the Chopin Berceuse and that of Grieg) romances, serenades (literally "evening songs," but indicating always the wooing of a lover, which Moszkowski, Chaminade, Drdla and Rachmaninoff have all celebrated melodiously), hunting, boating and pastoral pieces, and religious music. (A Barcarolle is strictly a boat-song. If you know Offenbach's, try the two by Rubinstein, and finally Chopin's.)

THIS IS FAIRLY OBVIOUS

Nature calls out loud for musical description and imitation. We have brook and river and sea and mountain and forest pieces, and every song-bird is fittingly idealized. (Look up the Glinka-Balakireff version of The Lark, as well as Leschetizky's Two Larks and other bird-music.) MacDowell's Woodland Sketches are simple but picturesque, and the various seasons of the year have all had their musical devotees.

Night and the moon inevitably inspire music, and the Chopin Nocturnes alone would be a monument to this seductive influence.

Liszt's familiar Liebestraum, no. 3, is really a Nocturne. Beethoven's Moonlight Sonata is beautiful, but it has nothing to do with moonlight, so far as the composer was concerned. Listen, however, to Debussy's Clair de Lune, as played by a good pianist!

DO YOU BELIEVE IN FAIRIES?

From actual Nature to the imaginary land of elves and fairies is but a step, and here again music finds a wealth of enticing material. Mendelssohn's Overture to the Midsummer Night's Dream is a classic of this type, and he also wrote a Scherzo of fairy-like charm. The piano is the logical interpreter of such music, for a light touch can make it absolutely realistic. (Look up MacDowell's Witches' Dance, in addition to the general run of supernatural suggestions.)

Stories as well as pictures may be translated into music, as witness the Peer Gynt of Grieg, the Danse Macabre of Saint-Saëns, MacDowell's Scotch Poem, the Ballades of Chopin, and the Edward of Brahms. Ravel, in his Jeux d'Eau, gives a continuous description of the play of a fountain, and Debussy's Afternoon of a Faun follows quite closely a poem by Mallarmé.

MUSIC OF A MOOD

More subtle, however, than purely descriptive or narrative music is that which suggests only a mood, perhaps with very little help from the title. All the Rhapsodies of the world are obviously mood-pieces, and Liszt has written the most popular ones, with the help of the Hungarian folk-music. Dohnanyi, another Hungarian, has followed in his steps with original Rhapsodies, and Brahms again contributes his share of the great examples.

Fritz Kreisler's little violin pieces are all significant of familiar moods, particularly his Liebesfreud and Liebesleid, depicting the joys and sorrows of love, while his Caprice Viennois sums up all the insouciance of the typical Viennese.

GROWING MORE ABSTRACT

Much "absolute music" has a definite individuality of mood, and this applies even to pieces whose titles indicate merely a formal experiment or a technical study. Chopin and Liszt both wrote Etudes which are far more than teaching helps, ranging from cheerful gaiety to somber melancholy. (Compare Chopin's familiar Butterfly Etude with that of Liszt in D flat, sometimes called A Sigh.)

There are Preludes also, particularly those of Chopin and Rachmaninoff, each establishing a distinct mood, and sometimes several contrasting moods (as in the Russian's popular Preludes in C sharp minor and G minor). Brahms called his quieter piano-pieces Intermezzi, and when he was in a cheerful mood he used the title Capriccio. Schumann's Soaring (Aufschwung) and Romances, Mendelssohn's Songs without Words, the great Chopin Scherzos, Dvorak's Humoresque and Indian Lament, all these are mood pieces of varying significance.

TOUCHING THE HIGH SPOTS

You will probably find also a consistent mood in the great sonata and concerto-movements as you come to them. Grieg, Mendelssohn, Schumann, Saint-Saëns, Tschaikowsky, Beethoven and Brahms are among the composers who succeeded in making such classic forms continually interesting to their listeners, whether they used the piano or the violin as their medium, in combination, or with orchestral accompaniment.

Even the smallest pieces of the masters may show something of this gift of expressing the abstract in concrete form, which is the ideal of all art. Note the serenity of Bach's well-known Air on the G string, the laughable excitement of Beethoven's Rondo Capriccio on the "lost penny," the contemplative absorption of Schumann's Träumerei, the sturdy courage of Chopin's chords in his C minor Prelude.

When you have arrived at an appreciation of the symphonies, the great choral works and the chamber music of the master-composers, you will grasp this abstract significance instinctively, even while you are feeling an intellectual admiration for their perfection of outline. When a symphonic masterpiece rouses your emotions at the same time that it stirs your reasoning faculties, you may be sure that you "belong," so far as musical culture is concerned.

A GUIDE TO THE SYMPHONIES

Schubert's Unfinished Symphony is the easiest for a start. Haydn's simplicity may seem a little dull, but Mozart's gem in G minor can never be dimmed. Beethoven's Fifth, with "Fate Knocking at the Door" and triumphantly subdued in the Finale, should stir your imagination without difficulty, and after that you may safely expose yourself to the still more dramatic emotionalism of Dvorak's New World and Tschaikowsky's fourth, fifth and sixth (Pathétique), all of which have a fairly definite "program."

Meanwhile do not overlook the charming symphonic works of Schumann, Mendelssohn and Goldmark, nor that great symphony in D minor by César Franck, if you have a chance to hear them.

Beethoven's Second and Fourth, his Pastorale (number Six), the sprightly Seventh ("Apotheosis of the Dance") and the Eroica (number Three) should all precede a hearing of the stupendous Ninth, with its unique choral Finale.

Brahms should become a part of your symphonic experience through his Second, in D major, followed by number One, in C minor. His

Fourth may prove difficult, although its slow movement is of overwhelming beauty; but once you find the Third, in F, you are its slave for life. There is nothing greater in all music than that symphony!

ADD SYMPHONIC POEMS

With your taste for orchestral music in the larger forms once established, you will listen with interest and considerable excitement to the symphonic poems of Richard Strauss, first Til Eulenspiegel, then Don Juan, Don Quixote, Death and Transfiguration, and finally the Heldenleben (Hero's Life). Liszt's Les Preludes, Wagner's Siegfried Idyl, and the extraordinary Romeo and Juliet of Tschaikowsky (probably his greatest single composition) will help to pave the way toward Strauss and the more extreme moderns, and you will find plenty of trick-pieces, descriptive and otherwise, to fill up unlimited orchestral programs.

Are you exhausted at the very thought of all these musical riches? Actually only a small part of the world's stock of tonal beauty has been mentioned!

PARTING INSTRUCTIONS

But have no fear. There is no hurry. The music awaits you whenever you are ready, and it can be assimilated a little at a time, "just one small piece after another," precisely as you feed the baby.

You cannot do it all at once, and you don't want to risk musical indigestion. But be assured that most of the music that has lasted is both palatable and digestible. Open your ears, as hungry young birds open their pink mouths, and let the tones slide pleasantly in.

You may not know it as yet, but your musical self-education is involuntarily going on at this very moment, and you are already, permanently and irrevocably, a factor in that inevitable response to Beauty which is in all truth the Common Sense of Music.

APPENDIX A

A NOTE ON THE SCALES AND LETTERS

Every key of the piano, and every note of music, has a letter of identification. Since the musical intervals repeat themselves in groups of seven, only seven letters are needed, ABCDEFG. The black keys have no letters of their own, and are not given official recognition in the fundamental counting of the scale. They are known as the "sharps" and "flats" in the musical landscape, and people call them "accidentals" when they appear unexpectedly.

A black key is the sharp of the white key just below it (*i.e.* to its left) and the flat of the white key just above it (*i.e.* to its right). Thus the lower black key of the pair is both C sharp and D flat; the second is D sharp and E flat. The lowest of the group of three is F sharp and G flat; the next is G sharp and A flat, and the last is A sharp and B flat. You can work this out on any section of the keyboard.

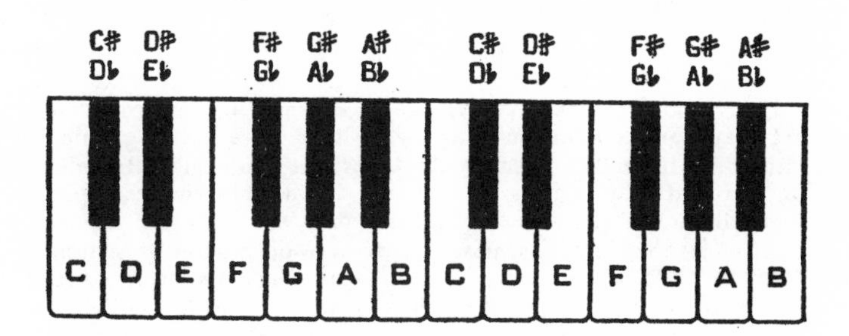

You will find that there are eight examples of C on the complete keyboard, counting the very top tone of the piano There are also eight B's, eight B flats (or A sharps), eight A's, and seven each of all the other possible intervals, including the sharps and flats. Musical notation can indicate these on paper by a system of lines and spaces, theoretically without limit, but actually grouped pretty closely around the center of the keyboard. You can tell in which section the notes belong with the help of a "clef" sign, distinguishing the bass from the treble. (There are also alto and tenor clefs, but they are seldom used, and need not bother the amateur.)

NOTATION

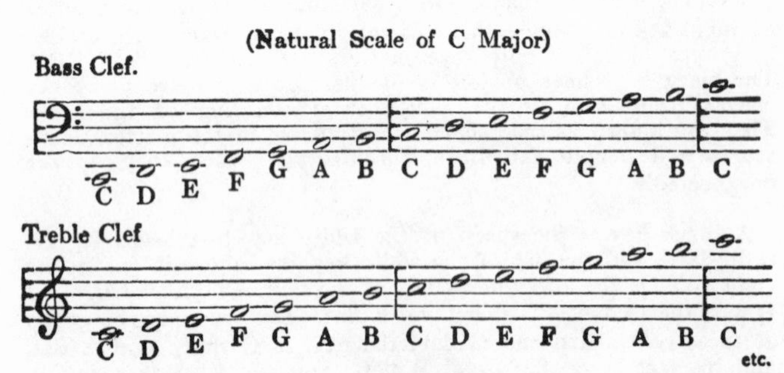

(Both bass and treble clef may add as many notes as desired above and below the regular five lines and four spaces, by simply adding extra lines.)

Every one of the twelve keys making up a complete set may have a scale built up, with itself as a starting point, either "diatonically" (using only the seven "natural" intervals) or "chromatically" (using all twelve). In the following examples you will notice that the sharps and flats are indicated at the start of all the diatonic scales, so as to save the trouble of writing them in front of each note. The note on which the scale starts is known as the "key-note" (how many platform politicians realize this when they use the term so freely?) and every piece of music is in some definite key, which is fixed by the starting point of the scale that is its basis. There are really only twelve scales, representing the twelve tones of the complete set, although you can add theoretically several more because of the possibility of reading each of the five black keys in two ways, as a sharp or as a flat.

APPENDIX A

DIAGRAM OF SCALES

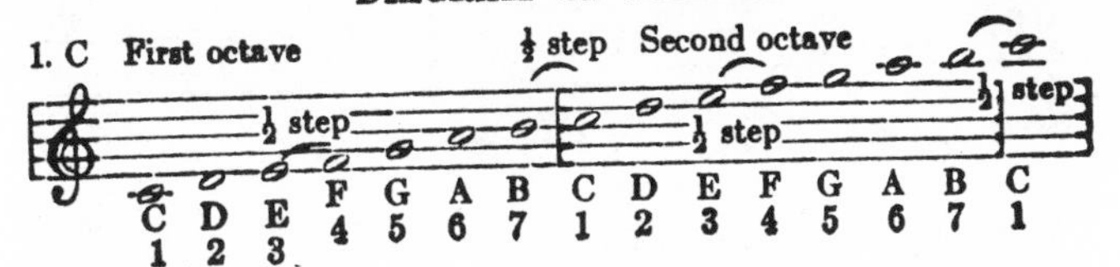

SAME IN CHROMATIC STYLE

CHROMATIC

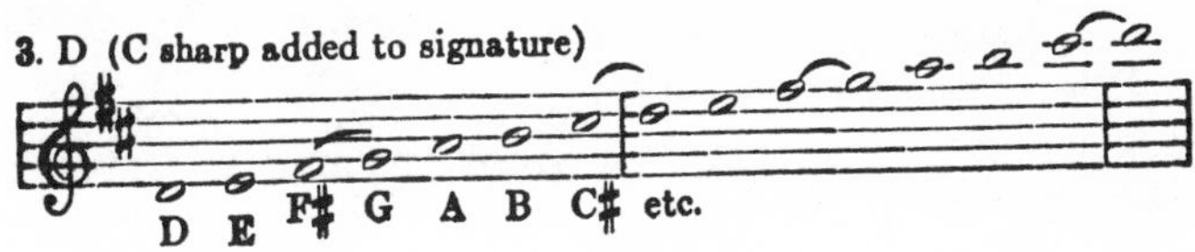

APPENDIX A

4. A (G sharp added to signature)
A B C♯ D E F♯ G♯ etc.
5. E (D sharp added to signature)
E F♯ G♯ A B C♯ D♯ etc.
6. B (A sharp added to signature)
B C♯ D♯ E F♯ G♯ A♯ etc.
7. F (B flat throughout)
F G A B♭ C D E etc.
8. B flat (E flat added to signature)
B♭ C D E♭ F G A etc.
(Same as A sharp)
9. E flat (A flat added to signature)
E♭ F G A♭ B♭ C D etc.
(Same as D sharp)
10. A flat (D flat added to signature)
A♭ B C D♭ E♭ F G etc.
(Same as G sharp)

APPENDIX A

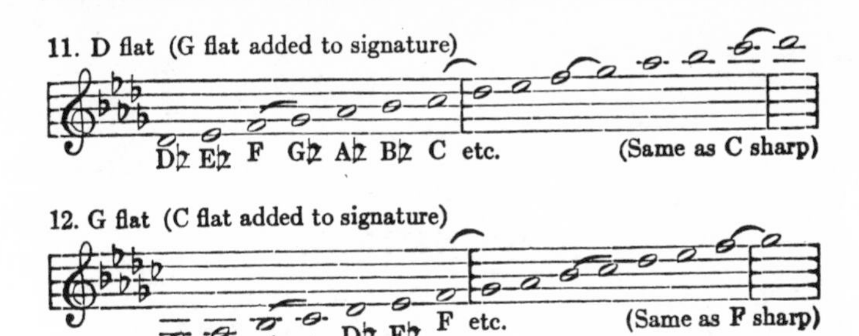

The diatonic scales above are all "major" scales, and they literally govern the majority of the world's music. Any major scale may be turned into a "minor" scale by simply dropping the interval of the third (step number three) half a tone lower, so that the progression involves only half a tone from two to three.

In all this welter of statistics, there are just two things to remember grimly and with everlasting determination: (1) The letters in music are constant, and represent always the same notes in their particular section of the keyboard. (2) The numbers of the intervals are merely relative, since a scale can start at any place on the keyboard, and its starting point is always numbered "one." You may have noticed that the diatonic scale of C major is the only one that can be played all the way through without using any of the black keys. (Hence its popularity with some amateur pianists.) But the system of numbering the intervals can be applied to any scale, no matter where it starts, and these numbers are in no sense fixed or constant. They are the equivalent of the Do, Re, Mi system, widely used in singing, and also merely relative.

TONIC SOL-FA

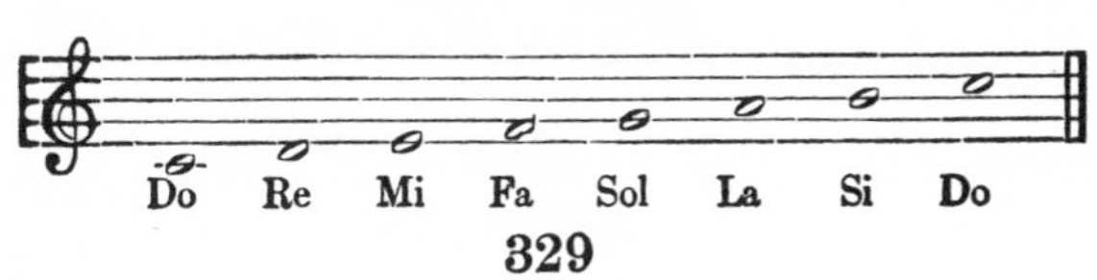

APPENDIX B

ROUNDS WHICH ANYONE CAN SING

Each group sings right through the round, over and over again, stopping finally on a given signal. Start the second group as soon as the first has finished the first line, etc.

1. ROW, ROW, ROW YOUR BOAT

(Three or four Parts)

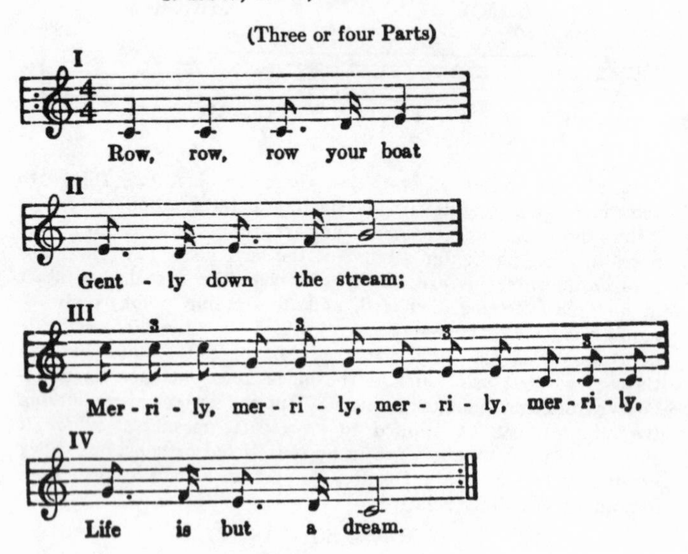

APPENDIX B

2. HEAR THE SONGSTER

(Three Parts)

3. I WANT TO BE A SAILOR

(Three Parts)

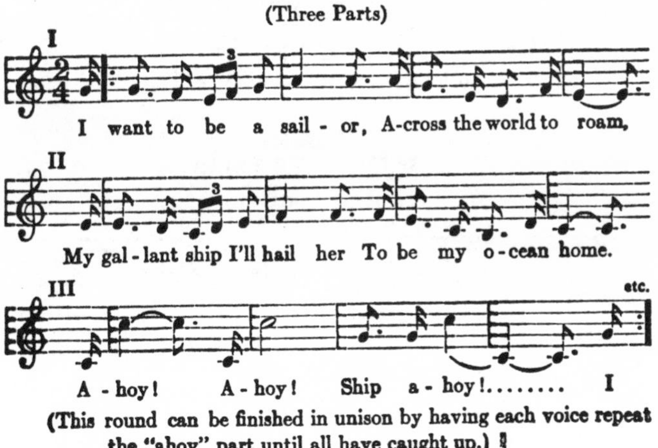

(This round can be finished in unison by having each voice repeat the "ahoy" part until all have caught up.)

APPENDIX B

4. THREE BLIND MICE

(Three or four Parts)

5. LIST TO THE BELLS

(Three or four Parts)

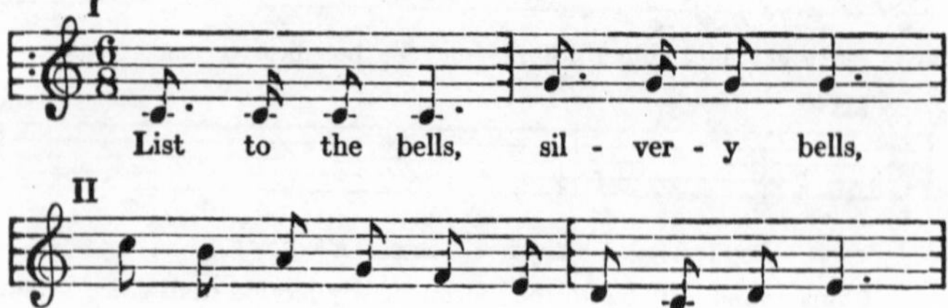

6. OH, THE CALM OF TWILIGHT SINGING

(Three Parts)

GLOSSARY AND INDEX

(Definitions and comments concerning some of the most important terms of music, used in this book and elsewhere.)

A: The tone that you hear a violinist play first when he tunes up. Also played by the oboe to get a whole orchestra in tune. A is the sixth note in the "natural" major scale, which begins with C, and the first in the relative (natural) minor scale. (The French and Italians call it "La.")

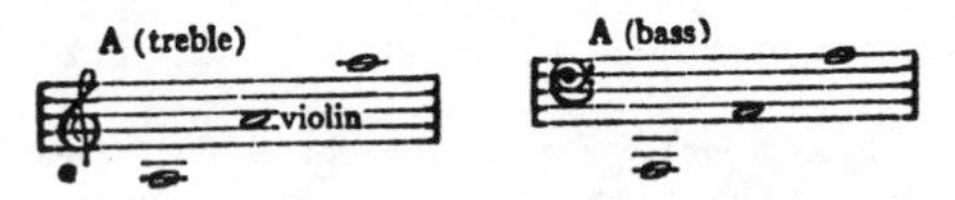

Absolute music: Opposite of "program music" (which see). P. 86 *ff*.

Accidentals: The sharps and flats that turn up accidentally, without having been included in the "signature" of a piece. P. 325. (See signature, etc.)

Accompaniment: The music that accompanies a solo voice or instrument, including sometimes the harmonizing parts added to a melody on the piano.

Adagio (*ah-dáh-joe*): Italian for "slow." Hence the slow movement of a composition.

Agitato (*ah-jitáh-toe*): Italian for "agitated." Hence, agitated. P. 89.

Allegretto (*ah-leg-réttoe*): A little Allegro, hence slower than Allegro time.

Allegro (*ah-lég-roe*): Italian for "cheerful." Hence, quick, lively, as applied to part of a composition.

GLOSSARY

Alto: Italian for high or loud. Now applied to the second part of a mixed quartet, and to instruments playing a similar part, originally sung by high male voices. P. 196 *ff.*

Amen: The end of a perfect hymn. Pp. 169, 170, 183, 205.

Andante (*ahn-dáhn-tay*): Italian for strolling, walking slowly. Hence, a quiet, peaceful gait or movement. (You may have noticed the Italian monopoly of musical directions. This is traditional, although there are perfectly good parallels in all other languages, including the Scandinavian.)

Anthem: A type of sacred or patriotic song, requiring a chorus or a crowd for its execution. P. 22.

Aria (*áh-ree-a*): Italian for "air." Hence, a song or vocal air. In opera and oratorio, a fairly elaborate solo. P. 302.

Arpeggio (*are-péd-joe*): Italian for "harp-like," meaning that the notes of a chord are played one after the other, as a harp would do it. (**Arpeggiáto:** Played in harp style.)

Augment: (1) To add a half step to a perfect or major interval. (2) To increase the length of the notes in a tune. P. 237.

Augmented Intervals

5+ 6+

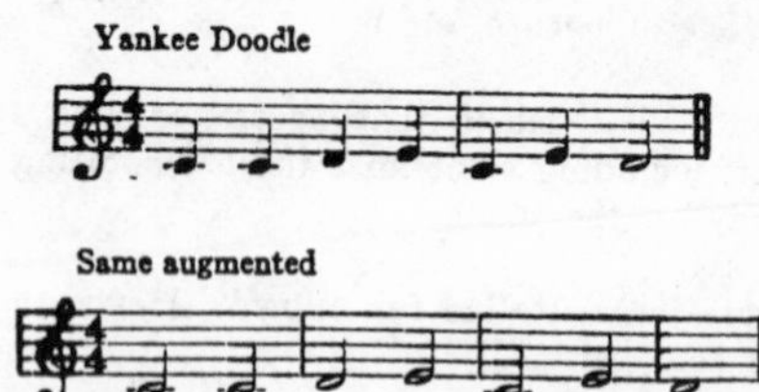

B: The seventh note in the natural scale of C major, and the second in its natural relative, A minor. (**B-flat:** The equivalent of "High C" for some tenors and sopranos.)

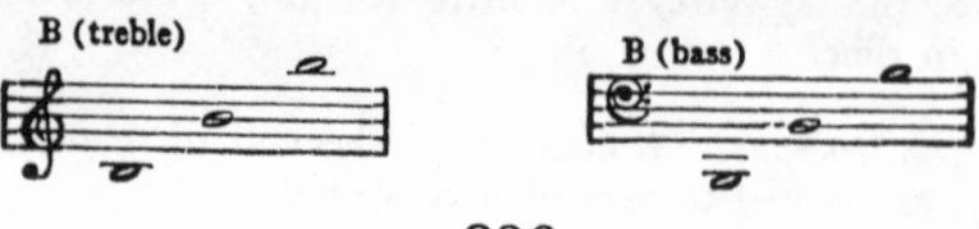

GLOSSARY

Bach, Johann Sebastian (*Bahkh*): German composer (1685–1750). Pp. 47, 63, 64, 68, 74, 75, 81, 94, 235, 257, 295.

Ballad: A simple song, originally connected with dancing. (*Cf.* ballet.) Also a song which tells a story, like the "Erlking" and "Edward." In popular music, a sentimental song.

Ballade (*ba-lád*): A composition for piano, of dramatic or lyric character. P. 319.

Ballet (*bal-eh*): French for a formal combination of music and dancing, sometimes with pantomime. Also used of the people who take part in such a performance. Fluffy skirts, pink tights and toe-balancing are characteristic of the classic ballet.

Bar: The line by which written music is separated into equal sections. Also used loosely for the "measure" itself, which is the portion between two bars. The first duty of an orchestra player is to "count the bars." P. 106 *ff*.

Bar Double Bar

Bárcarolle: French for a boat-song. Hence, a piece of music suggesting the rocking of a boat. (Best played sitting down.) P. 317.

Báritone: The medium male voice. Also used of the first bass part in a male quartet, and occasionally of instruments. P. 196 *ff*.

Bass (*base*): The lowest part in a harmony, used also of the singer of such a part. Bass voice: the lowest male voice. Bass viol: the bass fiddle or double bass, sometimes called "the dog-house," in an orchestra. P. 185 *ff*.

Bassóon: The bass instrument of the wood-wind choir in an orchestra, played with a double reed, by a mouthpiece coming out of the side. Pp. 285, 286.

Baton: The conductor's stick. P. 50.

Beat: A regular division of time, as it occurs in musical measures, or the motion of the hand or baton which indicates this division. Every bar or measure contains at least two beats, the down-beat coming first and carrying the accent, with the up-beat following. Waltz time has three beats to a measure, and "common time" has four, or two. P. 103 *ff*.

Beethoven, Ludwig van (*Báy-toe-ven*): German composer (1770–1827). Pp. 13, 18, 25, 35, 37, 38, 45, 46, 47, 59, 63, 66, 68, 74, 75, 81, 90, 94, 95, 161, 177, 226, 257.

Berceuse: French for lullaby. (Pronounce it your own way or page a Frenchman.)

Berlioz, Hector (*Béar-lee-oh*): French composer (1803–1869). Pp. 80, 95.

Bizet, Georges (*Bee-zay*): French composer (1830–1875). P. 80.

Bow: The stick strung with horse-hair, by which the strings of any viol are set in vibration. Also the verb meaning to use the bow. P. 280 *ff*. (Also, when pronounced as in "bow-wow," the contortion used by a musician to indicate that he likes your applause, and that if you keep it up he may do it again. "Take a bow": to come back unnecessarily on the stage without intending to repeat a performance.)

Brace: The elaborate parenthesis that joins two or more staves of music.

Brahms, Johannes: German composer (1833–1897). Pp. 12, 18, 25, 47, 59, 63, 64, 68, 74, 81, 161, 177, 227, 257, 314, 323.

Bravo: (Pronounced with the vowels and the mouth open.) The password of the professional claqueur. An Italian adjective meaning that the shouter thinks the performer a brave and good fellow, or that he got a free ticket or was paid to make a noise. **Bravissimo**: The same, but more of it. **Brava**: It's a girl. **Bravi**: There are several of them.

Bravura (*brah-vóor-ah*): A spectacular style of composition meant to encourage the bravo-hounds.

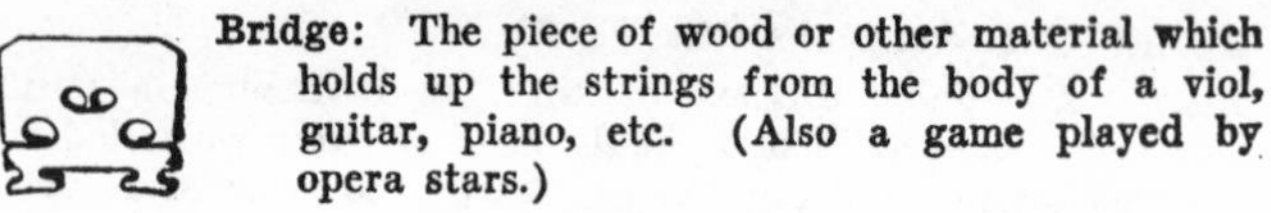

Bridge: The piece of wood or other material which holds up the strings from the body of a viol, guitar, piano, etc. (Also a game played by opera stars.)

GLOSSARY

Bugle: The goddess of army music. Pp. 19, 20, 22, 28, 137, 238.

C: The first note in the natural major scale, and the third in its relative (natural) minor (beginning with A). **"High C"**: The limit of the average soprano's ambition. **"Middle C"**: The starting point for all kinds of trouble in the middle of the key-board, also written midway between the two staves. P. 206 *ff*.

Cádence: The close of a piece or part of a piece. A full or perfect cadence ends on the key-note of the composition. A half or imperfect cadence has the fifth (or dominant) as the root of its final chord.

Cadénza: Italian for cadence, but generally applied to the interruption of a piece by a brilliant passage designed to show off the technical gymnastics of the soloist. P. 302.

Cánon: Literally Greek for law or rule. Musically the trick of making a melody harmonize with itself, by overlapping its repetition in the same key (as in a round) or starting it in a key that harmonizes with the original. P. 233 *ff*. Appendix B.

Cantabile (*conn-táh-bi-lay*): In singing style. (See the Andante Cantabile from Tschaikowsky's string quartet often played by orchestras.)

Cantata (*conn-táh-ta*): (1) A shorter form of oratorio. (2) A vocal solo, including recitative and aria.

Castanets: Clicking pieces of wood, accentuating Spanish rhythms. P. 290.

'Cello (*tshelloe*): Popular abbreviation of violoncello (which see).

Chadwick, George W.: American composer (1854–). P. 315.

Chamber music: Music meant for a small room. P. 261.

Chaminade, Cecile (*Sháh-mi-náhd*): French woman composer (1861–). Pp. 47, 63, 75, 79.

Chant: A form of sacred music.

Choir: A band of church singers. Also used of the different sections of an orchestra, as the "wood-wind choir," "brass choir," etc.

Chopin, Frederic F. (*Shów-pan*): Polish composer (1809–1849). Pp. 35, 36, 37, 47, 64, 68, 73, 74, 80, 95, 119, 310.

Choral(e): An old form of sacred song. Also the adjective referring to a chorus.

Chord: Three or more tones sounding together. (See major, minor, etc.) P. 180 *ff*.

Chorus: A band of singers, or the music written for them. The refrain of a song. P. 275 *ff*.

Chromatic: Moving by half-steps. Foreign to the regular key.

Chromatic scale: Any scale using half steps all the way. Pp. 53, 134, 326 *ff*.

Clarinet (*or* **Clarionet**): One of the wood-wind instruments in an orchestra or brass band. P. 253, 284, 285.

Clávichord: An ancestor of the modern piano, much used by J. S. Bach.

Clef: Literally, key. A sign by which the lines and spaces on the musical staff are given a definite pitch value. The treble clef is used for the higher voices and instruments, and the bass clef for the lower. There are intermediate clefs also, but they need not worry the musical amateur. Page 326.

Clefs
treble bass

Códa: Italian for tail. The closing section of a movement in sonata form, or some other formal composition. P. 247.

Color: Quality of tone, timbre, as of different voices. Pp. 251 *ff*. 298 *ff*.

GLOSSARY

Common time: The division of musical measures into two or four beats apiece.

Concert: Any musical performance.

Concerto (*con-sháre-toe*): A composition, partly in sonata form, for a solo instrument, with orchestral accompaniment. Pp. 320, 321.

Conductor: The leader of the band. P. 292 *ff*.

Contrálto: The low female voice, generally known as alto. (See alto.)

Cor anglais: English horn. (See horn.)

Cornét: An educated bugle. The most popular instrument of the brass band, sometimes substituted for the trumpet in an orchestra.

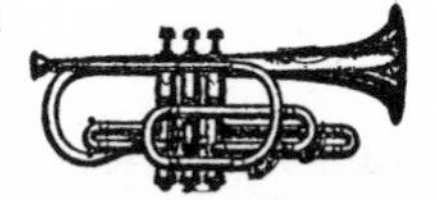

Count: To keep time by counting the beats. Also a noun mean- the number of the beat.

Coúnterpoint: The fitting of one tune in harmony with another. P. 234 *ff*.

Crescendo (*creh-shén-doe*): Italian for increasing. Growing gradually louder, increasing in volume. (Abbreviated cresc.) Also indicated in written music by an angle opening in the direction of the climax.

Cymbals: Brass noise-makers in a band or orchestra. P. 290.

D: The second note in the natural scale, and the fourth in its relative minor (A).

Da Capo (*dah cáh-poe*): Italian for "from the beginning," meaning "play it over again." Sometimes the repetition is to a sign, like an f, or to the word "Fine," meaning "finish." Abbreviated D.C.

Damper: A felt-covered bit of wood which stops the strings of a piano from vibrating after the hammer has struck them. When the fingers let go the keys, the dampers fall automatically on the strings concerned. **Damper pedal:** The pedal on the right side, wrongly called the "loud pedal," which raises all the dampers at once, and keeps the strings sounding to the heart's content of the emotional pianist.

Debussy, Claude A. (*Dé-bu-sée*): French composer (1862–1918). Pp. 74, 75, 81, 95, 116.

De Koven, Reginald: American composer (1859–1920). Pp. 62, 80.

Delibes, Leo (*Day-léeb*): French composer (1836–1891). Pp. 47, 80.

Diapason (*die-a-páy-son*): Greek for octave. Also the normal organ tone or stop. Also the standard pitch, according to which A consists of 435 vibrations per second. P. 295.

Diatónic: Concerning the conventional major and minor scales, with seven intervals to the octave. These seven intervals, with the five intervening half-tones (chromatic) make up the whole tonal material of music, merely repeating themselves in the same order, from the lowest to the highest pitch audible to the human ear. P. 326.

Diminish: To make an interval half a step less than perfect or minor, by subtracting half a tone.

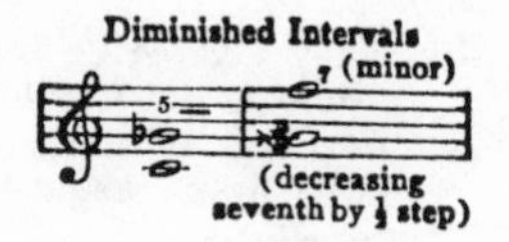

Diminuendo (*dim-in-you-én-doe*): Italian for diminishing, hence growing less in volume. (Abbreviated dim. and also indicated by an angle, narrowing toward the softest part.)

Do (*doe*): The Italian name for C, the first note in the natural major scale. In the "tonic sol-fa" system, Do is the key-note of any scale, and hence called the "movable do." P. 206 *ff*.

Dohnanyi, Erno (*Dokh-náhn-yee*): Hungarian composer. (1877-). P. 223.

GLOSSARY

Dominant: The fifth interval in the diatonic scale. Pp. 169, 181, 202, 205 *ff*. **Dominant Chord:** A chord built on the dominant as a bass or root. **Dominant seventh:** The minor seventh above the dominant, or a chord including this tone. P. 189.

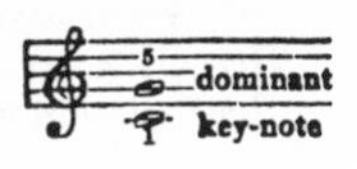

Donizetti, Gaetano (*Don-idz-étt-ee*): Italian composer (1797-1848).

Dot: A point after a note, increasing its length by one-half its original value. A dot over a note means that it is to be played short, or "staccato." Pp. 110, 111.

Drum: The commonest instrument of percussion, existing in many styles. P. 289.

Dvorak, Anton, (*Dvore-shock*): Bohemian composer (1841-1904). Pp. 62, 71.

E: The third note in the natural major scale, and fifth in the natural minor (A). The top string of the violin, and the bottom one of a bass-viol.

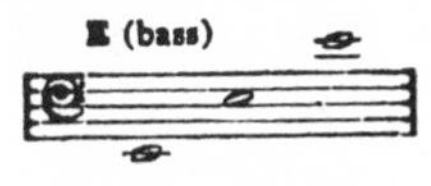

Elgar, Edward: English composer (1850-). P. 62.

Enharmónic: Containing intervals of less than half a step. Referring in modern music to a change of letter without technical change of pitch.

Ensemble (*ah-sáhmbl*): French for "together." The total number of performers in a piece, or the effect produced by them. A handy word for critics, who can call "the ensemble" good or bad without leaving anyone the wiser.

Etude (*éh-tude*): A study or exercise. Glorified by Chopin and Liszt into a musical form of real significance, fit for concert performance. P. 64.

Extemporize: To play extemporaneously, without previous preparation (so far as the audience knows).

F: The fourth note in the natural major scale (subdominant), and the sixth in the natural minor (A).

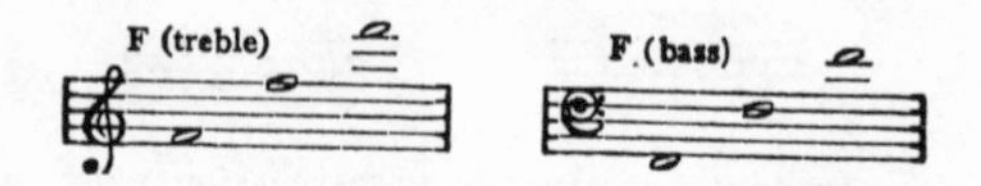

Fa (*fah*): The fourth interval of any scale, according to the "tonic sol-fa" system.

Falsétto: A false quality of voice in the high register, "breaking" the natural tone. A very present help to singers getting beyond their natural range, and the yodler's paradise.

Fántasie or **Fantásia:** A fanciful composition, not in strict form.

Fermáta: Italian for a pause. Indicated by the sign 𝄐 sometimes known as a "bird's-eye."

Fifth: A tone five steps above the key-note, in the diatonic scale. (Count such an interval on your fingers, including both the top and bottom tones.) The dominant in any scale.

Fifth (above) (below)

Figure: (1) A phrase or group of tones repeated a number of times without change, in melody or accompaniment. (2) That which is often sacrificed in the cause of vocal art. (3) The result of a press-agent's imagination as to salaries and box-office receipts.

Finale (*fee-náh-leh*): The last movement of a symphony, concerto, or sonata. The closing number in an opera or a minstrel show. P. 250.

Flat: The sign ♭ indicating the lowering of a note by half a step. The bugaboo of singers uncertain of their pitch. Verb, to sing flat. Pp. 271, 325.

Flute: An instrument of wood or metal, played by blowing across one hole and stopping others with the fingers.

Foote, Arthur: American composer (1853-).

Form: The technique of musical composition, or the systematizing of musical ideas. P. 217 *ff*.

Forte (*fór-tay*): Italian for loud. **Fortissimo:** Very loud. Often confused with such adjectives as "beautiful," "passionate," "soulful." Indicated by the sign *f*, *ff*, *fff*.

Foster, Stephen: American composer (1826-1864). Pp. 46, 61, 115.

Fourth: The tone four steps above the key-note, or tonic. The subdominant of the universal diatonic scale.

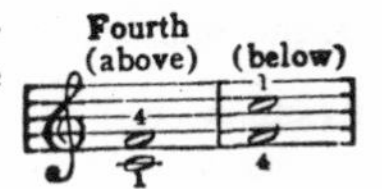

Franz, Robert (*Frahnts*): German composer (1815–1892). P. 80.

Fugue (*fewg*): A flight of themes, in counterpoint, developed according to formal laws. **Fugato** (*few-gáh-toe*): In the manner of a fugue. (A stock definition of a fugue is: "A composition whose themes come in one by one, and whose listeners walk out the same way.") Pp. 64, 235 *ff*.

Full cadence: Full stop. **Full chorus:** The whole chorus singing. **Full orchestra:** The whole orchestra playing. **Full organ:** The organ using all its regular stops.

G: The fifth note or dominant, in the natural major scale. The lowest string on a violin; the third on a viola or a 'cello, and the top string on a bass-viol.

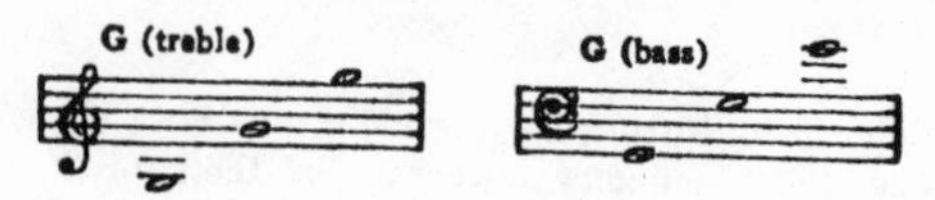

Glee: An unaccompanied composition for three or more voices.

Glee Club: A male chorus, flourishing particularly in schools and colleges.

Glissándo: A sliding effect gained by drawing the fingers along the keys of a piano or the strings of a violin.

Gluck, C. W. (*Gloock*): German composer (1714-1787). P. 80.

Godard, B. L. P. (*Gó-dahr*): French composer (1849-1895). Pp. 47, 63, 75, 79, 310.

Goldmark, Carl: German composer (1830-1915). P. 80.

Gounod, C. F. (*Góo-noe*): French composer (1818-1893). P. 81.

Grand manner: The stage deportment of an established artist.

Grand opera: Opera that takes itself seriously.

Grand piano: The large, flat type of piano, with legs, as distinguished from the upright style. (See pianoforte.)

Grieg, Edvard (*Greeg*): Scandinavian composer (1843-1907). Pp. 62, 80, 90.

Guitar: A six-stringed instrument, plucked by the fingers, popular for accompaniments, particularly with serenaders.

Half-note: A note having half the value of a full note.

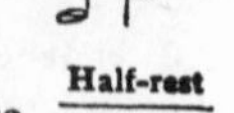

Half-rest: A rest of the same length as a half-note.

Half-step or **half-tone:** The smallest interval in the diatonic scale, and the regular step in the chromatic. Half a whole tone. P. 131 *ff*.

Half-tones

GLOSSARY

Hammer: That part of a piano which strikes the strings.

Handel, G. F.: German composer (1685-1759). Pp. 42, 43, 44, 80.

Harmónium: An organ deriving its tones from the forcing of air through reeds.

Harmony: Concord. The Greek word for system. Hence, the art of combining sounds systematically. Pp. 179 *ff*., 234 *ff*., 243.

Harp: A stringed instrument, plucked by the fingers, not much cultivated nowadays, perhaps because of heavenly expectations. P. 291.

Harpsichord: An ancestor of the modern piano, with quills instead of hammers.

Haydn, F. J. (*Hai-dn*)**:** German composer (1732-1809). Pp. 13, 18, 48, 80.

Herbert, Victor: Irish-American composer (1857-). Pp. 13, 62, 80, 119, 178, 309.

Horn: General name for various wind-blown instruments. In an orchestra, the **French horn**, of brass, with wide, bell mouth, and curved body, is conspicuous. **English horn:** One of the wood-wind, corresponding to an alto aboe. P. 284 *ff*.

English Horn
(*cor anglais*)

French Horn

Humorésque: A musical caprice. The most famous is by Dvorak. (See List of Pieces.)

Idyl: A short piece of a tender or sentimental character. (*Cf.* Lack's Idilio.)

Imprómptu: Extemporaneous. Hence, a piece giving the impression that the composer made it up as he went along.

Improvisátion: The art of playing "right out of your head," without previous preparation. Organists often develop this gift to a marked degree, and it has found its most practical expression in the movie theatres. MacDowell wrote a good piece called "Improvisation."

Improvise: To play extemporaneously.

Instrument: The medium for making music audible.

Instrumentation: The art of using musical instruments effectively in combination. Also same as orchestration (which see).

Interlude: A short musical passage coming between others of greater prominence. An interlude may separate the stanzas of a hymn, the acts of an opera, etc.

Intermezzo (*inter-méd-zoe*): A form of interlude, particularly applied to parts between movements of a sonata or symphony, and sometimes to opera (as in the famous Intermezzo from Cavalleria Rusticana, and the "Meditation" from Thaïs). Brahms called many a piano piece Intermezzo, for want of a more specific title.

Interval: The difference in pitch between two musical sounds. Intervals are counted from the key-note upward, including both the bottom and the top in the count. The term is applied both to the combination of two tones and to the top tone alone, figured if necessary from an imaginary key-note. The relationship of musical intervals is always the same, no matter where the key-note may be pitched. Intervals may be called by their numbers (representing the total number of letters included in their compass, as A to B, a second; A to C, third, etc.) or they may be given names, the commonest of which are Tonic, for key-note, Mediant, for third, Subdominant, for fourth, Dominant, for fifth, and Octave, for eighth. The tonic, subdominant, dominant and octave are "perfect" intervals, the same in major or minor key. The second, third, sixth, and seventh are major intervals in the regular major scale, and may be turned into minor intervals by simply dropping the top tone half a step. P. 138 *ff*.

Intonation: Playing or singing "in tune." The relationship of any musical performance to correct pitch.

Introduction: A preliminary manœuvre, of varying length and significance, leading to the body of a composition. In a popular song, the introduction is often part of the chorus, and followed by an infinite interlude marked "vamp till ready."

(Also a social formula of the green-room, which means nothing in the busy life of an artist.)

Invention: Bach's name for a piece of counterpoint, having two or three melodies. Also applied to the inventive or creative power of a composer. Its absence is always sincerely mourned.

Jig: A lively country dance, formerly the last movement of a classic suite. (Spelled also **Gigue**, with same pronunciation.)

Kettle-drum: An orchestral drum, consisting of a copper kettle, with a head of vellum, whose pitch may be changed by tightening or loosening, with the help of screws or braces around the sides.

Key: (1) The general level of pitch determined by the scale on which a composition is founded. Often used to mean the scale itself. P. 326 *ff.* It is a simple matter to transpose a piece of music from one key to another, keeping in mind the constant relationship of the scales. P. 212, Appendix A. (2) The lever on a piano or organ, by which the hammers are put in motion, or the valves opened. Some of the keys are white, and some black, to make it easy to distinguish them in their natural groups of seven and twelve. Each key represents an individual note, whose pitch never changes, so long as the tuner is on the job. P. 124 *ff.* (3) The stoppers of the holes in a clarinet, saxophone, etc., are also called keys.

Key-board: The lay-out of the keys on a piano or organ. Pp. 124 *ff.*, 203 *ff.*

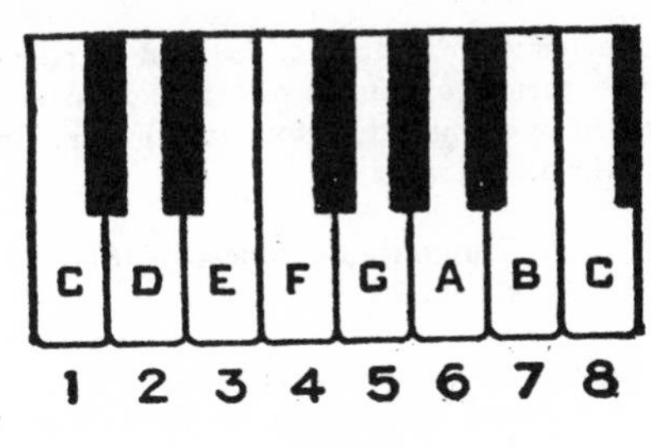

Key-note: The tonic of any scale, on which it is built up, and from which each interval has its number and letter reckoned.

La (*lah*)**:** The sixth syllable in the Do-Re-Mi system, and the sixth interval in the general diatonic scale. Used by the French and Italians to represent A.

Lárgo: Italian for large, broad. Hence, a slow, stately movement in music. Handel's famous Largo is really an aria from his opera, "Xerxes."

Legato (*leg-áh-toe*)**:** Italian for "bound," hence, smoothly, all tied together. The opposite of staccato, which refers to short, jerky notes, each for itself. Legato quality is much desired in both vocal and instrumental music. It may be indicated by a curved line, known as a slur. ⌒

Leger lines: Lines used for notes coming above or below the regular staff.

Leger lines

Leitmotif (*light-mo-téef*)**:** Wagner's term for a leading motive, *i.e.*, a group of tones labelling a particular character, episode or abstract thought in his operas, and frequently recurring as a means of identification. The practice has been successfully imitated by other composers.

Lénto: Italian for slow.

Leoncavállo, Ruggiero: Italian composer (1858-1919). P. 80.

Librétto: The book of the opera. P. 92.

Lied (*leed*)**:** German for song. It is used particularly of the characteristic form, combining melody and dramatic suggestion, perfected by Schubert, Schumann, Franz, Brahms, Hugo Wolf, and Richard Strauss.

Liszt, Franz (*List*)**:** Hungarian composer (1811-1886). Pp. 35, 41, 48, 62, 64, 74, 81, 90, 95.

Loud pedal: Really the damper pedal on the piano, which gives the effect of loudness by keeping all the strings vibrating as long as it is held down. It is usually worn quite smooth by constant use.

Lullaby: Cradle song. French, berceuse. German, Wiegenlied. The music is much the same in all countries, and affects adults as it does children. Pp. 18, 317.

Lyre: An early form of harp, supposedly invented by Apollo, and still used as a conventional decoration for concert programs. On a piano, the part to which the pedals are attached is called the lyre, from its shape.

Lyric: Literally, having to do with the lyre. Literarily, in song style. Used to describe tenor and soprano voices of the less robust type, also compositions of a melodious quality. Also the text of a popular song.

Ma (*mah*): Italian for "but," very convenient where reservations are necessary in giving musical directions. Also a popular syllable with writers of jazz lyrics.

MacDowell, Edward: American composer (1861-1908). Pp. 35, 80, 95.

Mádrigal: A kind of part-song, in counterpoint, popular in England about the time of Queen Elizabeth. Also loosely applied to various melodic pieces, such as Simonetti's Madrigal for violin, and the "Madrigal of May" in "The Jest."

Maestoso (*mah-es-tóe-so*): Majestically, with dignity (Italian).

Maestro (*mah-és-tro*): The Italian for "professor," as applied to musicians.

Major: Literally, Latin for "greater." In major scales, keys, chords, etc., the third interval is two whole tones above the key-note. In minor it is half a step lower, which completely alters the effect of the scale or chord. Pp. 205 *ff.*, 329.

Mandolin: A lute-shaped instrument (now made also in banjo and guitar style) tuned like a violin, but picked with a plectrum, hence easier to play. The mandolin club is the little sister of the college glee club.

Mánual: The keyboard of an organ.

March: A rhythmic composition in 2-4, 4-4 or 6-8 time, meant to keep people easily in step. French, Marche. Italian, Marcia. German, Marsch.

Mascagni, Pietro (*Mahs-cáhn-yee*): Italian composer (1863-). P. 80.

Mazurka (*ma-zóor-kah*): A Polish dance in triple time. Pp. 119, 311.

Measure: In written music, that which is included between two bars (hence, also called bar). It is used merely for convenience in keeping time, and the oldest music made no such division into measures. (Much of the ultra-modern music might just as well do the same.) The term has also been used for a dance step, and for rhythm or metre in general.

Measure

Médiant: The third interval in the diatonic scale, half-way between the key-note and the fifth (or dominant) and the necessary filler for a tonic chord. Pp. 169, 181, 208.

Mediant
(dominant)
(mediant)
(tonic)

Mélodrama: Words recited to a musical accompaniment. Also, more commonly, the kind of theatrical entertainment that the public will pay for.

Melody: A tune. The element in music most readily retained by the memory. See nearly every page of this book.

Méndelssohn, Felix (Bartholdy): German composer (1809-1847). Pp. 33, 34, 62, 68, 75, 80, 94.

Menuet: See minuet.

Method: A system of teaching singing or the playing of an instrument. It often reverses the saying, "There is method in his madness."

GLOSSARY

Métronome: The little wooden pyramid that stands on the piano and keeps time by wagging a metal finger at you and clicking rhythmically as you practice. Invented by a man named Maelzel, fortunately unconscious of the hours of misery he has caused. The abbreviation M.M. is often used at the start of a piece, with a number, to indicate the exact rate of speed, which can be gauged by corresponding numbers on the metronome.

Meyerbeer, Giacomo (*míre-beer*): German composer (1791–1864).

Mezza (o): Italian for half. **Mezza voce:** With half voice, hence, fairly softly. **Mezzo forte:** Half loud. **Mezzo piano:** Half soft. **Mezzo soprano:** Half a soprano, *i.e.* one that sings lower than a regular soprano, but higher than a contralto.

Mi (*mee*): The third interval or mediant in the "tonic sol-fa" system. Also the French and Italian name for E, which is the third in the major natural scale of C.

Minor: Latin for less or smaller. **Minor interval:** One which is half a step less than major. **Minor chord or scale:** One in which the third step is minor. Pp. 182 *ff.*, 205 *ff.*, 226, 329.

Minuét (Menuet, Minuetto): A slow, stately dance in triple time, or the music for such a dance. (Often used as a movement of a symphony, etc.) P. 311.

Mode: The Greek term for a scale or key, also used in church music. In modern music it is applied chiefly to the major or minor quality of a composition. **Neutral mode:** Neither major nor minor. P. 99.

Moderato (*mo-der-áh-to*): Italian for moderately, hence at a moderate speed.

Modulation: The process of moving from one key to another. This may be done diatonically, by using related chords on the way, or chromatically, by using unrelated chords. Organists

have to modulate constantly, and sometimes concert pianists modulate from the key of one piece to that of the next, when you think they are just showing off a little, and waiting for the crowd to quiet down. Composers find it a good thing to take daily exercise in modulation, and it is often the secret of their long compositions.

Molto: Italian for much, or very. Hence, a common word in musical directions.

Mood: Sometimes used for mode. Also the general emotional or intellectual atmosphere created by a composer, and transferred by him to his listeners, if any.

Moszkowski, Moritz (*Mos-kóff-skee*): Polish composer (1854–). Pp. 47, 63, 75, 79, 310.

Motif (*moh-téef*) (Motive): A short musical phrase, generally of decided character. (See Leitmotif.)

Motion: The progress of a vocal or instrumental part in music, by steps or degrees.

Moussórgsky, M. P.: Russian composer (1835-1881). P. 317.

Movement: An entire section of a sonata, symphony, etc. Also used of motion, and sometimes of time in general.

Mozart, Wolfgang Amadeus (*Mó-tsart*): German composer (1756-1791). Pp. 68, 80, 249.

Music: In its original Greek sense, any art sponsored by the Muses, priestesses of Apollo. Later restricted to the art of using tones in time. Now, in its best sense, the suggestion or active presentation of Beauty through Sound.

Mute: A little comb placed on the bridge of a viol to muffle the sound, or a stopper put in the horn of a wind-instrument for a similar effect. (But does it?) P. 279.

Natural: The sign ♮, by which a note is relieved of any sharp or flat attached to it in the signature, or previously added to

it in the same measure. Also descriptive of any note that is neither sharp nor flat. **Natural major scale:** That of C major, which has no sharps nor flats, and is played entirely on the white keys of the piano. **Natural minor scale:** That of A minor, also played without flats or sharps in the signature.

Nevin, Ethelbert: American composer (1862–1901). Pp. 47, 62, 80.

Ninth: An interval containing one more step than the octave. (Same as the second of the octave above.)

Nócturne: Literally, a night-piece (*Cf.* Schumann's "Nachtstück," which has been turned into a hymn.) Chopin's Nocturnes are unrestricted models of the form. P. 318.

Notation: The system by which musical sounds are put on paper, analogous to the writing or printing of language.

Note: The musical sign which indicates the duration and pitch of a tone. There are whole, half, quarter, eighth, sixteenth notes, etc., showing the exact fraction of a measure for which a tone is to be sustained. The pitch is fixed by the line or space occupied by the note on the staff (with a clef, treble or bass, for further guidance). Tones in general are often loosely called notes. P. 108. Appendix A.

Novelétte: Schumann's name for an informal and rather varied type of composition. Used to-day by music publishers for a dainty, melodious piece, in popular style.

Nuance (*néw-áhnce*)**:** Shading or expression, secured by variation of volume, tonal quality, speed, etc. A pet word with the harassed music critic.

Obbligato (*ob-blig-áh-toe*)**:** Italian for a necessary instrumental part accompanying a vocal solo, but actually not often considered obligatory. Notice the spelling, which is correct, strange as it may seem.

GLOSSARY

Oboe (*óh-bo-eh*) **(French, hautbois):** Literally, "high-wood" The instrument in the wood-wind choir from which the entire orchestra gets the A for tuning up. Pp. 253, 284.

Octave: The eighth interval above or below the key-note, which it really duplicates in a higher or lower register. Also two tones, an octave apart, sounded simultaneously. Pp. 126, 181.

Octave

Opera: A heterogeneous form of art, combining music, drama, dancing and publicity. Pp. 58, 91, 273 *ff*., 315 *ff*.

Opus (*óh-puss*)**:** Latin for work. Often abbreviated op., and used for cataloguing compositions in the order of their creation or publication. A composer is sometimes ashamed to call anything short of a symphony an opus, so you will find many smaller pieces listed as op.—, no.—, meaning that each one is only part of an ordinary job. P. 95.

Oratório: An elaborate form of sacred music, for solo voices, chorus and orchestra. Connected with the Latin word for prayer, but not necessarily with oratory. P. 275.

Orchestra: Originally the part of a Greek theatre where the dancers performed. Now the place where the instrumental musicians sit in a theatre. Also the band itself. P. 282 *ff*. Also, loosely, the seating-space for listeners on the ground floor of a theatre or concert-hall. (Orchestra circle is further away from the stage, so be careful when buying tickets.)

Orchestrate: To arrange music for an orchestra.

Orchestration: Instrumentation (orchestral).

Organ: A wind-instrument played by means of keys, pedals and stops, controlling pipes or reeds, and capable, in its most elaborate form, of a great variety of effects. P. 294 *ff*.

Overture (French, ouverture): The prelude to an opera, oratorio or play, often used as an independent concert piece. It may be in sonata form, or merely a potpourri of the tunes in the opera it precedes. Some overtures are so good that they are customarily played after one or two acts of the opera, so that most of the audience will be sure to hear them.

Paderewski, Ignace J. (*Pak-de-réff-ski*): Polish composer (1860–). Pp. 49, 50, 311.

Paraphrase: An elaborate arrangement, for some new interpreting instrument, of music originally written in simpler form.

Part: The tonal progression allotted to a voice or an instrument, or a group of voices or instruments. Also a section of a composition, marked off by a double bar.

Parker, Horatio: American composer (1863–1919).

Passage: A sequence of musical tones. Applied particularly to a brilliant run. **Pastorale:** Adjective or noun applied to music having to do with shepherds, or rustic scenes.

Pedal: A mechanism controlled by the feet of the performer, on the piano, organ or harp.

Phonograph: The most practical purveyor of music for the home. Also called graphophone, talking-machine, etc.

Phrase: An incomplete musical idea, as in language. **Phrasing:** The art of grouping tones in musical performance so as to emphasize their rhythmic and melodic significance.

Piano: Italian for flat, low, hence soft. Abbreviated *p*. **Pianissimo** (*pp*.): Very soft. **Piánofórte:** The full name of the popular instrument generally called a piano. Literally, soft and loud, meaning that you can play both ways on it, although this is sometimes overlooked. Pp. 124 *ff*., 254 *ff*., 296 *ff*.

Piánist: One who plays the piano.

GLOSSARY

Piccolo: A small flute, playing an octave higher than the regular instrument.

Piece: A musical composition. Also an instrument in a band or orchestra.

Pipe: A tube capable of producing musical sounds.

Pitch: The tonal level of a sound, as fixed by the number of vibrations per second by which it is caused. In the human voice, pitch is caused by the vibration of the vocal chords, in a violin or a piano by the vibration of a string, in other instruments by the vibration of a reed, a tube, etc.

Pizzicato (*pits-i-káh-toe*): Plucked by the fingers, instead of played by the bow, on a violin. Abbreviated *pizz.* P. 278.

Player-piano: A piano capable of producing music mechanically, by foot-pumping or electricity. Often called "player" and "pianola."

Poco: Italian for a little. **Poco a poco:** Gradually.

Polka: An old-fashioned dance, in 2-4 time.

Polonaíse: A stately Polish dance, really a march in triple time, made famous by Chopin. Pp. 119, 312.

Polyphónic: Literally many-voiced, referring to music in which each part or voice is an independent melody, instead of having a single melody with accompaniment. Pp. 235, 295.

Pótpourri: A medley of tunes.

Presto: Fast. (Which is exactly what magicians mean by the term.)

Prima (o): Italian for first. **Prima donna:** Leading lady. A term often substituted for "singer" in general. **Primo:** The upper part in a piano duet.

Program music: Music which indicates in some way that it has a definite program, in the shape of a story, picture, etc., as opposed to "absolute music," which receives no help of any kind. P. 85 *ff*.

GLOSSARY

Progression: Sounding one note or chord after another.

Puccini, Giacomo (*Poo-tshée-nee*): Italian composer (1858–). Pp. 15, 39, 40, 47, 80.

Púrcell, Henry: English composer (1659–1695).

Quality: Same as timbre. That which distinguishes individual tones, voices and instruments. (Also known as color.)

Quarter-note: A note lasting one-quarter as long as a whole note.

Quartét: A group of four solo performers, or a composition written for them.

Quintét: Same as a quartet, but with five instead of four.

Rachmáninoff, Sergei: Russian composer (1873–). Pp. 27, 34, 67, 96, 177-178.

Rameau, J. P. (*Ra-móe*): French composer (1683–1764).

Re (*ray*): The second note in the "tonic sol-fa" system, and the French and Italian name for D, the second interval in the natural major scale. P. 209.

Récitative: A declamatory way of singing, without any particular melody, and only a fragmentary accompaniment, usually introducing an aria, or filling up the holes in an opera, when the composer runs out of material. Pp. 301, 302.

Reed: A small strip of cane, metal or wood, whose vibration causes the tones of certain wind-instruments.

Reel: A lively dance, popular in Scotland and Ireland.

Refrain: The chorus at the end of each stanza of a song.

Repeat: Indicated by two or more dots before the double bar, or Da Capo (D.C.) if one is to go all the way back to the beginning of a piece.

Repeat

Reproducing piano: A piano capable of reproducing the performances of pianists. Also known, in its highest form, as "re-enacting piano."

Réquiem: A mass for the dead.

Rest: A sign indicating silence for a certain part of a measure. There is a rest corresponding to the length of each note in music. P. 111.

Rests

Rhápsody (ie): An irregular form of music, rhapsodic in character. P. 12.

Rhythm: The organization of accents in music. Pp. 51 *ff.*, 102 *ff.*

Ritardándo (*with broad ah's*): Italian for slowing up the time, slackening the speed. Abbreviated *rit.* Also Ritenúto, and sometimes Rallentándo, *rall.*

Rondo: A musical form, similar to the Rondeau in verse, used in sonatas, symphonies and independently. P. 250.

Root: The fundamental note in a chord.

Rossini, G. (*Ross-ée-nee*): Italian composer (1792–1868). P. 80.

Round: A part-song in which each voice sings the same melody, starting at different times, so as to harmonize instead of sounding in unison. P. 236. Appendix B.

Rubato (*roo-báh-toe*): Taking liberties with the rhythm of a piece, usually to indicate individuality and "temperament."

Rubinstein, Anton (*Róo-bin-stine*): Russian composer (1830–1894). Pp. 34, 62, 80, 310.

Run: A scale passage, usually at high speed.

Sáxophone: A brass instrument with a clarinet mouthpiece.

Saint-Saens, Camille (*Sán-sáh-uh*): French composer (1835–1921). P. 317.

Scale: Literally a staircase. A succession of musical tones, in regular order. (See Diatonic, Chromatic, Major, Minor.) Pp. 18, 22, 212. Appendix A.

GLOSSARY

Scarlàtti (*with broad ah's*): Two Italian composers of the same name. The father, Alessandro (1659–1725). The son, Domenico (1685–1757).

Scherzo (*scáre-tso*): Literally a jest, hence a piece or movement of playful character. (Chopin's piano Scherzos, however, are very serious.) P. 250.

Schúbert, Franz: German composer (1797–1828). Pp. 12, 34, 47, 48, 62, 68, 176, 302.

Schúmann, Robert: German composer (1810–1856). Pp. 47, 62, 66, 68, 74.

Score: The copy of a composition containing all the vocal and instrumental parts, used by the conductor. P. 292.

Second: An interval whose letters are adjacent (only one degree apart). P. 209.

Secóndo: The lower part in a piano duet.

Sémitone: A half-tone, or half-step. (See half-tone.)

Serenáde: An evening song, usually with sentimental associations. P. 317.

Seventh: An interval including seven letters. Pp. 184, 209.

Sextét: A composition for six solo voices or instruments. The one from "Lucia" (*Loo-chée-a*) is a famous example.

Sharp: The sign ♯, indicating that the pitch of a note is to be raised half a tone. Also as a verb, to sing or play sharp, *i.e.* too high. P. 325.

Si (*see*): The seventh interval in the "tonic sol-fa" system, and the French and Italian name for B, which is the seventh in the natural major scale.

Signature: The marks at the beginning of a piece indicating the sharps or flats that are to be played throughout, as well as the time. Pp. 109, 212.

Sixteenth note: A note worth one-sixteenth of a whole note in time.

Sixth: An interval including six letters. P. 209.

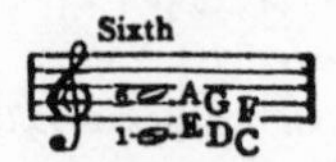

Sol: The fifth in the "tonic sol-fa" system, and the French and Italian name for G, the fifth in the natural major scale.

Solfeggio (*sol-féd-joe*): A vocal exercise.

Solo: Italian for alone, hence a piece in which one instrument or voice takes the principal part.

Sonáta: (*broad ah*): A composition in several movements, at least one of which is in sonata form, representing the highest development of absolute music. P. 244 *ff*.

Song: A vocal composition. Pp. 265 *ff*., 314 *ff*.

Soprano (*broad ah*): The high female or boy's voice.

Sordino (*sor-déen-oe*): The mute used by violinists, etc. (See mute.)

Sostenuto (*sos-ten-óo-toe*): Sustained.

Space; The room between every two lines of the musical staff.

Staccáto: Cut off short. (Indicated by a dot over a note.) (See dot.)

Staff: The fence on which musical notes are written, consisting of five lines and four spaces.

Staff

Stop: Noun, part of an organ. Verb, to press on a string so as to give its tone a certain pitch.

Strauss, Johann (*Strouse*): German composer of waltzes (1804–1870). Pp. 35, 55, 177.

Strauss, Richard: German composer (1864–). Pp. 89, 93, 95, 316 *ff.*

Subdominant: The fourth degree of the scale. Pp. 186 *ff.*, 202 208 *ff.*

Subdominant

Suite (*sweet*): A set of pieces, written around a central idea.

Sullivan, Arthur: English composer (1842–1900). Pp. 45, 62.

Symphony: A sonata for orchestra. Pp. 12, 18, 243, 247.

Syncopate: To shift the accent by artificially lengthening certain tones, producing the effect called "rag-time." Pp. 114 *ff.*, 242.

Tambourine: A small drum, with jingling metal pieces, played by the hands alone.

Technic (Technique): The mechanics of singing, playing or composing music. P. 269 *ff.*

Temperament: Really the division of the octave into twelve half-tones, as it is now standardized in music. Also a convenient substitute for artistic ability. P. 50.

Tempo: Italian for time. The speed at which a piece is played or sung.

Tenor: The high male voice. P. 191 *ff.*

Theme: A melody.

Third: The tone three steps above the tonic or key-note. The mediant in the universal scale.

Timbre (*tambr*): Quality or color of tone.

Time: The division of music which provides for a regular distribution of the accents. P. 51 *ff.*, 101 *ff.*

Tom-tom: The drum of the savage, ancient and modern. P. 54.

Tone: A musical sound.

Tonic: The key-note of any scale. Pp. 169, 181, 202, 207 *ff.*

Tonic sol-fa: The system of syllables, Do, Re, Mi, Fa, Sol, La, Si (Ti), Do, which can be applied to any scale, using Do always for the key-note or tonic. (Hence, "movable" Do). P. 170, Appendix A, 329.

Tonic Sol-fa

Do Re Mi Fa Sol La Si Do

Touch: The manner in which a pianist strikes the keys.

Transcription: The arrangement of a composition for some other instrument, voice, or combination than was originally intended.

Treble: The highest part in mixed vocal music.

Treble clef: The high clef.

Tremolo: Trembling. An effect used intentionally by organists, and unintentionally by singers. P. 295.

Triad (*try-ad*): A chord of three tones.

Trill: The rapid alternation of two adjacent tones. Indicated by tr ~~~~~~~~~~

Triad

Trio: A composition for three voices or instruments. Also a certain section in a piece.

Triplet

Triplet: Three notes played in the same length of time as two of the same value.

Trombone: The long trumpet with a slide, seen in bands and orchestras. P. 287 *ff*.

Trumpet: A brass instrument, like a cornet, but harder to play. P. 288 *ff*.

Tschaikowsky, P. I. (*Tchai-kóff-skee*): (Also spelled Tchaikovsky, Chaikovsky.) Russian composer (1840-1894). Pp. 41, 47, 62, 80, 90, 95, 310.

Tuba: The bass horn in the brass section of an orchestra. P. 287 *ff*.

Tympani: (*tim-pan-ee*) (Also spelled timpani): The kettle-drums in an orchestra. (See kettle-drum.) P. 289 *ff*.

Unison: Identity of pitch.

Valse: Waltz.

Value: The duration of a note in its relation to the time of a piece.

Variations: Elaborations of a melody, in various styles. P. 223 *ff*.

Verdi, Giuseppe (*Váre-dee*): Italian composer (1813-1901). Pp. 45, 48, 80.

Vibration: The rapid motion of a surface which starts the air-waves that produce sound.

Vibrato (*Vi-bráh-toe*): A vibrating effect, used by violinists and singers.

Viol: The ancestor of the violin, and a family name for all its relatives.

Viola (*vee-óh-la*): The alto violin, but playing tenor in a quartet. Somewhat larger in size and deeper in tone than a regular violin, with a very individual quality of tone.

Violin: The best known of the viol family. P. 278 *ff*.

Violin or Viola

'Cello

Violoncello (*vee-o-lon-tshéll-oh*): The bass of the string quartet, generally called 'cello. P. 277 *ff*.

Vocal: Having to do with the voice. "Take vocal": To study singing. (Provincial.)

Vocalise: Practice singing (verb). A vocal exercise (noun).

Voice: (1) The sound produced by the singing and speaking mechanism. (2) A vocal or instrumental part. P. 265 *ff*.

Vox humána: An organ stop, imitating the human voice. P. 295.

Wagner, Richard (*Váhg-ner*): German composer (1813-1883). Pp. 23, 27, 47, 48, 58, 63, 80, 87, 90, 177, 302, 316.

Waltz: A popular style of dance-tune, in triple time. Pp. 37, 119.

Weber, C. M. von: German composer (1786-1826). Pp. 22, 48.

Whole note: A note worth four quarters.

Wood-wind: The orchestral choir of wind instruments mostly made of wood, such as the oboe, clarinet, bassoon, etc. P. 283 *ff*.

Xýlophone: An instrument of percussion, able to play all the notes of the scale. P. 289.

Zither: A stringed instrument, like a small harp, laid out flat and plucked by the fingers.

LIST OF PIECES

MENTIONED IN THIS BOOK, WITH PAGE REFERENCES

(Most of these are available in the records of standard phonographs and reproducing pianos)

LIST OF PIECES

LIST OF PIECES

LIST OF PIECES

LIST OF PIECES

LIST OF PIECES

LIST OF PIECES

LIST OF PIECES

THE END